MYSTIC WARRIOR

MYSTIC WARRIOR

Stephanie L. Hamer

CreateSpace

CreateSpace Edition, 2018
An Amazon Company
Copyright © 2014 Stephanie Hamer
All rights reserved.

Published in Canada by CreateSpace, an Amazon Company

To everyone who has stood by me; For everyone who needs to know the goal is within reach.

Preface

The tale of the Realms' origin is one that has been passed along generations for many millennia. It is said a lonely Spirit awoke from a slumber, bored with the medial happenings of the current worlds and desiring new companions and adventure. Its kin had spent their time discovering new ways in which to cause mischief amongst one another. Not one had seen or taken the opportunity to feel the preserved ingenuity deep within. This lone, harmoniously mystic Spirit thought its passion and desire to create unbearable and did not understand how the other Spirits had ignored such a reluctant force. Perhaps, it reasoned, they could not or willed not to feel the same urgings. *How stale*, mused the Spirit. Beings interested in nothing more than their own existence. Did they not wonder? Dream? Yearn? Should the young Spirit expend the same passionless, worthless energy? That inner struggle was soon dispelled. This Spirit had something substantial stirring in its soul.

When the new Plane of Existence was established, the Spirit allowed one world to birth all manner of life, in its waters and upon its land; while other Worlds were inhabited with only a few species or simply sculpted for the purpose of inquiring minds. Still others had been designed at times of great emotion, from ecstasy to malice, and were therefore living images of whatever emotion the Spirit portrayed at a given time as it meticulously sculpted our complex planet. These planes, as they are to be known, for they are not simply other planets, are not realms to be eagerly sought. Such places, such scenery, are enough to drive any creature mad into the farthest reaches of the dark chasms within the mind. The impossibilities of our world, of our plane, are all too possible on these planes. A world dedicated to the cultivation of horrors only known to inhabit our nightmares. Another so divinely exquisite, one would forget all the love and passions within his or her heart, simply to have the ability to embrace the radiating wonderment for a mere moment.

As centuries passed from the birth of the planet, the creatures wandered throughout the broad landscape and when the first millennium had reached its end, all volcanoes across the Earth erupted in sync as a celebration of time. Only one volcano was reluctant to release its pyroclastic, smoldering excitement. Curious of this phenomenon, animals and humans slowly made their way to the peak to investigate. It was a mystery awaiting discovery. Without hesitation, pulled by the magik of a world beyond, each creature braved the danger and leapt into the narrow opening, where only molten earth is meant to pass yonder. One by one, animals and humans alike found their selves gently landing onto the pillow-soft turf of the Core World.

The whole of the Withering World, as earth had been so aptly named, had not discovered this gate to the Core World beneath, but those that stumbled upon it or felt its call, slowly migrated and settled into its rich, colorful, aromatic atmosphere. The radiance of this tropical world slowly began altering the beings now populating it. Within mere months of entering, one would find his or her body – brighter – than it had previously appeared. Their bodies, their very beings, emanated a soft glow. Other creatures had also adapted to the wonder and mystery of this Core World by evolving to more peculiar and – well – *magikal* beings. Those that had lived at the dawning of the Core World established a Council and had exhumed from their spirits a natural dialect. The words of this ancient language can be found in scrolls or engraved in objects scattered through-out both the Withering and the Core World. One of the ancients of the Core World that continues to thrive is an unusually small Cherry tree. It was of the first few that found its way to the Core World. As a seed it tumbled along the meadow beneath the opening until stopping in a welt next to a giant redwood. There it remained and grew only slightly, despite the assumption of growing larger rather than smaller in this mysterious world. Its roots stretched far beneath the surface to the iron river at the World's bed. Being of the eldest and connected to the river, this Cherry tree grew in wisdom and was thus called Wise Bright. All the creatures were soon referred to as Brights. That is, all but the few that had allowed their evolution into dangerous, malicious creatures. They had given their minds, not their hearts, wholly to the magik of the Land, desiring not to feel the permeating warmth of the Core World to become Brights, but rather wanting the power and strength to control what they considered to be weaker beings. Some of the

Brights were intrigued by the differences and gradually spent more time interacting with the beasts. As time continued, the Brights that had befriended these dark beings lost their glow and were but smudges of their old forms. They were aptly referred to as Shadows and, in their resentment towards their once fellow Brights, grew cold and offensive. One such Shadow, named Nitris, was exceedingly bitter and before the Bright Council, of which she was once a part, could officially exile the Dark beings to another region, the Shadows, comprised of animals, Griffins, and humans, attacked the Council and took dominance of the land they called Minaleth. Wise Bright and the surviving Council members devised a treaty with Nitris to deter her from waging further battle, stating all Brights were to remain in the outskirts of Minaleth. The valley of Minaleth was to belong to Nitris and her followers.

Over the following years, Dark beings searched the valley, forests, and mountains of any Brights yet to abandon their homes. Once discovered, their territories were ravaged and they were forcefully relocated beyond the agreed borders. As time went on, Griffins had destroyed most of the land with their sulfuric breath. The valley that had once been luscious and captivating with color was now a desolate landscape crawling with threat. While the Withering World continued in its natural development, the Core World maintained its mystical and magikal environment, for it was not merely a world *beneath* or *within* our own but it was an entirely separate Plane that had manifested itself as part of ours. Animals that we know to be dumb and threatening had become capable of speech, learning the words to speak as they observed those around them, as well had become close companions to other beings. Though most creatures were comfortable with how the magik allowed them to grow and evolve, many humans that ventured below willed to remain in their natural form. Time was slower in the Core World and all that lived there far exceeded natural ages of death. The eldest surviving ancient is Wise Bright, the Cherry tree, who is known to be nearly as old as the World itself.

Meanwhile, in the Withering World, life flourished at times and suffered in others as all Worlds do, even worlds within worlds. Though history texts and literature pertaining to the

World's past have, for the most part, accurately recorded and described various pertinent events, individuals, and milestones, they failed to mention one very intriguing concept. When the Core World had settled, the ancient Council felt it would be of the World's best interest to – safeguard – their existence. In the possibility of war surely to awaken, the Council decided the best defense would be from a powerful warrior of the Withering World. It is said that they believed a warrior of their own kind, though mighty indeed, would lack particular strengths necessary to attain victory. It would have a kinship to the World that could cause it to falter that much more easily. So in their magikal way, the Council chose a spirit of the Withering World to protect them. *The* Cherry Blossom was born.

PART ONE
CALL TO THE WARRIOR

Chapter 1
The Ancient Law

"I feel something beyond our understanding is imminent. An odd sense that all we know will unravel to become something new. " Grenig observed while drinking in the beauty of this world atop his perch at the peak of the volcano. He looked down, across the expanse of land below, to focus his view on the people he could see far in town. "I feel they, too, are in the clutches of change beyond recognition. If only they could see."

"I agree, friend, but their world has become numb to the intricate gift of their minds. The children possess the necessary sight but are taught to conceal it once they have reached adolescence." Serian rested his head on his outstretch arms, austerely gazing below to the world he dreamed would soon relinquish its hesitant nature and enter into his beloved home. After releasing a thunderous yawn, he raised his end while bringing his head low and wriggling his shoulders as he kneaded the soil beneath his claws. With a flick of his tail, he regained his composure upon all legs and turned, tossing his captivating, rust-colored mane, to summon Grenig.

"Come Grenig. The hour is late and we must return."

"My dear cousin should not mind our late arrival, Serian. Must we leave so hastily?" Grenig whined, not wanting to leave the surface just yet. He adored the beautiful…what were they called?...*sunsets*… he had before seen atop the volcano.

"Our Commander is expecting our company at the Council. The urgency of the meeting implies a serious matter to be sorted. As warriors, it is our duty to attend, especially at the Commander's bidding." Serian spoke with wisdom and authority, unintentionally causing his younger cousin to feel insolent.

With a meek roar, Grenig rose from his paws and lurched toward Serian, "Yes, yes. Your words are true so let us make way." But not before Grenig took one last gaze at the silhouetted-mountainous horizon, tickled with wisps of cloud against the blazing, sundrenched, ocean-blue sky.

The two massive warriors approached the mouth of the volcano and candidly leapt to none other than their fate. Nearing the end of their freefall to certain doom, both glanced at each other before vigorously fixating their eyes on the rock landing fast approaching. The surrounding walls and volcanic floor trembled as Grenig and Serian unleashed a heart-stopping roar in unison only seconds before hitting the bed of the vertical tunnel. Instantly, a light so intoxicating that one could stare in awe while enduring the pain of such brightness, shone from beneath the rock. The bed seemed to writhe and boil as if it had turned into a sort of bubbling custard. Without so much as a blink, Grenig and Serian plunged head first into the bubbling rock and within seconds their bodies had vanished, the light had diminished, and the rock returned to its natural state. They were gone.

Upon the greenest, softest grass they landed, with no more than a quiet thud. Both shook their bodies as if shaking off water and began walking through the serene meadow. Serian lowered his head while walking, allowing the floral blanket to brush his face. He looked to his friend in fascination. Grenig's orange-covered, black-striped coat absorbed the warm, brushed sky. One would think him to be a lovely painting, each stripe a mesmerizing stroke, strategically yet effortlessly placed. His heavy, crimson, orange, and cream-colored body a mimic of the sky encompassing their world.

Upon reaching the hilltop, the two feline warriors leapt over the oversized tree root into the massive welt just below. Boulders had long ago been chiseled away into magnificent stone seats, each appropriate for its Council member. The intricate markings covering each stone seat depicted the journey thus travelled by its Council member. Grenig took his seat upon the long stone, low to the ground, next to his cousin. It depicted images of him and his cousin finding one another in the Core World after facing daunting trials. It was beautifully bordered with flame-work of swirls. The artistry conveyed a heart of loyalty and vitality. The Commander's stone was simple in shape but elaborated in the most mesmerizing images and words of the ancient language. Serian settled in his cup-shaped stone that was inundated with an array of words and proverbs of the ancient language (he always had been the wise, historically-studious

Bright). The other four Council members had already been settled into their stones as they waited for the two overdue warriors.

"Cousin, have I not beseeched you a hundred times over to be more punctual?" Fayden, the Commander, said gruffly with a twitch of her tail and the faintest hint of a growl.

Grenig ceased his bathing, looking up rather embarrassedly to the other Council members, and then to his cousin, "I apologize, Fayden. It was not intended and I beg your forgiveness. Serian and I were caught up observing the Withering World...and I – dawdled – as usual."

At those words, Serian gracefully lowered his head while making eye-contact with the Commander, "We humbly apologize for our insolence, Commander." He then closed his eyes for a brief moment before lifting his head and poising his self upon his stone. "You are forgiven but in light of the very present danger we must move on to greater issues." Fayden turned her head slightly downward to her left, "Sire, please enlighten us with what you understand to be unraveling."

Each Council member turned their attention to a tiny Cherry tree – no higher than five feet. Its bark was soft and luminescent and the cherry blossoms were so rich in color, one would be certain the particular shades had never before been seen. Its miniscule yet robust roots were firmly if not indefinitely planted and the two, symmetrical branches two-feet above the ground were in every aspect its limbs. An intoxicating aroma of vanilla bean or, cinnamon, ameretto...lavender maybe? Every beautiful scent that has ever tickled one's nose emanated from the tree's every particle. It spoke in almost a whisper, sounding not unlike a grandfather, yet every breath held the power and magnitude of Kilimanjaro.

"My dear Council! Thank you for assembling with such haste. As you well know, since Nitris seized our country, Minaleth and its surrounding ranges have endured degradation and hostility. The sulfuric dust of the Griffins has devastated the forests and turned our kingdom of ancient redwood to nothing more than kindling. The concealed nests of the Hawk lords have even been discovered and ravaged. Most escaped unharmed but there are still a few that remain captive. Despite the Treaty of Minaleth, stating Nitris and her followers possess the valley and

Brights are to remain on the outskirts, she remains adamant that every inch of the valley and forests are her territory and any Brights remaining are in clear breach of the treaty. Though these truths pain us all, we have lived the last centuries relatively content in these outskirts." Wise Bright sullenly blinked his button-like, midnight eyes as he lowered his head and clenched his tiny arms. He continued, with immense distress in his voice, "But the time has come to relinquish our opponent of her guile and reclaim our land. If we do not," he released a drawn-out sigh, "it will surely be our end." He looked up, aware of the questions certainly stewing in the minds of the Council members.

Ostel, a Grostel – an enlarged, platypus-like creature in appearance with oak-colored fur and a sapphire undercoat; a black bill, large, half-webbed ebony feet, and a mellow voice – looked around the circle, ending his gaze on Wise Bright, "Sire, what do you mean, 'it will surely be our end'?" He turned to his lifetime friend, Klum, who was just next to him, with a look of eagerness to understand what gloom was erupting from its dormancy.

Wise Bright smiled with understanding, "My roots are deep into our Core World. They skim the very surface of the magma-heated, iron river buried leagues below. This river is a conductor of thoughts. Specific thoughts however, of torment, and only when the individual is in any way cradling granules of the soil. Traces of the iron river are found in every grain of our rich soil and carry such thoughts to the river. Any creature with the tiniest connection to the river is conscious of the dangerous thoughts that travel its current." Wise Bright had been looking around at each Council member as he spoke but now he focused his stare in front of him, at no one in particular it seemed, "Nitris is plotting to apprehend the remaining land of the Core World and eliminate any creature unwilling to follow. I believe she is planning something much larger than we could have anticipated. I believe once she has taken the Core World, she will move on to another - likely the Withering World because of our over lapping existence. We have reached a point of war."

There was a hushed silence all around until Klum – a giant, resembling a human body but covered in iridescent silver scales, like armor, and having wiggly, elongated tapered tube ears, a wide mouth and a ball nose and enormous, round eyes as well as a surprisingly harmonic voice – spoke in concern, "We must assemble the Bright Army and take victory upon Nitris before it is even expected!" Ostel, Strike, and Flutter agreed without hesitation. Grenig lay silently on his stone, looking as though he were calling to some ally in his mind.

"Members of the Council," Serian raised a paw, ushering calm, "it seems it has escaped your minds that the very tree we meet below displays a law we must abide by in such tremulous times." Serian rose from his stone to walk just behind Wise Bright where the ancient language had been etched into the mighty redwood. As he passed Wise Bright, he caught the slightest grin stretching across the Cherry tree's face. On reaching the trunk he raised a paw to rest it on the bark as he began reading the lawful engraving,

"To those of the Core World: Fail not to keep this land abounding in beauty and honour. Should any Darkness prevail, only a warrior of the Withering World can achieve victory on our behalf. This warrior will feel as a faceless, voiceless entity to its race but its destiny to conquer awaits within its soul. The warrior needs only to hear our cry upon the wind to venture forth unbeknownst to the quest ahead. Let fly upon the wind with our cry the cherry blossoms of the cherry tree of Old. Lest impending Darkness entrench our World."

Serian lowered his paw and walked back into the circle, stopping next to Wise Bright and, still standing, spoke with authority, "My fellow Council members, the ancient law is now set in motion and we must not falter from it. Fayden – as the Commander of our Bright Army, it is by your authority that we proceed in summoning this warrior and preparing for battle. As the Council we assuredly may discuss the matter but the choice will be yours."

The Council members looked to each other pondering the law and what alternatives could be at hand. Each perplexed with uncertainty of this unknowing warrior, Fayden alone was devoid of hesitation and lifted her head to speak, "Serian is wise and right. We must not stray from the ancient law. I can see the worry on your faces but if our ancient lords bestowed this course of action, it was with good reason and best intent." She looked strongly into the eyes of each member and gave a faint purr as she looked to Grenig.

"Serian and Fayden have shown truth. We must observe such a law engraved in the eldest redwood by the ancients that settled our World. I will surely follow wherever your command leads, dear Fayden." Strike – a dragonfly, emerald and sapphire in color, with the ability to breathe out the sharpness and radiance of diamonds and move with the speed of light – echoed his voice as he buzzed around the center of the ring. Flutter, Ostel, and Klum expressed their accordance with nods and shouts of accordance. Grenig then lifted his body from its reclined position to stand, grinning as though he had just been knighted, to express his allegiance. Serian simply gave a single nod and at that, Fayden stepped from her stone to stand before Wise Bright. Perfectly erect with propriety and resolve, she spoke in a resounding, melodious voice, "Sire, in accordance with the ancient law and in agreement of the Council, I propose and request to pluck three blossoms – carrying in them the words *conquer, truth,* and *valor* – to release to the winds to bid aid to our human warrior." Fayden then bowed, awaiting Wise Bright's reply.

"It is with honour and pride that I consent to our Commander's proposal." Wise Bright turned to face Flutter, "Sweet faerie, I ask that you take three blossoms of your choice and then fly to the peak to meet the winds."

Flutter gracefully approached the Cherry tree and while hovering through the small branches, serenely plucked three of the richest blossoms. She then flew to the center of the Council and raised her arms, cupping the cherry blossoms in her petit hands. Each member then cast a gentle breath towards Flutter before she lowered her arms to place the cherry blossoms in her shoulder sac, bowed her head to Fayden and Wise Bright, and departed through the meadows to the gate. Her slender, kitten-sized body glistened in the golden, crimson daylight. Her tiny, magenta feathered wings shimmered as she flew across the infinite meadow with few scattered trees. Her jewel-like wings stood out against her soft, cream-colored body. Every part of her, perfectly proportional. Her adorable, short hair was just long enough to catch the breeze and wave through the air. As every faerie, her eyes were an enchanting ice-blue. She came to the landing of the gate and increased her speed. Higher and higher, she climbed through the air until she was only inches away from the rock-sky above her.

Seconds before penetrating, she uttered a single word in the ancient language, "Terecluse" – meaning *break through*. In the blink of an eye she was through the rock bed and climbing higher through the volcanic spout. She reached the peak and took a moment to rest on a small stone of granite. As graceful as faeries are, sometimes flying with such speed and determination justifies…sloppiness. Flutter hovered slowly down upon the stone and as if she fainted, collapsed completely with her little arms and legs spread wide and limp and her face hidden behind her wind-struck locks.

The Withering World was just welcoming dusk. The sun was brilliantly casting distinct rays upon the nearby town. The oranges, yellows, and reds swirled and danced, serenading the population and landscape with vivid beauty, casting a sweet spell of tranquility. While gazing at the sky, Flutter noticed the winds had offered a current blowing toward the quaint town. She caught her breath then spread her wings to catch an updraft and effortlessly drew nearer to the current visible only through her faerie eyes. Once next to the current she lifted her shoulder sac over her head to pull out the three cherry blossoms. Holding the blossoms in her hand and lifting them to their taxi, so to speak, she tenderly spoke words of prayer in the ancient language,
"Litsu finay kualih rol ihe sactir. Drit ahmi hep friv rol ihe Duhlan. Pru ihr okahn seep lemire ihu corr."
Meaning:
"Let this current carry you to our warrior. Descend upon it then guide it to our World. May your words of hope caress its heart."

She then cast the flowers to the wind's current and watched as they sailed high above towards the inner-right edge of town. Twirling in the directional breeze, the cherry blossoms gently descended to flow through the buildings and trees. Once reaching the property of the high school Grenig and Serian had been observing earlier, they shifted course to graze along the blades of the lusciously, green field. The current carried them high again, circling above the mid-sized school. Moments later the current caused the flowers to quickly fall towards a series of bike racks cluttered with dark-clad teenagers. Across from the racks was a cemented alcove littered with cigarette butts, wrappers, and pop bottles. Secluded in a corner, veiled by shade, a young girl sat cross-legged with her back perfectly erect against the wall. Her eyes were shut, showing her dark, shadowed lids. Her long, midnight and scarlet locks fell over her shoulders and outlined her face. Her tender, defined arms brushed across her loosely-fitting kaki cargo pants. Her slender hands calmly gripped the white, rubber toes of her high-top Converse sneakers. Her fingers were decorated with white-gold and silver rings of various designs. A tiny stud sparkled from the right side of her nose and a blue barbell from her left eyebrow. The rich, soft cherry blossoms clung to the breeze as it drifted toward the solitary teen then released their bond to sink one by one into the girl's lap. The last blossom brushed, ever so slightly, across the very tip of her nose before falling upon the other two flowers. She opened her eyes.

Chapter 2
The Warrior Awakened

Dorian was invisible – at least to everyone around her. It may have been that her appearance deterred company. Perhaps having a black belt in nearly every martial art offered in the city was cause for uncertainty or her lack of attendance in every class despite the ability to maintain a constant 4.0 GPA every term. No matter what the reason, no one ever seemed to desire Dorian's company. She didn't mind, though. She was intelligent, strong and quite content in her solitude. Of course she yearned for just one close companion with which to trust, love, laugh, and cry but she wasn't going to alter her persona in order to appease the people around her and find such a friend. In every class and at every break, one could find Dorian sitting alone in a corner either daydreaming about who-knows-what or writing inimitable tales and poetry expressing her desire for – something different. She had always longed to see rich, warm colors that could be felt as well as seen. She would often escape to an eternal sunset in her mind where she was welcomed with grins rather than shunned with inquisitive glares. Her teachers were her only allies but even then they would incessantly urge Dorian to join clubs and teams, like Mathmagicians, Debate Squad, Writers' Guild, Law Lovers. Of course, as socially outcast as she already was, she was less than eager to pursue membership to any such club. She hadn't the time anyways. Her walk home took over an hour and once there she would have to change for which ever martial art class she had that particular day. A few hours later, she would be home again to eat dinner before wandering the forested gully behind her house until all hours of the night. Her parents didn't mind and never worried. Their daughter had proven her intelligence, strength, individuality and trust. They didn't care whatsoever if she went to school or not because they saw she was quite capable of learning on her own.

Dorian's mother and father were certainly out of the ordinary. As a young woman, her mother had been beaten and stabbed in a mugging, leaving her with a large scar on her left shoulder. Her father had volunteered in the army before the two had married. It was in Sudan, India, and even the streets of L.A., that her father witnessed atrocities he vowed never to befall his family. Once they married and became pregnant, both agreed their child should never suffer at the hands of monsters. They decided at the age of five, their little boy or girl would be put into every martial art available in their city until the age of eighteen – unquestioned. It seemed harsh to their family and friends but when little Dorian was six and excelling in her training, they knew she would be able to defend herself no matter what threatened her and so trusted they had made the right decision. Being at every lesson, every day was the only rule Dorian ever had to follow. The classes had taught her discipline and obedience, so her parents rarely struggled with back-talk or inappropriate behavior. It did pain them to see Dorian alone all the time, knowing the other kids were a little frightened of her, but they were glad to see their daughter used the time she had to "play" to instead excel in her academics. With her father being a foreman, engineering military vehicles and her mother a partner at a law firm, Dorian only occasionally saw her parents briefly at night or during the weekend. Her parents certainly loved her and said it as often as they could and Dorian never doubted it, so she never fussed about the lack of attention they gave her. For her 18th birthday, her mother and father surprised her with a breath-taking katana, made by *the* Masamune Okazaki, known as one of the world's greatest swordsmiths of the 14th century. His works were superior in quality and beauty and were considered to represent an internally peaceful and calm warrior. They had tracked it down in a rundown School for Samurai still in use in Japan. It had been a treasure and inspiration to the students and sensei but Dorian's parents were insistent and assured the Samurai that the sword was going to be well-appreciated by their daughter, a Western Samurai. It was their way of showing Dorian how proud they were of all she accomplished in school and in training. Dorian was astounded. She had other katanas of both forged and folded steel but to now have a sword that had been made by the greatest swordsmith – she was ecstatic! Though her parents made clear that she was now free to cease her martial training, Dorian chose to continue for two more years – enough time to attain her final black belt in muay tai and kendo.

***

Now, when she opened her eyes to see three astoundingly colorful blossoms resting ever so perfectly on her lap – she hadn't a question in the world! No inquiries of where they came from, why they landed on her lap or why one brushed her nose. No questions of how they came to be such a brilliant color. No – Dorian looked down, gently picked up the three blossoms and held them close to her face to study them. She certainly had never seen those shades of pinks and reds before. And she had never known a cherry blossom to look so – alive – after having fallen away from its tree. The entire understanding of cherry blossoms is that when they reach their prime they then fall from the tree to wither away. It is at the height of their glory and beauty that they face death. The life of cherry blossoms has been a philosophy for centuries in the East and especially to Samurai. So having *three* very healthy blossoms in her hands, Dorian couldn't help but believe it must mean something. At least she desperately hoped it meant something. She needed to escape society's black hole of technological dependence and tolerance for ignominiously raised future generations. She looked around to see if there may have been someone who placed them but she could see no one that stood out. She did however notice an unusual streak of what looked like smoke above the school heading towards Mt. Solace. She had never seen anything quite like it before and assumed it had something to do with these flowers now in her possession. Of course it was not a common assumption most people would have swimming around their mind but Dorian's imagination and optimism for a more accommodating life beyond the borders of the tangible world were too much to contain. Before she could think too far into the mystery, Dorian noticed the fading sunlight and glanced at her watch. She had waited long enough for the crowd of students to dissipate (she couldn't stand having to maneuver through large groups of people). Dorian put the cherry blossoms in the front pocket of her bag and started heading home.

When Dorian got home that day, before heading to Tai Chi, she carefully removed the cherry blossoms from the pouch and placed them on her bed. As she took them out, she caught a very subtle scent of what seemed like a variant of vanilla. She softly ran her fingers over each petal – completely captivated by such immense beauty. But *beauty* was an understatement. She could not think of the exact word but they were beyond anything she had ever smelled, seen, or touched. Her senses were utterly elated. Gazing at the precious flowers, she noticed a peculiar marking on each one. Focusing more clearly, she saw that they were words! Imprinted on one petal of each flower! They were very faint but discernible as the words *conquer, truth,* and *valor.* The very words breathed into the cherry blossoms by the Council of the Core World. She could not believe what she saw! Her dad had been home that day to catch up on a few things so Dorian ran downstairs to show him. But when he looked at the flowers he saw nothing out of the ordinary. He didn't see the words, notice the aroma, or see the magnificent colors. They were ordinary cherry blossoms to him. It upset her slightly that her father was unable to enjoy something so profound and mysterious. Dorian couldn't understand the phenomenon but she knew she wasn't crazy. She went back upstairs to put them in a treasure box she kept hidden behind a loose baseboard in her room before changing and heading to Tai Chi. She desperately wanted to understand everything possible about the cherry blossoms but she was hesitant of whom to inquire. After class she found the head Master and told him how they fell on her lap, had brilliant shades of color, emitted a succulent aroma, and had words imprinted on the petals. "What were the words, Dorian?" Master Hakira looked a little suspicious but intrigued.

"Conquer, Truth, and Valor. And only I can see them. I showed my dad but they looked normal to him."

Master Hakira raised his eyebrows and turned his head in thought, bringing one hand up under his chin. "Interesting. Hmmmm. I can't explain exactly what it means, Dorian, but it would certainly seem that these magical cherry blossoms carry in them a part of your destiny. But of course, dear girl, it is a person that makes their destiny. No man, nor deity. All else I can say is be sure to keep them safe. You will know the time you are to respond to their mystery." Having neither alternative ideas nor logical explanations, Dorian did as Master Hakira advised. She kept the flowers in her treasure box to wait until she felt what to

do. When she would feel lonely, tired, or uncertain, she discovered that simply looking at the flowers brought her a sense of peace. Should couldn't explain or understand how, but she felt a warmth when she looked at or touched the flowers.
***

Nearing graduation, Dorian received a surplus of scholarships to prestigious universities around the world. While most graduates would be plagued with such a defining decision to make Dorian found no interest in any of the schools requesting her attendance. She had decided to continue at the Martial Academy. When graduation did roll around, Dorian had been named Valedictorian but was uninterested in being any sort of spectacle. For the first time in her school's history, Dorian passed the privilege on to the next best candidate. It wasn't much of a shock to the faculty or graduates but it was still, no doubt, a horse of a different color. Everyone expected something out-of-the-ordinary from their estranged peer.

After the convocation ceremony, Dorian was approached by numerous alumni from various universities nearly begging for her to attend their school. She just swatted them away like flies until she was finally approached by Master Hakira of the Martial Academy.

"Dorian! Congratulations my dear." He stretched his right hand forward for a hand-shake and pat Dorian's shoulder with his left. Master Hakira had been Dorian's Head Master since she was five. They considered each other family. She was glad to see him and gave him a warm smile, "Master Hakira! Thank you, sir. You're certainly a pleasant distraction from all these university hounds."

He let out a course laugh, "Hahaha! My dear, you always have been quite the unique girl. I have a proposition for you, Dorian. Your parents told me you had no intentions of going to school and I know you mentioned continuing your final black belt but how would you like to teach a class of your own?"

Dorian certainly was caught off guard. She was certainly aware of her skill level but never planned on *teaching* anyone. "Sir, I was looking forward to using my new Masamune katana in the Kendo class I want to take."

"Of course! Of course! I couldn't ask you to give up any classes, Dorian! You teach the beginners of any martial art of your choice, attend Kendo and muay Tai class as often as you can, and in two years I will present you with your final black belt. Also, being a teacher, you will certainly be paid for your instruction." Hakira patiently waited for Dorian to respond but she seemed utterly perplexed. "I can see you need a bit of time, dear. When you have made a decision, come find me. I'll be just by the refreshment table." He smiled and began walking away.

Dorian didn't know what to do. This was an amazing offer that she was actually interested in – but teaching? Could she teach? Could she handle being at the front of a class everyday with students having no choice but to listen to her? Then again, how could she not agree!? She would still get to take her Kendo class, be paid to do what she loves, and she would now have something to occupy her time. She shook away her fear and rushed to stop him, "Master Hakira! I'll do it. I would be glad to take your offer, sir!" Drawing a breath, with a smile stretched ear-to-ear, Dorian looked up to see her excitement reciprocated across Master Hakira's face.

"Fantastic, Dorian! I'll discuss more with you after your lesson tomorrow and get you started next week."

"Thank you again, sir." Dorian gave him a hug before turning to find her parents to tell them the news.

"Well that's fantastic, sweetie!" Dorian's mom gave her a hug then embraced her daughter's face with her hands, "We're so proud of you."

"We are, Dorian. And if this is what makes you happy then *we* couldn't be happier! Congratulations!" Her dad drew her in for a bear hug before scruffling her hair.
***

The next week, Dorian met with Master Hakira to set up a teaching schedule. She had decided to teach Jiu-Jitsu. It was her best art and one of her favorites. Hakira and Dorian agreed that she would work three days a week, teaching one morning class of beginners and one afternoon class. That left her two days for Kendo and Muay Tai class and she could also use any time she would like to teach private lessons.

When she started, she found her morning class consisted primarily of teens and adults. She preferred her afternoon class because it consisted of little tykes which made it extremely amusing. At first, she was nervous standing at the front giving instruction. She wasn't sure if her students would listen to her, especially those that were her age or older. But she soon found that her students were respectful and eager to learn from a young lady that had attained so many black belts. The first few weeks of classes were a little rough around the edges. Everyone was inexperienced and some of the more mature students did nothing but complain of back aches, leg cramps, stiff knees – pretty much whining about every muscle! Dorian had to kindly explain to a few of them that perhaps it was just not in their body's best interest to continue in martial arts. Thankfully, only one older woman was offended…the others simply hobbled away, moaning. The younger kids, on the other hand, were catching on rather quickly. The youngest kids had a bit of trouble focusing and would often get caught up in their punches – jabbing forwards incessantly rather than just once with each arm. It wasn't too long though before most of her students from both of her classes displayed progress. One girl, about thirteen, from her morning class had even asked Dorian to give her private lessons along with attending public class. Her name was Reilly and incidentally had gone to the same school as Dorian so she felt she already knew Dorian…a little. Dorian however hadn't a clue who this girl was but she certainly was not about to say no – even if she did feel slightly awkward. It was summer so Reilly came to the morning class and had her private lesson when Dorian was finished her Kendo class on Thursdays. It didn't make much sense to Dorian why Reilly wanted the private lessons. She was one of the best in the morning class.

"I just…I just want the extra practice." As Reilly finished her sentence she brought her right leg down from Dorian's neck. "Plus, it's fun and gives me something constructive to do." Reilly was a petit girl with long, straight-as-a-board dirty-blonde hair that fell just past her shoulder blades. Even with her toned muscles, her arms and legs were quite small though, she did have a bit of a tummy bulge. She was just about five feet tall, had large, copper-colored eyes, and had an armband tattoo on her upper-left arm of a vine with thorns and one blooming, black rose. She was exceptionally strong but her size was, to her, a disadvantage, making it easier for Dorian to overpower her.

"Well I can't exactly oppose extra practice. What made you want to take Jiu-Jitsu?" Dorian asked through her heavy, controlled breaths as she demonstrated a low kick.

"Why did *you* take Jiu-Jitsu?" Reilly retorted, mimicking the low kick after Dorian.

Dorian raised a brow, "My parents had me take every martial art since I was five years-old so I could defend myself against…well, against anything." Without warning, Dorian lunged towards Reilly and with her left arm square in front of her body, rammed Reilly's chest then rolled behind her, slipping her right leg around Reilly's right leg while in motion and brought both of Reilly's arms back in a lock before knocking out her left knee. Reilly was now on the blue mat with her left knee down, her other leg locked in Dorian's leg and her arms tangled behind her back.

"I'm taking it for the same reason. I want to be able to defend myself."

"Fair enough."

Reilly pulled herself up and repositioned herself in front of Dorian again, "Why did you always sit alone? How come I never saw you with anybody at school?"

That was certainly out of nowhere. Dorian stumbled with her words for a second, "Uh – I guess…I guess I never fit in with the social conformity. Nor did I want to. I preferred spending my time alone so I could write or just relax. Besides, for whatever reasons my peers were never too eager to befriend me."

"Fair enough."

Dorian squinted with a crooked grin then jabbed Reilly with her right arm, "I guess so."

Reilly immediately reacted. She blocked the jab by bringing her left arm up and continuing with the momentum, wrapped her arm around Dorian's then pulled her in as she wrapped her other arm around Dorian's other arm, "So what are you going to do now that you're out of school?"

Without flinching, only returning Reilly's stare, Dorian answered, "I'm going to keep teaching and writing short stories. I'm also working on getting my black belt in Kendo and Muay Tai." Dorian smiled, "Now, would you like to know how to get out of this knot you've got us in?"

Reilly chuckled, "Yeah – I didn't think this far ahead!"

"Alright, this will hurt slightly but if you relax and *do not* resist, it will hurt less." Without a moment of hesitation, Dorian swayed her body back before bringing it forward and *leaping* onto Reilly! In just a matter of seconds, she *ran* up Reilly's small body, kicked off her shoulders into a back flip, and forced Reilly to release her arms as they were now being wrenched from their sockets. Dorian landed a couple of feet away from Reilly and caught her breath, "Are you ok?"

Reilly was rubbing her shoulders but stood completely wide-eyed at her sensei, "Holy crap! I'm totally fine but how the hell did you pull that off without killing me!?"

"Thirteen years of training, my dear grasshopper!" Dorian said with an accent and a bow, bringing a bout of giggling.

***

Days turned into weeks and weeks turned into months as Dorian faithfully attended her classes, taught classes, and gave Reilly private lessons. Being finished with school gave Dorian all the time in the world (aside from martial arts) to do as she pleased but Reilly had actually become quite the tag-a-long. She said she hadn't many friends and really admired Dorian's eclectic lifestyle...being a kind, dark-clad genius that possessed various black belts and spent her free time writing, meditating, and hiking. Not too many people seemed to have much interaction with Reilly, so Dorian started inviting Reilly along when she went for her walks. She taught Reilly botanical remedies for all manner of wounds and ailments. She explained the meaning and practice of meditation to Reilly and helped her understand how to free one's mind and focus on one particular concept or interest. Dorian even brought two of her bokkens (blunt katanas made of wood, rubber, or other non-metal material) on a hike once to show Reilly a bit of what she had learned in her Kendo class. When Dorian was able to escape her obligations in the world, she was immersed in her decorative poetry and prose. She wrote gracefully of the visions that came to her mind. Scenes like enchanting, sun-drenched skies creating silhouetted landscapes to dust-smeared caverns, hollow of vitality; the words she penned reached out to grip one's heart. She often wrote short stories of the fantasy worlds she longed to discover and the journeys she imagined...beneath the surface of oceans or in the depths of an undiscovered rainforest. It did not matter what she wrote. Dorian's mind was saturated in utterly captivating concepts. She even found herself writing of the cherry blossoms she still had hiding in her treasure box:

Upon my lap, so gently they descend
Bearing a mystic whisper of confidence
I quiver at
The delicacy of their nature
Wrapped in unfathomable splendor
Conjured from within my spirit the innate understanding
That such brilliance is borne of a distant soil
The place of their origin
And why they were cast unto me, I have yet to discover
The aroma is intoxicating
The plush texture, sobering
The magnificent colors are mesmerizing
I am but lost in their tranquility
In their silent cry of harmony
But what?
The tiny petals cast forth a faint, melodious resonance
It permeates my essence,
Pulling me to a world beyond that of my perception
Awakening to its harmonies
I shake free of the world's woes
To bask in the radiance of this gift that befell me
They are not but cherry blossoms, dear friend
They are messengers

It wasn't long before Dorian's first year out of high school had come to an end. Many of Dorian's students were now wearing yellow or orange belts and a few had even progressed to green belts. Dorian had never really felt so proud before. She too was moving along quite swiftly at her progression in Kendo and Muay Tai. In what normally would take the average person about three years to achieve, she had earned her purple belt in just one! Master Hakira had not just shown partiality to Dorian in order to fast-track her to a black belt as he promised. Dorian had truly demonstrated exceptional skill and determination and it is by ability that belts are awarded. There was a zeal about her that Hakira was displaced about. Whatever the reason, her demonstrated fervor was astounding for anyone that watched. She now had one year left to help her students advance as much as possible before they would have to move on to another sensei. That was one more year to figure out what she should move on to next.

***

Meanwhile – in the year Dorian had spent training and teaching, only a month or so had passed in the Core World. The Council had spent that time organizing infantry, weapons, armor, and strategies. Each Council member had been given the task of going to their kind with news of the oncoming war in hopes of obtaining as many soldiers as possible. Worthy females and youngsters of each – species – were even called to participate in the campaign. Fayden always said it did not matter if one was male or female in a battle. What mattered was his or her ability to fight and defend. That being said, when Flutter had announced the immediate need for all capable faeries to bear arms with their fellow Brights, the men were just nearly outnumbered by the women and teens. More than half of Faerie Willows agreed to serve with Flutter. Klum, Ostel, and Strike had also beckoned their fellow Giants, Grostels, and Dragonflies to join ranks against the Shadows and Griffins. Grenig and Serian walked the land, gathering all manner of Minalethin creatures to defend the Bright race and reclaim Minaleth.

"Has Wise Bright spoken to you of the Warrior?" Grenig casually glanced at Serian then returned to scanning the meadow for potential soldiers.

"Dorian? Yes. He has shared with me the progress of her training and the status of the cherry blossoms. She is nearly ready. He believes it will not be much longer before the winds carry them once again to the gate where Dorian is sure to follow." Serian said with optimism and hope.

"Serian, I feel as though there is something amiss. As though – as though something has gone awry since the cherry blossoms found Dorian." Grenig looked at Serian with sincere concern.

"Impressive that you can feel such displacement. Friend, you are not wrong. Just after Dorian had first spoken to her head Master about the flowers, Fayden and Wise Bright learned that Nitris had vanished from Minaleth. Not one Bright or Shadow has yet to locate her." Serian said in a steady, monotonous tone.

"Where could she have gone? And why do you think she would leave at the brink of war…war that she initiated??" Grenig had lost his composure and come to a stop.

"We do not know, Grenig. But you must not worry. As we have devised a plan, so has Nitris. We may not know exactly what she is up to or where she may be, but one thing is certain: we need not fear, for our army grows each day and Dorian grows stronger in body and heart." As Serian spoke with courage and passion, he looked to the sky as if to allow his words to stretch through the air.

This certainly seemed to reassure the anxious tiger. At Serian's words, with a surge of confidence, Grenig rose to his hind legs and let out a mighty roar that echoed beyond the meadows. Serian smiled as Grenig fell to the ground and continued walking alongside him. He chuckled as he nudged Grenig's body with his own in delight. Grenig shoved back with a smirk. It was then that two blue jays flew down to glide beside Serian and Grenig.

"Hello, friends!" Said the one on Serian's left.

"Fantastic day, is it not?" Said the one on Grenig's right.

Serian chuckled, "Why, hello feathered friends! What brings us the pleasure of your company?"

"And not to disagree but why do you find the day to be fantastic?" Grenig followed the two birds now with his eyes as they flew across each other, up and down, sideways, and around.

Dekel gleefully spoke as she twirled above the warriors, "We were in the neighborhood…"

Adalei continued Deki's sentence as she, too, twirled about, "…and thought we would tell you of our spectacular news!"

"Sweet Wise Bright has asked us…" Deki went on.

"…to welcome the Warrior, Dorian, when she arrives…" Adi continued again.

"…and be sure she is treated with superb hospitality…"

"…and answer any questions she may have! Us! Simple blue jays!" Adalei was now gliding backwards as she hovered between Serian and Grenig.

"Well now. That certainly is cause for celebration! Congratulations, girls." Serian smiled at each of them as they zigzagged just ahead.

"That is wonderful to hear. Wise Bright couldn't have chosen two better subjects!" Grenig stood, waving his paws at the birds as a kitten would to a butterfly.

"Thank you, sirs! Come Dekel. We should be getting back to our nest." Adalei started to ascend.

"Good-bye, friends! We will see you soon!" Dekel followed Adi up and off through the meadows.

Grenig and Serian laughed as the birds flew away, "Farewell, ladies!"

***

Back in the Withering World, Dorian was half way through the year when she found out Reilly was moving. It came as a shock and quite to Dorian's surprise, she felt rather affected by the news. Reilly may have been five years younger than herself but the two had grown close in the past year and a half. She felt like an older sister to Reilly...teaching her Jiu-Jitsu, helping her with school work, taking her on walks. What confused Dorian was not only the swiftness of Reilly's move but also how distraught Reilly *did not* appear when she left. Though it caused Dorian to feel lonely she did not allow her emotions to prevent her from teaching or receiving instruction. She had successfully awarded over half of her students from both classes with green belts and a few had even earned purple belts. Dorian was even now wearing a dark blue belt for her Kendo class (only two grades from black) and she had been given the privilege of bringing her Masamune sword to train with. She was spending even more time now meditating in the woods and often she would bring along the cherry blossoms. She couldn't resist the feeling they brought to her. When she looked at them or touched them, she couldn't drink in enough of their sweet serenity. She was actually rather enchanted by them. It seemed as though the melody she heard emanating from the flowers had gradually grown louder over the many months, but of course inaudible to any other. Often, she would dream of the flowers being cast upon the wind to take her to a new life. She surely enjoyed having that dream more than once. Her parents even noticed her obsession with cherry blossoms and, as corny as it may be, they had conspired together to buy a cherry tree for her 20th birthday that wasn't too far away. In fact, the last few months before her birthday flew right by! Master Hakira had awarded Dorian a black belt in the art of Kendo only a week prior to her birthday. It was a marvelous accomplishment for her. On top of that, *she* had awarded all of her students with either a green or purple belt in the art of Jiu-Jitsu and, at the graduation ceremony, gave two of her best students the privilege of demonstrating combat with the use of bokkens. It really was a splendid week as Dorian introduced her students to their new sensei, resigned from the Martial Academy (for now at least), and celebrated her 20th year of life. She was thrilled to receive the young cherry tree her parents had given her! It puzzled yet excited them to see their daughter so delighted with something as simple as a plant. Immediately after giving it to her all three of them found a spot in the backyard and planted it. Family tree-planting may certainly be a remarkably cheesy pastime…but her parents would inevitably cherish the moment as one of their last with their beloved Dorian.

The day after her birthday, while she was in her room writing, Dorian was disrupted by a sensational sound coming from the cherry blossoms. It wasn't the usual tune she heard but more of a continuous tone. It wasn't in the least bit irritating but she could not understand why it had changed. She pulled open the baseboard concealing the priceless blossoms then opened her treasure box. The moment she opened it a gust of wind passed through her window, sweeping the flowers along with it. "Wait! No!" Dorian cried as she rushed to the window with an outstretched arm. But to her astonishment, they seemed only to hover in the wind just outside her window. *What?* Dorian didn't understand. She searched her mind for a logical explanation but what she was witnessing defied numerous scientific laws and she was left utterly dumbfounded! However, she could not deny the pull of her heart that she felt towards the flowers. Staring up at the flowers, she thought of the many dreams she had. She thought of her fantasy tales. She thought of her daydreams of somewhere else, somewhere better, where she truly belonged…a place that would understand her. With just a moment of thought Dorian turned back into her room and sat at her desk. After writing a note to her parents she packed a few things in a small pack, swung her Masamune scabbard with the katana over her back, and headed outside determined to follow the cherry blossoms wherever they took her. *I'm a bloody moron. I'm a crazy bloody fool!* An hour or so later, Dorian's parents arrived home from shopping to find a note on the kitchen counter:

Dear Mom and Dad,

I knew if I had spoken to you first, you would have either locked me in my room or sent me to an insane asylum! Believe me, I even thought of admitting myself to one! Instead I chose to listen to my heart. I guess you can say I've gone off on an adventure. I'm not a little girl anymore, so you can trust I will be just fine. I wish I could tell you where I am going...but quite honestly I'm not too sure myself. I haven't a clue when I'll return but know that I love you both deeply and I'll carry you always in my heart. When the time comes I will return home and tell you of the adventure I seem to be now embarking on. Please don't consume yourselves with worry and take care while I'm away!

All my love,

Dorian

Chapter 3
Welcome

The cherry blossoms travelled a current of wind close enough to the ground for Dorian to keep them in eyesight. When she first left her house it was around two in the afternoon. At first she followed the flowers down a few main roads then they took Dorian through a couple of parks and down streets no longer in use. By the time she reached a playground, a few miles from the base of Mt. Solace, twilight had arrived and brought with it a crisp greeting. The cherry blossoms fell from the current onto a platform of the playground – the top deck with the Captain's wheel to be precise. Dorian climbed up the tiny ladder and snuggled herself in the corner of the little, wooden structure. Pulling off her pack, she grabbed an apple, bottle of water, and pita she had packed. She then pulled out a tiny blanket she brought along and made herself comfortable…well, as comfortable as she could get, sleeping on wood and using a near empty pack for a pillow. With her arms brought back, supporting her head, Dorian gazed up to the stars and imagined what lie ahead for her. She questioned her sanity in following three cherry blossoms to god-knows-where for whatever bizarre purpose but then thought of how often she dreamt of this very thing happening to her. She was finally escaping from the routine life she loved yet hated. She was finally on a mystery adventure she was sure would bring to her life something new and desired. Though Dorian was twenty, there was not a seven-year-old child on the earth that could have anticipated with their imagination the very quest she had begun. *Am I on a quest? A voyage…journey…adventure? Am I exploring? What on earth am I going to tell people if and when I return, "Oh, I just spent the last while on an escapade with three cherry blossoms"??* Despite her inquisitive, sarcastic state of mind, Dorian was exhausted and it did not take long before she was fast asleep with the flowers safely beside her.

When she awoke the next morning, Dorian had another apple and a bit of water before tossing the cherry blossoms in the air so they could catch a current of wind once more. Off they drifted, still heading east towards Mt. Solace. Within about a three hour hike along a back road, she reached the base of the dormant volcano. As she stretched her neck in order to glance up to the peak, Dorian realized just how difficult this was really going to be. She decided a five minute break to rest and have water would be the best idea before engaging the mountain where the cherry blossoms hovered in the wind just above the peak. *I can do this. I CAN do this.* Dorian gathered her nerve and began the climb. It started out as any mountainous hike would. The grade of ascent was gradual as a path wound through out pines, shrubbery, and overgrowth. She passed a few small creeks, harmless deer, and too many berry bushes to count. About an hour or so into her hike, the path curved sharply to the left, looping back down but in order for Dorian to reach the top, she had to leave the path and travel through and further up the forested mountain. At first it wasn't too hard but she soon encountered steep inclines, tight edges, loose rock…everything an amateur would hope NOT to experience on a hike. Four hours had passed by since starting her hike and looking up she noticed there was still a nauseating distance between her and the peak. *Aw hell! I'm out of my mind.* She was just at a drop-off, making eye contact with the tips of a few of the lower trees, when she sat in the shade of a crevasse to rest once more, eat a little, and rehydrate. That's when she noticed it. She couldn't believe what she was seeing. Only about twenty yards ahead of her, crouching under a tree, was a terrifyingly large tiger. *Dear god, no! What is a tiger doing HERE!?* Dorian dared not look away yet she knew not to bring herself to look directly into its eyes. It was beautiful, no doubt, and clearly a male. It certainly seemed powerful and quite a bit larger than any tiger she had ever read about or seen. It also seemed…more exuberant in color…and his charming, inquisitive stare only complimented the oaf-like grin, she could swear she noticed across his face. Uneasy and unsure of whether to feel safe or terrified, Dorian slowly and very quietly continued along the rocky edge before gripping the spaces above her, to climb the remainder of the small cliff vertically, rather than risk passing the tiger…despite its luring composure. Only about an hour later, to Dorian's surprise, she reached the peak of the volcano. It was warm even though air is supposed to be colder the higher the altitude. The trees, grass, and display around her appeared very healthy and she saw no evidence of it having ever erupted. Trusting it was dormant, she confidently walked to the edge of the ¼ mile large diameter of the opening to its black depths. The cherry blossoms had ever hovered above Dorian and now, turning to ensure their presence, she watched all three at once fall from the sky as if weighted and disappear into the volcano. *You have GOT to be kidding me.* A river of thoughts flooded her mind as she felt the adrenaline rush through her body and her nerves tighten. On the one hand, she was eager to continue and discover what lie ahead but on the other hand, leaping into the spout of a volcano was irrefutably and no less than psychotic! Dorian turned to appreciate the breath-taking view of her city as the sun began to set. The landscape was drenched in a deep orange and serenaded by the songs of robins, herons, and tiny birds thanking the sun for a glorious day. Dorian contemplated turning back. She was afraid. Scared of what might not lie ahead. She focused her gaze in the direction of her neighborhood and with a deep breath uttered a farewell to her parents before turning back to face her doorway. She recalled a lesson once with Master Hakira, when he told her the secret to relinquish fear, one needs only to clear one's mind. Fear cannot consume where it cannot dwell. Remembering this, Dorian closed her eyes and imagined her dreams of finding an enchanting world. She let her poems and stories of eternal sunsets and vivid colors and aromas come alive in her mind. She basked in the splendor of a divine peace as her heart rate slowed, breathing steadied, and muscles relaxed. With her mind now clear as a glacier lake, she opened her eyes and leapt into the darkness.

Plummeting to the bottom, Dorian noticed the hard rock bed but instead of fearing for her life, she stared at the barrier and with a cry from her heart cried, "Please! Open to somewhere new!" She immediately had to close her eyes for a blinding light crept from beneath while the rock moaned and boiled. Dorian was only seconds away from impact. *Well...at least I'll be the only person to ever die in bubbling volcano pudding!* She reached the bottom and sank right through. Not unlike quick sand, the rocks enveloped her body and drew her further down. Before she knew what had happened, Dorian found herself looking across what seemed to be a never-ending meadow. She dropped from the sky (though it seemed only inches) onto down-soft, luscious green grass. She took in a deliciously warm breath of cinnamon-sweet air then opened her eyes to see a canvas of golden, crimson sky, emerald grass stretching for miles, and a lurid floral tapestry that would most certainly constitute as a bee's paradise. Dorian's mouth gaped. *I knew it.*

"Helloooo!" Dorian looked around to find the voice but saw only a blue bird.

"Welcome!" Said another voice but again Dorian saw only two blue birds swooping here and there. One of the birds perched itself on a tree branch a few feet from where Dorian was standing.

Again, a feminine phantom spoke, "My name is Dekel!"

"And my name is Adalei!" Dorian heard as the second blue bird joined the other on the branch. Then, in unison, the two voices proclaimed, "We're here to greet you!" It was then that Dorian noticed the birds' beaks and reactions had perfect timing to the voices speaking to her. *Is it possible?* Dorian stepped a touch closer to where the birds were perched and tilted her head slightly while focusing her attention on their little faces,

"Hi…" Dorian said with uncertainty, "I'm Dorian." The blue birds smiled and Dorian's suspicions were confirmed. *Fantastic!* She continued but spoke more assuredly now and looking around asked, "So what or where is this?"

The bird on the left, who seemed to be Dekel, perked up, "This is the Core World…"

"…beneath the surface of the Withering World!" Adalei finished.

"…though a separate world, another realm…" Dekel added.

"Wise Bright sent *us* to greet you!" They exclaimed enthusiastically in unison as they smiled, rocking their little bodies, as a child does when he or she is nervous or excited while sitting.

Dorian was now quite amused by her new animated friends. She returned their smile and inquired further, "Who is – Wise Bright?"

Adalei answered swiftly, "He is the small cherry tree of whom the cherry blossoms that led you here were plucked."

Dekel went on, "He is an ancient: one of the first to enter and establish the Core World. He has been on the Council for over two millennia!"

"But conversation is best left for walking now. We must get Dorian to the Council!" Adalei left the branch and Dekel followed suit. Dorian joined them as they headed east along a carpet of greens, yellows, pinks, reds…every color imaginable but luminescent and richer; and each flower, berry, blade of grass – everything! emanated its own aroma that was divinely enchanting. And it was not a nauseatingly suffocating chemical-rich scent. No. This was subtle. Desirable. A stream bordered the north of the meadow. Its water was clear and calm as an untouched, country lake and it glittered with tropical beauty of turquoise and white. The sky was brushed with warmth and with no apparent sun there was still a brilliance that shone all around.

"So how did this Core World come into existence, if you don't mind my asking?" Dorian asked the birds.

Dekel spoke first, "We expected the question, my dear."

"O yes! How could you not wonder?" Adalei added. Taking turns in speech, Adalei and Dekel went on to explain to Dorian of the Spirit that formed the Withering World, the eruption of volcanoes in the first millennium, the migration of humans and creatures alike to the *gate*, and the establishment of the Council. They also explained the course of change many creatures undertook and how after only a few months of living in the Core World, one would find he or she had a glow – which was why they were called Brights. With both girls explaining the story in divided thoughts it was somewhat difficult to comprehend as well as time consuming. By the time they came to their conclusion, Dorian looked ahead to see an enormous redwood with a pocket at the bottom where it seemed this Council gathered. She stepped over and down the large root to join the circle.

"Well done, ladies. Well done." Serian said to Adalei and Dekel. Together they responded, "Thank you, Serian!" But seeing as how they knew they were neither part of the Council nor privileged to bear witness to any of its proceedings, they smiled at Dorian then flew away. Dorian stood in the center of the ring, casually studying each of the members. All were eye-catching but she found herself captivated by the power and loveliness of the tiger standing upon a stone next to a small cherry tree. *That must be Wise Bright that the blue birds spoke of.*

"Welcome, Dorian. I am Wise Bright, the ancient of the Council of the Core World. Welcome to Minaleth. You need not be afraid, sweet girl." Wise Bright spoke as a grandfather would speak to a friend of his granddaughter.

Dorian met the little black eyes of Wise Bright and smiled, "I'm not afraid, sir. Not at all! I think this is all wonderful." She smiled as she looked around to each member (she had to tilt her head to catch the eyes of Klum). Her eyes then fell once more upon Grenig and she knew exactly why he seemed familiar, "You're the tiger I saw on the mountain near the cliff, aren't you?"

All eyes, particularly Fayden's, turned to Grenig, "Grenig! What were you doing alone in the Withering World without anyone's knowledge?" Fayden asked not angrily but rather concerned and annoyed.

"I was only ensuring the girl was safe and in the right direction, sister." Grenig drew a surprised expression of shock from everyone's face as he, instead of cowering with a whine, stood erect with his head high. Serian couldn't help but smile with pride. Even Fayden smiled (almost giggling) after her immediate displeasure of course.

Fayden turned to Dorian, "Dorian, glad to see you arrived, *safely...*" Fayden turned her head subtly towards Grenig as she said this with a smirk, "...my name is Fayden. I assume you are curious as to the nature of your presence here. Did the blue birds give you any briefing regarding the reason for us calling you?"

"Travelling cherry blossoms certainly are a unique way of summoning someone." Dorian smiled again while a few of the members released a chuckle, "Adalei and Dekel told me of how the Core World was established, how you're known as Brights, and how some creatures have evolved."

Fayden asked, "Did they not tell you of the exact reason to why we have called you here?"

"No ma'am. Just as they were finishing explaining the Core World we arrived here at the Council."

Fayden turned to Wise Bright and without saying anything, Wise Bright said to her, "You may tell her, Commander."

Fayden is the Commander. A female tiger. That's fantastic!
Fayden faced Dorian again and went on to explain how some of the creatures had turned into Dark beings and were since called

Shadows. She told of how Nitris was once part of the Council but now the leader of the Shadows and was currently devising a war against the Brights to claim all of the Core World – not just the valley of Minaleth and possibly more.

Wise Bright broke in for a moment, "In the establishment of the Core World, the ancient Council created a safeguard against the outbreak of war. We set a law that a warrior from the Withering World was to aid us if we hoped to be successful. That is where you come in, dear."

"Yes. Now more than ever we are in a state of detriment. Nitris has disappeared and we know not what she is scheming. Our desire is to train you so you may fight with us against the enemy." Fayden looked as though she slightly bowed to Dorian.

Dorian's first thought was *why me?* but she found the situation intriguing and was quite honored to have been the chosen warrior of the Withering World to help reclaim Minaleth. After a short pause of mind stirring, Dorian clapped her hands together with a smile and looked around at the Council members, "Super! So what's the plan?"

The Council seemed unprepared for such a response. Each were looking at one another in confusion and slight concern, "Are you not – frightened – or nervous or in disbelief? " Asked Strike. "Do you have no other inquiries or concerns?" Asked Ostel.

"Not really. I have longed for a beautiful world beyond my own and a journey of importance such as this for many years. My poetry, stories, dreams…I don't know how but the concept of the Core World, Brights, and Shadows has always consumed my mind." Dorian was now slowly walking around the circle speaking to each member and making hand gestures of enthusiasm.

Wise Bright let out a laugh, "Afraid? Confused? We have all watched this young girl grow in age, beauty, and strength since infancy. We are all aware of her capabilities. Dear girl, I see that you *are* a *warrior* in all aspects." He smiled then discreetly winked at Dorian.

"Well then! What more needs be said?" Fayden proclaimed, "Our young warrior, Dorian, is sure to bring pride and hope to all our hearts!"

The Council cheered (rather roared, shouted, squawked, and moaned) and left their stones to personally introduce their selves to Dorian, now that formalities were swept aside. Dorian shared a good laugh with Klum and Ostel, expressed admiration to Flutter and Strike's amazing colors and ability to fly, unreservedly embraced Grenig with a hug and gentle kiss on his whiskered cheek, and gracefully embraced Serian, as one would a past professor or old friend. She bent down to shake Wise Bright's – *branch* – but he pulled her in softly to give her a surprisingly gentle hug. Then she stepped in front of Fayden who was still on her stone seat. Fayden smiled down to Dorian and gracefully walked to stand directly in front of her. For a moment, they only exchanged stares of wonder and gratitude, then, because of Fayden's magnificent size, Dorian wrapped her arms around Fayden's neck without even bending. As she did this, Fayden glanced over Dorian's shoulder to see Wise Bright delightfully observing the sincere expression of trust. Fayden thoughtfully smiled back to Wise Bright before briefly shutting her eyes to accept the gesture then pulling away to speak.

"Flutter, would you kindly take Dorian around the meadow, perhaps introduce her to a few Brights, then show her where she will be staying?"

Flutter flew up beside Dorian instantly, "Of course, Commander! I would be delighted. Come on, Dorian! The meadow is beautiful and I can take you to the Faerie Willows!"

***

Each creature that Flutter introduced to Dorian was as enthused to see her as the next. Dorian was quite taken aback by the Faerie Willows. So many vibrant colors of wings and hair (some of which she had never seen before) and their icy-blue, piercing eyes were almost hypnotizing. In the first few centuries, the faeries had converted a cluster of willow trees into communities. Of course these willows were much larger than they naturally are in the Withering World. The trunks had been hollowed and a system of tunnels and caverns had been built beneath the ground. The majority of faeries nearing or beyond the age of one thousand years lived in the caverns. They preferred the dimmer, quieter atmosphere apart from the younger, energetic generation that occupied the trunks and branches. The faeries were superior carpenters. Not just the men either. The women, teenagers, and even the older children demonstrated remarkable skill with their unique tools and methods of construction. Their fascinating tools were such as the *hitrum, squeezely, corkin, and sever.* Dorian couldn't help but snicker at how adorable they all looked with their tiny tool belts attached to their waists. It seemed all the men and boys were clothed in coffee-colored trousers of an unknown soft yet durable material. They wore loose pants with the sides ripped from hip to ankle then laced back up with a lighter shade of material. All displayed a bare torso. Each male faerie had a small dagger in a holster around his waist and wore a small necklace made of a round solid iron medallion depicting a cherry blossom with words of a different language around the circumference. The female faeries wore coverings of the same coffee-colored material over their chest, exposing their naval and collar bone while their bottom half was covered with a slightly more fitting version of trousers. They, too, wore the same iron necklace but instead of carrying a dagger around their waists, each female carried a small bow and quiver wrapped over one shoulder and around the back. Neither female nor male wore shoes of any kind, strictly barefoot, and all had short, flipped out hair littered with layers that came just below the chin. And of course they all had angel-like wings of feathers which were an identical color to each faerie's hair.

Dorian very much enjoyed meeting the faeries and after visiting the Faerie Willows, Flutter took her around the meadow to meet other animals and creatures. She also showed Dorian around the forest as well as the Rainfalls. The Rainfalls were a series of waterfalls that came down as rain would, in a curtain of drops, rather than in a thunderous avalanche. The sight was breathtaking and the sound of thousands of little drops gently falling into calm, clear pools was relaxing; a wild stallion could not have resisted standing in silence to soak in the splendor. Eventually Dorian and Flutter made their way past a group of Giants where Klum introduced them to a few friends. Ostel and the Grostels of the Lake along with Strike and his fellow dragonflies also crossed paths with the girls on their little adventure of introductions. Flutter eventually steered herself and Dorian back to the gate in the Eastern Absent (it was called this due to its lack of inhabitants because it was simply a pathway to travelers).

"Look up, Dorian. Do you see the rock sky? Here, it is the sky but from above, it is the bedrock of your Mt. Solace. This is what you passed through to enter the Core World." Flutter explained as she and Dorian tilted their heads upwards to examine the portal between Worlds.

"How *does* one pass through, Flutter? I mean – I understand the rock basically liquefies – but *how* does it liquefy?" Dorian asked. Flutter shook her head, "I wish I could enlighten you, child, but it is unknown how or why the rock transforms. Some conjured a theory that it is the heat of the molten core that creates our warm, climatically and in color, atmosphere and it is this atmosphere that somehow causes the rock to become malleable. Of course, there are holes in this theory, which is why we let the matter be. What we do understand is that somehow, by the will of magik, those that are meant to pass through the gate are capable."

Dorian was still quite curious but satisfied knowing she was not alone in her curiosity. They turned to continue west and followed the North Stream for a short while before reaching a fort…if one could call it that. The outer wall was formed by an enormous ring of redwoods while cabins of large river stones speckled the inner landscape. Countless creatures of all sorts lived in the protection of what they called Redwood Wall. When the Brights were exiled from heart of Minaleth to its outskirts, Redwood Wall was settled as their new home. If you can picture a mid-large sized island, that is approximately the size of Redwood Wall. With the exception of the faeries and Grostels, all Brights were neighbors to one another which made it necessary for the fort to spread so far. A smaller forest within Redwood Wall acted as a canopy over the stone cabins and provided homes for smaller animals. Flutter led Dorian near the center where, in no shape in particular, a group of cabins were shadowed and encompassed by dense maples trimmed with hemlock. They were neither ornamented nor labeled in any form but it was clear to Dorian that this was where the Council made home. Flutter pointed out which member occupied each cabin then directed Dorian to what seemed to be one newly made next to that of Fayden.

"This is your cabin, Dorian. A committee of faeries and I built it just last week for your use. I hope it is to your pleasure." Flutter said looking proudly over the small architecture.

Dorian let her mouth drop slightly as she walked the perimeter of the cabin before examining inside and peaking out again, "This was built for me? My goodness Flutter! It is absolutely sensational. Why on earth did you all go to so much trouble just for me? I would have been glad to sleep under the stars…well…under the sky, I guess, or in a tent."

"We are more than willing to comfortably accommodate our warrior. And you know we faeries adore construction! Anyhow, Fayden suggested it would be best suited for you to have your own private quarters. She said 'we all need solitude at times'."

"Thank you so much Flutter! You will let the others that helped build it know that I am thoroughly impressed and sincerely grateful!?" Dorian said with glee.

Flutter smiled, "Of course I will. They'll certainly be glad to hear how thrilled you are." She discreetly followed as Dorian studied the artwork of her cabin in amazement. It was of simple construction but given the finest detailing that would have astounded even Michelangelo. The stones used were taken from the river that ran from the Rainfalls which left them smooth as a ping pong ball. Engraved in the stones around the entrance-way, about the size and shape of a regular door-way, were words of the ancient language. She lightly let her fingers absorb the beautifully obscure language as she grazed each letter – keeping her eyes closed to exaggerate her sense of touch. She continued admiring the cabin, discovering sporadic stones engraved of words or phrases of the ancient language or symbols that she could only assume had profound meaning. The stones were not simply grey but naturally colored of onyx, sienna, chestnut, and cream and each was laid upon another with a thin layer of what Flutter called "pudd". The roof was domed with ebony wood that came a ¼ part lower than the top of the cabin's body all around. Inside was illuminated by a single candle-lit lantern hanging from the center of the ceiling. The stone walls of the circular room were fixated with wooden hooks and rods while the ground had been overlaid with sheets of a straw that, with the plush grass beneath, created a wonderfully soft floor. A mammoth-sized hammock made of material Dorian was unaccustomed to spread across the right side of the room with a nicely folded sheet at one end and a pillow resting on top. Across from the hammock was a chair carved of a linwood-sort of tree and adorned with a full map of Minaleth – its heart and surrounding regions. Resting on the seat of the chair was a pair of black, leather-like, knee-high boots with a guard built into the shin. Hanging on one of the hooks above the chair was – a garment of sorts – made of gentle, suede-like material but with the sustainability of folded steel. The top was a black and deep navy blue, over-one-shoulder corset-style that met fitted trousers, of the same coloring at the hips and was connected with a red and black marbled belt that was fitted with a holster for a dagger. In the center from the ridge of the chest to the bottom edge of the corset-top was a navy-blue strip that tapered from top to bottom. This was bordered on each side by thinner silver strips. Dangling from the top of the hanger was a pair of black, elbow-length leather-like gloves, also fitted with armor along the forearm and knuckles, to complete the outfit. Seeing no reason why not to make use of her new home, Dorian removed the katana still slung over her back and placed it between two hooks on the wall and hung her pack on another hook. Turning to see a thoughtful smile from Flutter, the two girls left the cabin so Flutter could continue their tour. Fayden's cabin was to the left of Dorian's, then Wise Bright's (it was much smaller), and to her right were Serian's, Grenig's, and Klum's (his was rather gigantic, for obvious reason). Strike may have been an animated dragonfly, but he was still a bug nevertheless, so he set up home in the leaves of silver birches with the rest of his kind. In the middle of the ring of Council members' cabins, Flutter and Dorian spotted Fayden sauntering past the fire-pit.

Flutter flew to the Commander for a moment then back to Dorian, "I'm going to leave you in the company of Fayden now," she smiled, "I will see you tonight at the fire. Enjoy acquainting yourself with your new home!"

Dorian waved as Flutter flew off towards Faerie Willows, "Thank you, Flutter!" She shouted.

***

Fayden approached Dorian neither smiling nor frowning but with a look of contentment. Dorian was not afraid but she couldn't help but feel a hint of nervousness towards the tiger. With good reason too! Not only was Fayden the Commander but she was an overwhelming, robust display of power and beauty of phenomenal contours and color. Even her eyes grasped one's attention with their sharp, olive green and amber luster. Without speaking, just a twitch of her head, Fayden motioned for Dorian to follow her back to Dorian's cabin. Dorian stood once more at the doorway, entranced by the incomprehensible writing surrounding it. It was then that she heard Fayden dimly utter words Dorian had never heard before. When Fayden was silent, Dorian inquired, "Commander...what was that you were just speaking?"

Fayden faced Dorian, "Please, Dorian, call me Fayden. It was the ancient language. Beautiful, is it not? I was reading the script the faeries engraved surrounding your doorway:

Nokun terr reyh yevir kuna vodan; nokun corris reyh yevir kuna terr. Kelden reyla bej ihn rol wilrev."

"What does that mean?" Asked Dorian.

"Without fear, there can be no courage; without love, there can be no fear. Grasp that which leads one to victory. It is an ancient proverb to encourage. The faeries were wise to bless your cabin with such words." Fayden's voice rang with profound insight.

"How fantastic. Can you tell me what these other words and symbols around my cabin mean?" Dorian led Fayden to each of the sporadic stones depicting symbols, words, and phrases of the ancient language. Fayden certainly didn't possess the same comprehension as Wise Bright concerning the text but she was rather successful in translating the outside of the cabin for Dorian. It seemed the faeries took the liberty during construction to endow the cabin with words of confidence, phrases of protection, and symbols representing Dorian and her journey thus far (including her years in the Withering World). It was all marvelous.

"I trust you noticed the armor that has been made for you?" Fayden questioned after the last stone translation.

"Oh, yeah, that black – suede-ish outfit hanging inside?" Dorian appeared bemused with the subject, still drenched with fascination at the engravings.

"The material used to fabricate your armor is derived from the iron riverbed of the Core World. It can withstand any puncture, impact, tear, and even the sulfuric breath of Griffins. The plating in the boots, gloves, and abdomen are for added resilience. It,too, was designed by the faeries and pieced by their most skilled seamstresses." Fayden broke from her factual explanation, "And I mustn't forget, there are less restraining garments in the trunk just under your hammock. There is no need to wear your armor at all times and you'll find the trousers and tunics to be most comfortable." She smiled and shifted her weight, lifting one paw and batting her tail a few times.

"Well thank you, Commander – er – Fayden. This is really wonderful." Interrupting her sentence was a distinct tune Dorian knew she had heard before but she couldn't put her finger on where. Stepping outside with Fayden she was quick to realize the familiarity. The sound was coming from Wise Bright. It was the same melody Dorian heard from the cherry blossoms that brought her here. It was a call to all the Council members and others perceptive to the tune who were interested in gathering for dinner. Within minutes a group of around twelve, the Council as well as a few friends, gathered around the fire pit where a succulent feast of veggies, fruits, cheeses, and meat waited to be eaten. With arms spread wide in welcome, Wise Bright greeted each Bright as they joined company seated on the grass and directed Dorian and Fayden to sit near himself. With a wonderful introduction of gratitude to "Dorian, dear warrior and treasure of Minaleth" from Wise Bright, Dorian was applauded then shared a cup of sweet wine with the Brights before everyone indulged in the delectable meal. As the night went on music was played, tales were shared, and simple peace from the crackling of the fire was appreciated in silence. Time was a little different in the Core World, but what would have been the equivalent of around two in the morning was when everyone exchanged pleasantries before settling into their cabins to drift into still slumber.

Chapter 4
Prepare

It was shortly before dawn that Dorian awoke anxious to better acquaint herself with the landscape and history of Minaleth. She strolled down to the stream for a bath in the delightfully refreshing water, after which she dressed herself in a tunic and trousers that she pulled from the trunk under her hammock. They were exceptionally comfortable, neither itchy nor dense, not unlike fine linen. She casually made her way through the meadow until she came to the redwood where the Council meets. She circled the massive tree in awe, letting her fingers graze the bark, when she felt a change in consistency. She opened her eyes to see the engraving Serian had read to the Council before sending the cherry blossoms to the Withering World to beckon Dorian; the engraving that had been laid down by the ancient Council regarding the necessity of a foreign warrior. To her luck her intrigue was not abandoned to the morning mist, for a moment later Fayden quietly appeared just behind Dorian. She looked to the script then to Dorian who remained elated.

"It is a protocol established by the ancient Council. It explains how victory for Brights is only attainable with the aid of a warrior summoned from the Withering World." Fayden spoke gingerly, "It was written for the very time upon us…for the very life you have sought."

Dorian remained silent staring at the tree. With no sun to rise the sky just gradually grew brighter, warmer, and richer, accompanied by songs of birds and creatures meeting the new day. Rays of brilliance shone from the north, behind the tree, highlighting Fayden and Dorian's faces, particularly their eyes, causing them to slightly squint for a moment to adjust.

"In your world," Fayden began, "the sun rises in the east to greet the day. Minaleth does not have a sun, yet each new day is welcomed by outstretched rays. It is the magik of our world."

Fayden glanced down to see the girl contemplating the logic. She spoke again, "Do not entangle your mind with logic that will never be sound, dear girl."

Dorian's perplexed expression settled to contentment as she let go of what her mind so desperately wanted to explain. It was then that Dorian finally spoke, "It would be amazing to learn the ancient language."

Fayden smiled at the engraving, directing her words to Dorian but keeping her focus on the tree, "The majority of Brights are illiterate to the language. Only a handful is capable of recognizing words and speaking the dialect *nearly* correctly but Wise Bright is the only known Bright today to have full knowledge and understanding of it."

Dorian pursed her lips to the side and pointed to a word, unwilling to forfeit her interest, "What is this – **rol** – it's quite common?"

"**Rol** means *to*." Seeing the delight swirling through Dorian's eyes, Fayden continued, "This here, **ih**, as well as its variations, **ihe, ihr, ihu,** and **ihn** are generally possessive pronouns (as you may call them) meaning *mine, you, our, your,* and *one* (pertaining to an individual)."

"In my world, foreign languages are comprised of masculine and feminine words. Is it the same here?" Dorian asked.

Fayden smirked, looking a little puzzled, "How can a word be female or male? That seems odd. No, words of the ancient language are just words – neutral to the sexes." She couldn't help but chuckle to herself. For the following few hours of the early morning, Fayden helped Dorian understand many of the frequently used words and concepts of the ancient language. She also tried to teach Dorian the pronunciations but unfortunately the results were not so successful. It was not a supremely difficult dialect, void of the hacking associated with the French accent and the rolling tongue used in with Russian, but it was spoken with a slight whisper and hiss, much like a snake. Not to mention Fayden's roaring accent made for a few confused interpretations.

"Is there a term the Brights use in regards to the ancient language? I mean – instead of saying 'ancient language' – is there a name for it?" Dorian asked as the two began walking back to Redwood Wall for breakfast.

Brushing the grass with her paws, Fayden answered, "Yes. The ancient language is referred to as Silethin. It is derived of the words silek, meaning *whisper* (describing the manner in which it is spoken) and Minaleth, our beloved country."

"*Sigh-leth-een* – wow!" Dorian looked as though she had just returned home from the candy store.

***

Breakfast, consisting of eggs, some sort of bird, cheese, fruit, biscuits, and milk, had been prepared and quickly devoured by the still-waking Brights and the two early birds that had spent the morning learning Silethin. After eating, Wise Bright inquired as to the quality and comfort of Dorian's rest and garments while Serian and Grenig invited her on a walk through the meadows. Fayden however intervened to insist Dorian begin training sooner than later. Wise Bright, understanding she was neither slave nor servant, allowed Dorian the decision and in the end it was decided that she would train for the better part of the day then relax with Grenig and Serian. The Commander laid out quite the lesson plan:

- Learn names and locations of regions of Minaleth
- Learn offensive and defensive strategies of Shadows, Griffins, and other creatures following Nitris
- Practice endurance in running, swimming, and climbing
- Know the advantages and disadvantages of the Brights
- Learn edible flowers, berries, and plants and
- Weapons practice

Of course Fayden was not so daft to believe it was possible to complete the list in a single day, but she was certainly eager about, at least, an introduction to each task. Fayden led Dorian through the meadows towards the Lake, stooping at times to discuss the benefits of particular plants or flowers, all of which Dorian was certainly unfamiliar with. The *Swellip*, a plant resembling the marshmallow flower, was useful in reducing inflammation of wounds if one mixed it with cream as a drink. Cream, oddly enough, was produced by another plant. There was a type of moss, *Tynif Moss*, which grew on the west side of some trees that was rich in protein, making a great meal when cooked, as well, it was frequently used to mend torn skin. There were many flowers rich in nutrients, trees that provided perfect kindling or shelter, and even leaves capable of cleansing one's body. With each new botanical description came a story of its history and a time its particular attributes had been utilized in a dire situation.

When they reached the Lake, they were greeted by a school of Grostels that was not like a school of fish but quite literally, a *school* of young Grostels learning to dive for a period of time, tread water, float, and call to one another under water. When the youngsters caught sight of Fayden and Dorian, they all shouted greetings and splashed about as they made their ways to the shore to properly introduce their selves to the famed warrior. In high pitch, duck-like voices the boys and girls ooed and awed at Dorian and the privilege she had of spending her time with the Commander. The lot of them even permitted Dorian to tousle their fur when she commented on the superb distinction of their sapphire undercoats. The supervising Grostels exchanged polite greetings with Fayden and Dorian before urging the students to return to the lesson.

"Grostels are swift on land but under water one could miss them in a single blink. They are also capable of causing their surface fur to stand on end, exposing the colorful undercoat, which they use to blind and deter attackers and also to reflect the radiance of the sky to create the illusion of water (so they can swim unseen if need be)." Fayden leaned in to inform Dorian as they continued walking the perimeter of the Lake. It was not exceptionally large, about ten miles in diameter, but it did take the better part of a two-hour stretch on their stroll to reach the far end where a single willow tree stretched over the water. It was here that the two came to a rest beneath the dismal, flowing vines. Its bark was a deep, chocolate brown while the leaves were a matted, clove color. The two took a few moments to quench their thirst and refresh their stomachs with bread they brought along in Dorian's pack. Fayden then became sullen and focused a stare into Dorian's eyes.

"I remember once, an impossible many years ago when I was not quite so strong, a Griffin thought it amusing to surpass the boundaries in order to taunt some unfortunate Bright. Well, the misfortune took its course upon me. I had gone for a walk in the evening hours when the beast caught wind of my presence and unexpectedly attacked. I was smaller and weaker, so there was only so much I could do to defend myself against such a monstrosity of a creature. For a moment I was caught off guard and it took the opportunity to blind me with its sulfuric breath. Afraid I was at my end I decided to flee and in my desperation I hid within this very willow. I concealed myself at the top of the trunk, clinging for life, and crying a plea of salvation from my heart. The Griffin came to me. Glaring into my eyes with a grin, it crept closer to me and when I thought the end had come, a wave of arrows struck its side. I turned to see a small army of faeries armed and coming my way with immense speed. Well, I needn't express my relief and gratitude when the Griffin retreated in fear. When I asked how they knew where I was and that I was in need, they told me Wise Bright informed them of my urgent situation. When I returned to Redwood Wall, he explained that the roots of willows stretch to the iron river-bed, as do his, and the thoughts of one connected to the bark are carried along the river, just as the soil carries thoughts of torment. He felt my cry for help in his roots and told the faeries where to find me."

Dorian was wide-eyed and silent.

"Dorian, if there is ever a time that you are in desperate need for help, you simply need to lay a hand upon the bark of a willow tree, *any* willow tree, express your need, and someone will come to your aid without fail, as long as your need is of genuine peril or importance." Fayden brought her paw to Dorian's shoulder.

"Thank you Fayden. I will always remember that. And thank you for being so honestly vulnerable. I can imagine most beings here believe you have always been mighty and fierce."

Fayden brought her paw back down, "It is true but as you well know, strength and courage are acquired, not instilled at birth. And I believe you are one who is trustworthy and of noble character." They smiled to each other then made their way from the tree, back around the Lake, to return to Redwood Wall.

***

Upon returning to Redwood Wall, Dorian and Fayden were enthusiastically greeted by the rambunctious Adalei and Dekel. Together they carried a large document made of woven paper. As they got closer, Dorian was able to see that it was a map of some sort, complete with a legend and rose.

"Adi...Deki! How are you today?" Dorian called.

"Dorian!" They cried in unison then Adi began their ritualistic sharing of sentences, "Dorian! We took the liberty last night..."

Dekel continued, "...to create a personalized map of Minaleth for you!" Their excitement was nearly overwhelming and rather entertaining.

Fayden lowered her head in laughter, "Hahaha! Well aren't you girls ahead of the game! Let's take a look, shall we?"

Adalei and Dekel proudly smiled to one another as they lowered the map to the grass for Dorian and Fayden to inspect. For a couple of birds writing and drawing, it is understandable that the map was a little crude. It had been cleverly titled, **Dorian's Map of Minaleth**, with the lettering outlined in black and filled with a blue mineral. In something like child's writing, the Core World was quite accurately displayed and labeled. Each region was accompanied by either a symbol or picture pertaining to it and each symbol or picture was accented with color. Adi and Deki explained this was to add appeal. The bottom, right-hand corner read, **Created by Adalei and Dekel: blue birds of Minaleth**. Beneath this both girls had signed the document with impressions of their little bird feet.

"Well done, ladies. A finer map could not have been produced from even the Hawk Lords!" Fayden smiled and laughed as they landed to strut along her back.

"Thank you so much! I'll be sure to keep this with me always." Dorian said through her laughing.

Reaching their cabins, Dekel and Adalei parted while Fayden and Dorian joined Wise Bright and a few others for a mid-day meal. Grenig and Serian were not around and Fayden said she and Dorian had spent plenty of time in training for the day. So afterwards, Dorian retreated to her cabin and made herself comfortable on the hammock as she opened her specially-made map to study and memorize it. She also reviewed in her mind the variety of botanical remedies as well as Silethin words she learned earlier that day. She was just about to meander down to the Council's meeting place in the Eastern Absent when Grenig and Serian poked their heads into her cabin. The two invited her to the Rainfalls for a splash before supper. At first, she was confused as to what she would wear but Serian explained that humans in the Core World were accustomed to swimming in their clothing. Armor was best because it was water resistant but other garments dried quickly anyhow. So the trio made their way down to the Rainfalls where Dorian was introduced to completely alternate versions of Grenig and Serian. They acted as kittens, scratching, splashing, pouncing, diving, and dunking each other, as well as Dorian. Serian was like an uncle, paddling under the water to emerge with either Dorian or Grenig upon his back. Dekel and Adalei had heard the commotion nearby and joined in the fun; swooping here and there, clasping onto ears and hair or fur, and using the heads and shoulders of the others as personal rafts. Nearing nightfall, the dragonflies weaved through Redwood Wall, shimmering in the glow of numerous fires. Serian, Grenig, Dorian, Adalei and Dekel made their way back to join the others for dinner. Serian had not been exaggerating about the quick-drying garments. Within minutes, Dorian's clothes were fully dry and the only thing remaining soaked was her hair.
***

Reilly? What are you doing? Where did you learn to do that?

Aahh! That sword isn't blunted now knock it off! Damn it, Reilly, what the hell is your problem!? Why are you attacking me?

Fine! Have it your way!

What did you expect? You could threaten me unjustly without consequence?

Reilly stop! Faeries LIVE in those willows! Stop, STOP!
Flutter!!!
Why is no one listening to me? Grenig! Get help! Ostel,
get all the Grostels and bring the Giants!! Grenig!!
Ostel!!!
Reilly! What have you done? Why is no one aware that
I'm here!? AAAHHHHH!
Fayden! Fayden, watch out behind you!!! Please,
PLEASE, hear me! Reilly don't!! I'm begging you, no!
Fayden!!! NOOOOOO! NOOOOOOOO FAYDEN!!!!!
You can't be!! Please no!! Fayden get up!!! GET UP!!!!
Wise Bright!? Wise Bright where are...no...my god,
REILLY WHAT HAVE YOU DONE!?!?! Wise Bright!!!
Serian!? Klum?? Deki! ANYBODY!?!?!?!
No, no, no, NOOOOOOOOOOOO!!!
***

Dorian awoke drenched in sweat with Fayden's beautiful, enormous head only inches from her own.

"Dorian! Dear! It's ok! It was merely a dream." Fayden had one paw gently resting on Dorian's right arm as she sweetly leaned in to graze Dorian's face ever so gently with her tongue.

Dorian sat up to immediately embrace Fayden as she sobbed into the tiger's thick, soothing fur. She explained her nightmare with great distress, commenting on the absurdity of Reilly's involvement, but Fayden kept the girl close and reassured her everyone was in good health and this girl Reilly hadn't the ability to enter the Core World. This comforted Dorian's trembling nerves but it still took most of the morning hours to regain her composure. To help calm her young friend, Fayden went around the cabin translating the Silethin words and symbols inside, so Dorian would have better understanding of the inside now, as well as the outside. She also wanted to take Dorian's mind away from the nightmare. When she had become completely calm, she and Fayden joined Wise Bright and Serian for mid-day meal. They were concerned about Dorian's state but Fayden explained she was simply distraught from a dream. Wise Bright and Serian offered their condolences but Dorian insisted she would be fine as the day went on.

Not wanting the young warrior to dwell on the dream, Fayden suggested they get started with the day's training. So the two finished their meal with Serian and Wise Bright then headed back to Dorian's cabin. At first, Dorian was unsure as to why they were going to her cabin again but Fayden explained she would need her armor today to properly grasp the lessons. Well, without say, this made Dorian slightly nervous but most definitely intrigued. She changed into her pristinely mint outfit of armor, with plenty of squeezing, wriggling, and zipping, then pulled on the boots and slipped on the gloves. Fayden nudged the katana, hanging on the hooks, with her nose so it dropped into her mouth then gave it to Dorian to put over her back. Fayden was astounded by the metal work and detailing of the sword and asked Dorian about it. Dorian explained how she had received the katana as a gift for her birthday then gave a brief history of its maker, Masamune Okazaki, and its significance. The Commander was thoroughly impressed, commenting that such a remarkable piece of weaponry was destined for a remarkable warrior, such as Dorian. After the sentiments, she and Fayden travelled over to the Rainfalls where Fayden explained that today Dorian was going to practice swimming, diving, and climbing with her armor. Not as difficult as one may think – her armor did not weigh that of a medieval knight's armor – however it was constricting and added a few extra pounds which made the tasks challenging. Hopping into the pool beneath the falls, Dorian soon discovered just what Fayden had meant when she said she was going to teach her endurance. She was not overwhelmingly heavy of armor but her body was unable to exercise the usual flexibility in swimming. The boots caused problems when kicking and her sword continuously knocked at her bum. Fayden just wanted Dorian to be able to tread water smoothly for at least five minutes but even that took over an hour to accomplish.

"You'd think the magik of this world would cause this armor to be weightless and comfortable as silk!" Dorian commented, sputtering as she spoke.

"You need to allow your feet to sway slowly, forward and back, because if you kick in a hurry the density and bulkiness of your boots will not only cramp your legs but also bring your body deeper." Fayden shouted to Dorian through the splashing and coughing. "Don't forget to tilt your sword back a bit so when you are treading, the scabbard flows along the contours of your back rather than at the sides or high enough to hit your head."

Through her spitting, Dorian replied, "I…I think… [cough]…I've got it!" Dorian shouted in delight, "How's that?"

"Excellent, dear, excellent! Now try to swim a bit. Just a few feet." Said the tiger.

Dorian did so brilliantly and with the newly developed confidence in her system, she even managed to swim the diameter of the pool instead of simply a few feet. Fayden was supremely impressed and called Dorian back for more instruction.

"By the way," Fayden added, "the magik of this world HAS been used in the construction of your armor. Consider how it would compare in your world, as it is made of iron with integrated plating."

Dorian couldn't argue.

Once again, she swam the distance with little disruption and a sense of ownership over the water. Of course, she was not perfect in the strokes and grace had not yet set in, but she was travelling at a decent pace without being tangled or dropping beneath the water's surface. Fayden gave Dorian a rest before challenging her to swim around the whole of the pool, under the curtain of rain drops as well. Before setting off to accomplish the task, Fayden offered a few tips about breathing patterns and movement that would make it a little easier. Dorian made it around the pool wonderfully. She incorporated a touch of grace this time as she made use of the butterfly stroke. When she reached Fayden again, the Commander had her circle the pool once more but this time using the forward stroke. She explained that there may come a time when the butterfly stroke would prove a disadvantage and it would be best if she were capable of various strokes. Dorian had no objections but this time really was a challenge. The constriction of her armor made it difficult to bring her arms around and over her head (due to the breastplate digging slightly into her bosom). But nevertheless, she succeeded and took another break when she returned to Fayden. A couple of hours now passed and Dorian had successfully learned to tread, swim using the butterfly stroke as well as the forward stroke, breathe in a way to conserve air, and kick in a way to conserve energy. All while in her armor. Fayden thought the day had been more than reasonably productive and was ready to pack it in to head back to Redwood Wall. Dorian, on the other hand, was eager to continue her exploration of aquatic movement.

"Can you teach me to dive?" She asked, climbing out of the pool to sit with Fayden on the grassy shore.

Fayden raised her feline brows, "You really want to learn that today? We can always return and continue another day if you would prefer."

"No, no! I would really like to learn now! I'm exhilarated and focused and you even said you wanted to teach me endurance. What better way than to show me how to dive in my armor while I'm spent?!" Dorian insisted.

Seeing there really was no way to dissuade the young warrior, Fayden submitted to Dorian's request, "Alright! You truly are much more spirited than we expected!" She motioned for Dorian to return to the water, "Now, when you're diving with armor, you need to remember that the added weight will cause you to sink with more ease. So if you relax your body while under, you will not float to the surface as you are accustomed to." She went on to explain that Dorian need only propel herself by kicking her feet once she was underwater. Using her arms for more than steering would only cause her body to jerk, thus frustrating her endeavor. She also mentioned that should Dorian run out of breath before being able to surface there was a particular coral that behaved as an air pocket. Fayden reassured her they were very kind and Dorian need only point to her mouth for the coral to allow her to breathe through its porous surface.

"Excuse me?" Dorian was not so much surprised as she was confused.

"The corals are very kind creatures and understand that many animals and humans are incapable of breathing underwater. Just be sure to make it clear you are in need of air otherwise you may just find yourself engorged by bubbles."

Dorian raised both brows in astonishment but then noticed Fayden turning her head ever so slightly to hide a smirk. She then lowered one brow while keeping the other raised in disillusionment, "Is that so?"

Fayden displayed a completely alternate persona than that most had known her for. She was no longer able to contain her laughter from her *almost* deceptive notion of irritable coral. She burst out laughing, purring as she did so, while with one paw she clenched her side, "Oh dear! I couldn't resist! All this training must be getting to my head."

Dorian also laughed, for the sight of an enormous tiger of the highest rank losing control to look more like an orange, cartoon kitten than the mighty Commander she was, was far too entertaining not to, "'All this training'! You haven't even gotten wet!"

"Well then! Perhaps I'll join you this time." Fayden leapt into the pool with Dorian and both immediately twisted their bodies to disappear beneath the surface. Maneuvering upright, both relaxed their bodies and faced each other, while gently treading the water in order to stay in place. Fayden glanced at Dorian then pointed downwards, indicating they should try going deeper. Dorian turned herself over and following Fayden's previous instructions, kept her arms pointed forward while using only her legs to propel forward (or down, rather). Fayden certainly brought new meaning to 'water-loving cats'. Her two front legs were outstretched with her paws overlapping each other and her hind legs dangled behind her as she kicked her back paws the way a duck paddles its feet. It undoubtedly looked amusing but at the same time one would find utter fascination in the sight. The two swam deeper until they reached the bottom then allowed their selves to drift directly beneath the gently churning falls. Impressively, about five minutes passed before Dorian expressed the need for more air. Unexpectedly, Fayden paddled to a nearby coral and waved Dorian over. Completely aghast with uncertainty, Dorian remained floating where she was, but Fayden kept looking back and forth between the coral and Dorian until Dorian made her way over. She raised her arms in question but watched as Fayden gripped the sides of the coral with her paws then placed her mouth to it. She was astonished to see a jet of bubbles protrude from the other side as Fayden inhaled. Dorian decided to do the same and found herself dumbfounded as air flowed into her lungs. She looked to Fayden then pointed to the surface and both ladies swam upwards. Bursting from the water without gasping for air, Dorian inquired about the coral phenomenon, "I thought you were only joking!?"

Fayden smiled, "I was joking about asking for permission from the coral and the coral potentially attacking, but as you now know, coral truly is porous and capable of providing air."

"That *is* remarkable!" Dorian exclaimed.

Now that they had experienced basic diving, the two agreed it was time to call it a day, so they climbed out of the water to return to Redwood Wall. Perfect timing too because by the time they would arrive it would be time for dinner. They hadn't touched on climbing yet (Fayden planned to get Dorian to climb the Rainfalls) but Dorian would need more strength than she had to safely learn. She was once again amused as her armor dried entirely within only moments of walking. Fayden however, being of cat origin, appeared as a rat, despite her constant shaking. She was still relatively damp when they reached the fire pit but looked less of a rodent and more like a large cat again. During the course of the meal, Fayden and Dorian regaled the group of their friends with their adventurous day of swimming and diving. Numerous jokes and chuckles were passed regarding Fayden's unkempt coat but she rebutted with fearsome glares (that were only teases of course). Everyone seemed to notice a subtle change in the Commander's mannerisms. She was less domineering and more unreserved. And though she had always been pleasant, she now appeared to have an extra sparkle in her eyes and smile to her face. She seemed to have been struck with a different form of happiness she had been slightly hollow of. Dorian, too, was brighter even though she had been in the Core World for only a few days. But even her increased internal composure was evident. Seeing his long-time friend, whom he considered family, and the cherished warrior both infused with delight, brought gladness to Wise Bright's heart. He always longed to see Fayden let loose her reserved personality but it appeared Dorian was the only individual capable of enticing the Commander's childhood characteristics.

***

Little did the Brights know the Shadows had been busy boring through the surface towards the iron riverbed. They hoped upon reaching it, they could disengage Wise Bright's connection, thus greatly diminishing chances of foresight or aid in the midst of battle. The Griffins had spent their time imprisoning the Hawk Lords as well as improving the range in which their sulfuric breath could travel. They had yet to discover the whereabouts of their leader, Nitris, but it did not faze them. The Shadows and Griffins made practical use with their time, forging weapons, establishing ranks and regimes, and formulating methods of attack that would surely be cause for victory. Humans of Minaleth had always remained relatively neutral to Shadows and Brights but the Griffins threatened most into joining Nitris' army and persuaded the others that had it not been for the Griffins, the Hawk Lords would most certainly have ravaged their communities (this of course being a lie). Many humans had willed to remain human while others developed the Bright glow. But even those that retained the glow were still dimmer than other Brights. This not only gave reason for them not to be referred to as Brights but also to be occasionally unaccepted by Shadows. Bitterness drove many to join the Shadow army while morale moved the others to oppose them. Sadly, if and when any Griffin discovered a human that had been living nearer to the heart of Minaleth wanting to flee to the Council to divulge the preparations being made by the Shadows, it immersed the individual in a cloud of sulfur, leaving the unfortunate victim dead. Griffins were known for being merciless while Shadows were infamous for their covert and rather malicious attacks. Though the Griffins were merciless, they refrained from killing the captive Hawk Lords because they believed the birds would, by way of torture, inevitably succumb to disclosing any useful information regarding the Brights, particularly Wise Bright. The unfortunate but loyal Hawk Lords endured severe brutality, having blood-feathers plucked, wings and ears sliced, and beaks bludgeoned all while being chained in a cavern hollowed from a group of trees, as they refused to surrender the integrity of the Council and Bright army. One Lord, a young male by the name of Tukiund, had been set free, only to act as a guide to Redwood Wall and the Council's meeting place in the Eastern Absent. Lord Tukiund's wings had been repeatedly sliced, as well, a talon had been ripped out, so he made his way to his home territory hopping along the ground (because he could not flap his wings enough to lift more than a foot or so off the ground).

A militia of Shadows followed Lord Tukiund from a distance as the injured Hawk made his way across Minaleth's terrain of hills, meadows, and forests. Along the way, he came across a hospitable family of boars that provided him a place to rest and eat. He was also kindly welcomed by an elderly Owl by the name of Duynik who gave Lord Tukiund a meal, nest, and enthralling conversation of ancient customs, inevitable demise of Nitris, and the unfortunate inability to trim those pesky, overgrown feathers.

The reason the Griffins and Shadows had released Tukiund with the intent to follow him was because though they knew the land of Minaleth, the redwoods of Redwood Wall were both a natural cloak to its inner forest as well as an enchanted covering, masking the haven of cabins. When the Brights had been exiled, Wise Bright believed it safest to allow the faeries to enchant the trees. He trusted the natural misguidance of the redwoods but knew a little extra protection would prove helpful in the unlikely event of discovery. So, while Fayden, Dorian, and the Brights were preparing to defeat Nitris, Lord Tukiund was unknowingly offering the Griffins and Shadows an advantage as he was leading them to the protected Redwood Wall.

Chapter 5
The Wood of Willows

Where is everyone?

I know I'm in the Eastern Absent but – where is the Council's meeting place? It should be here.

The grass – it can't be – crispy and brown?

O my god...what could have made the sky look like that? How? Why?

It's cold, too. This doesn't make any sense.

Wait a minute. Who are you? Do you know what happened?

You seem kind of familiar...

What do you mean, 'Perhaps we've met before'? Either we have or haven't. Can you please just tell me what's going on?

Whoa! Alright, now who are all of you? Don't you DARE breathe anywhere near me.

Now – I've had enough of this...back away! Don't you come any closer!

My katana? Where'd my – where the hell did you come from? How'd you get behind me?

I can't do this on my own. I can't do this on my own.

Fayden? Where could you be? Serian?

***

Dorian woke again covered in sweat and convinced what she had just experienced was not a dream. She sat up on her hammock with her legs dangling over the edge as she held her head in her hands and rubbed her eyes. Gentle tears began rolling down her face as she recalled the immense sensation of loneliness and fear she felt in her dream. She wanted to understand what was provoking such disturbing dreams but she couldn't wrap her head around it. She dressed then stepped out of her cabin, stretching as she took in a deep breath of the sweet, warm morning air. She looked up to appreciate the marvelous sky then bent down to stroke the wonderfully soft grass. She felt no desire to eat and only a few others were up at that time anyways, so rather than going to the fire pit, she took a walk to the Rainfalls. Along the way she came across a berry bush that Fayden said was a good, natural source of energy. With no coffee down here in the Core World, and certainly needing a pick-me-up, Dorian picked a handful of the dark pink berries and tossed them in her mouth. They tasted refreshingly, deliciously sweet. She continued and when she reached the falls realized she felt more awake. At first, Dorian sat quietly on a rock, meditating to the sound of the Rainfalls and early morning birdsong. She escaped to yesterday, in her mind, recalling the joy and laughter she and Fayden shared. A smile stretched across her face as she thought of the warmth and protection she felt whenever she was with Fayden. Allowing her mind to be momentarily saturated with the delight she felt thinking about magnificent tiger, then emptying her conscience of all thought, she drifted into clarity and stillness. She harnessed the peace she grasped but let go of all else. Listening, smelling, hearing – she immersed herself in the immediate, natural surroundings.

Time disappeared in her tranquility that settled then drifted off. Opening her eyes, she felt an eagerness to direct her freshly derived energy to something productive, so she stood from the rock and jumped into the pool. She was not wearing her armor but she knew it would be useful to strengthen her muscles and lungs by swimming. She swam normally as if back in her own world. Practicing all strokes, holding her breath, diving, and floating. Surfacing, she gazed up at the curtain of drops falling from above and decided to attempt climbing up the rock wall behind it. She raised an arm out of the water to grip a space in the rocks then pulled her body up to grab hold of a protruding stone. Dangling, she looked up and around to find her next hand placement before lunging upwards to another space with her left hand. She continued pulling her body higher, gripping holes and stones with her hands, balancing with her feet, as the gentle mist from the drops clouded her body and course. Half way up, she glanced below then looked above, realizing just how high the Rainfalls really were. The one she was climbing was just the last in a series of five falls. She reached about one hundred feet skyward before coming to a level plateau of water that led to the next rainfall that was about half the size of the first. Ascending up Rainfall Mountain, Dorian conquered the first four falls but coming to the fifth and final fall, she found herself exhausted and uncertain about continuing without someone else around. This last (or first) fall was, by far, much larger than the others and more vigorous despite its being a collection of rain drops. She also noticed the color of the sky had already turned to a darker scarlet and orange with a sprinkle of pink, meaning it was probably past mid-day meal. She didn't want anyone to worry so she started the descent back to the initial rainfall.

***

While Dorian had been off swimming and climbing in the morning, Grenig had gone to Wise Bright, commenting that Dorian was neither in her cabin nor near Redwood Wall. Wise Bright had previously encountered a teenage faerie, Kayfin, who informed him that she had seen Dorian walking alone in the meadow then swimming at the Rainfalls. Kayfin said, by request of the Commander, that Flutter asked her to keep an eye on Dorian. In order to do this she had to cast an enchantment upon herself to perceive Dorian's movement. When she felt Dorian rise so early then head off alone, she felt it necessary to find out where she was going. Wise Bright gave account of this to Grenig, easing the tiger's concern, before calling to Fayden.

"Pleasing to know our Dorian is being carefully protected." Wise Bright said.

Fayden immediately understood, "After her nightmare I thought it wise to have someone keep watch over her in case anything was to threaten her."

"Kayfin is an intelligent young faerie. She was sharp to notice from her enchantment that Dorian left early this morning to the Rainfalls." Wise Bright commented.

Fayden began to casually saunter around Wise Bright, not in a menacing or nervous manner; she just wanted to move, "Yes. I was glad when Flutter informed me she had chosen young Kayfin."

"Wise decision - having a faerie keep watch. But I'm interested…what led you to believe Dorian needed further protection?" He asked.

Fayden answered, "I believed Nitris was in Dorian's dream and poisoning her mind with fear. Her powers can be devastating and

I did not want to witness Dorian's dream come to reality. Even if it was simply benign."

Wise Bright smiled.

Fayden bowed her head then turned to join her younger cousin at the fire pit. They pushed each other around in good fun and then sat calmly, swishing their tails in contentment. Just as Grenig initiated a conversation, asking what Fayden had in store for the day, Dorian appeared just beyond her cabin. She made her way across the grass to where Fayden and Grenig were sitting. She couldn't help but notice that both seemed slightly – off – than their usual countenance…they had a peculiar expression on their faces. They, too, could see she was uneasy. They explained they were a little worried when they found she was neither in her cabin nor near Redwood Wall. She told them about her dream and how she just needed to find a bit of peace which was why she went to the Rainfalls to meditate. She smiled after a moment then went on to say she had climbed the first four falls with little difficulty. This clearly surprised both tigers. They widened their eyes and glanced at each other in amazement when she said this.

"That's amazing, Dorian! You didn't slip at all?" Grenig asked.

"Not really. It was actually a lot of fun but I wish I had been able to go up the last fall. I was tired, though, and I knew it wouldn't have been safe."

"Well done. We should go back there today to climb all of the falls. I was also thinking we could get in some weapons practice." Fayden was eager to teach Dorian how to use the weapons of the Core World. The faeries and Giants were spectacular blacksmiths. Dorian gripped the back of her neck to stretch it, "That's sounds great. I just want to get a bite first and maybe relax a bit."

"That's a fair negotiation. Grenig, want to join us today?" Fayden turned to her cousin.

"It'd be a pleasure!" He smiled excitedly.

***

After a long, hearty lunch of wine, cheese, and rabbit stew, Grenig, Fayden, and Dorian made their way to the Rainfalls. This time Dorian was wearing her armor and carrying her katana. To make it fair, Grenig and Fayden had put their armor on as well. It was plating, made of forged metal from the iron riverbed, of course, which tightly covered their underbellies, backs, and forelegs. They also had helmets but wearing them would have been a bit much. First, Fayden had Dorian recap the previous day's exercises, having her swim around the pool in the butterfly stroke then the forward stroke. She and Grenig swam alongside her, paddling their paws like dogs. Then the three of them dove for a while as they played games of holding their breath without using corals. They surfaced in order to rest before climbing the falls. When they started Dorian went up the way she had before but Grenig and Fayden, being tigers, went up the flanks, as mountain lions may. The ledges were narrow and slippery with mist so they had just as much of a struggle as Dorian had. Upon reaching the first plateau, the tigers switched sides for a little variation in terrain while Dorian continued up the center of the wall. By the time they reached the final fall, all three were tuckered out and dripping from the mist. The expressions on their faces conveyed the desire to call it quits and head back but the whole reason for coming today was to climb all five falls. Anyhow, Dorian mentioned their goal for endurance and that clenched it. There was no way two warriors and the Commander were going to appear weak and incapable. All three took a deep breath as they stared up at the overpowering wall of rock before reaching up to begin the climb. There wasn't much difficulty to begin with but Dorian still wasn't completely used to having her armor while she climbed, or her katana, so nearing the top, about ¾ of the way up she made the mistake of grabbing a loose stone. It plummeted down, very nearly bringing Dorian with it as she dangled with one arm, but thankfully she was quick to spot another place to grab. She anchored her body then looked down with a worried expression. As all of this occurred, Fayden and Grenig had each cried out to her and scurried further up as fast as they could, hoping if they reached the ridge they would be able to reach down far enough to grab hold of her and pull her up. Fayden reached the top but not until Dorian had already secured herself to the rock behind the fall. When Dorian felt she was no longer in danger of dropping, she turned to face Grenig, who looked more disconcerted than she did, and let him know that she was alright and going to continue. Grenig looked down as well, shocked that he and the Commander had just come frighteningly close to losing their warrior, and then kept climbing till he took a leap over the last few feet to land the same time Dorian was pulling herself over the edge. The two tigers examined Dorian, making sure she was not injured, then sighed with whistles to ease the tension. The summit of Rainfall Mountain was glorious. Overlain with shrubbery, a forest of willows overhanging the water, and scads of a type of flower Fayden called *Green Serdies*...which made absolutely no sense to Dorian because they weren't even green. They were a soft blue, really, almost lavender, and they looked more like open berries than flowers. They were beautiful, nevertheless. Looking over the calm river flowing beyond the edge, forming a curtain of raindrops as it submitted to gravity, and coming from nowhere really, one could gaze across the entirety of Minaleth. Its desolate land, the mountain range where the Hawks were held captive, and the forests and meadows where the rich soil and magikal splendor was being smothered each day by the Griffins' sulfuric breath carried in the wind.

Breaking the silence of the glory serenading the landscape, Flutter appeared, not in a hurry, but with determination. She slowed her pace as she drew nearer then came to a stop on the ground in front of Dorian, Fayden, and Grenig.

"Commander. The faeries and I have constructed a weapon that should be of great use when battle ensues." She said, through controlled breathing and a proud, inquiring smile.

Grenig spoke first, "A weapon? What is its nature and how does it work?

Now Fayden, "Is it of consequence to Nitris and her minions?"

"Yes, ma'am! Its main function is the destruction of Griffins but it could prove useful against Shadows as well. Come and I will show you, all of you!" Flutter began to hover.

Dorian tilted her head slightly in thought, "Hey, Flutter...how did you know we were here?"

Kayfin, of course, had been concealing herself within the trees and when Flutter was curious as to Fayden's whereabouts, Kayfin told her exactly where to find all three. Dorian was the only one present who was unaware of her – guardian faerie – causing the others to exchange glances of nervousness. It was not that they were eager or proud to hide such truth from Dorian but they feared if she knew of Kayfin's presence, she would feel provoked to mislead them if ever she wanted to wander off on some premise of challenging a Shadow, Griffin, or even Nitris.

"Oh – I had been flying through the forest, looking if you were near, when I heard Grenig and Fayden shouting." She met eyes once more with Fayden before receiving Dorian's.

Clueless, or dismissive, "Oh. Well that was a lucky coincidence! Let's get goin' then, shall we? Now I'm curious to see this weapon." Dorian smiled, looking at each of the others.

"Right. Flutter, should we meet you in Faerie Willows?" Asked Fayden.

"No, no. We figured it would be safer to build it where Nitris and others would not think to attack. It is here, in Willow Plateau. Follow me."

Grenig, Dorian, and the Commander followed quickly behind as Flutter scurried in the air through the trunks and branches. From a distance they could hear the sound of celebrative shouts and clapping. They were nearing the end of the plateau, where it sloped downwards into a hill that led to back to the meadow. As the willows and green serdies became fewer and less dense, Dorian could see a wooden structure that at first glance, appeared crude and obnoxious, but nearer it was really a work of art and craftsmanship. Quite impressive really. The group of four arrived at the site to be welcomed by a group of about ten male faeries, each equipped with tool belts, with the tools strewn across the grass, and looking gleefully to and from their creation and Fayden. They waited in expectation of praise or scornful reproach. Dorian and Grenig remained where they now stood, next to a willow, facing the – whatever it was - while Fayden slowly made her way closer and around the structure. Flutter accompanied her, explaining its purpose, proper usage, materials used…everything a contractor might explain.

"This wood…of willows?" Fayden asked as she reached to it with her paw.

"Yes. It is lighter than redwood which was necessary if any are expected to move it with at least a morsel of ease." Flutter spoke matter-of-factly.

"And this?" Fayden motioned to, what appeared to be, an extendable, thin and narrow sheet of lumber and tynif moss.

"You see these holes? They are meant to hold arrows and when this band is pulled back, it fires an ambush of arrows yards farther than any archer could dream of." Flutter was excited.

It was then that Dorian looked over the structure again, then without really meaning to, laughed, "This is a slingshot! Well, in a manner of speaking. We have these in my world. They are shaped like this (here, she drew in the air the shape of a wishbone) and have a rubber band across the space and a pouch in the center to hold a rock, marble, or whatever."

Fayden, Grenig, and Flutter looked at her in amusement, "I think I know what you're describing. We've watched younger human boys use them in menacing ways. This is different. Obviously by size but also in its ability to shoot many arrows of larger size with speed and power. Our intention was for it to be used against Griffins."

"Well, get on with a demonstration tiny!" Not Grenig's usual behavior but he was in an interesting mood.

Flutter flew up to him, trying to control a smile as she glared, and wacked him right in the schnoz. He crinkled his tingling nose with a sarcastic "ow" then swapped at Flutter while she turned her back. She and the other faeries loaded the band, though Dorian referred to it as the sling, made a few quick adjustments, then positioned their selves along the length of the band and gripped it tightly. The nirfen, as it was named, faced northwest, further into Minaleth, as it was the safest direction and least likely to be inhabited. Everyone stood anxious and thrilled to see just what this enormous weapon was capable of. Flutter looked to Fayden, who nodded in approval, then looked back to the faeries that were prepared to stretch the band back. She called out to them to "PULL and FIRE" and they did just that. All at once, in a masculine roar, the men and teens cried out as they stretched back the taught band then released it. Predictably, it sprang forwards, shooting the arrows far and high through the air. Only the faeries, because of their magikal eyes, were able to follow the distance and height of the arrows. Jaws dropped, eyelids failed to blink, as everyone stood stunned. In a moment, all the faeries shouted in awe and excitement, cheering to each other and exchanging high-fives.

"My GOODNESS! That was unbelievable, Flutter! It's fantastic. Those Griffins are certainly in for a surprise now!" Grenig's expression was complete amusement.

"Well agreed!" Fayden added.

"That was so awesome, you guys!" Dorian was smiling, nearly laughing, with her teeth bared as she joined the faeries in their celebration without hesitation, swapping miniature high-fives and cheers.

***

Fayden and the two warriors returned to Redwood Wall. Flutter stayed with the faeries to help with a few alterations. Fayden was just on her way to tell Wise Bright of the faeries' nirfen but she caught Dorian heading to her cabin to change out of her armor.

She stepped away from Wise Bright, "Hold on there, you. Keep that on. We've still got a bit of weapons training to go through this evening!" Fayden gave a sideways smile and squinted her eyes.

"Ugh! Well then you better prepare yourself, cat, because I'm not going to go easy just because you're the Commander!" Dorian shouted back and laughed.

Fayden turned back to Wise Bright, "You two are certainly getting along well, I must say!" He commented.

Fayden was unsure of how to respond, so she just jumped to her reason for speaking with him, "Yes, we are. Sire, you must see what the faeries have constructed! They call it a nirfin and it is capable of firing over two dozen arrows at once, farther and higher than the best archer in the Core World!"

"Is that so? It sounds fantastic! Are they building more?"

"I'm not sure. I would imagine so. The faeries are well in logic." Said the Commander.

"This is great! And training? What have you and Dorian accomplished thus far?" He looked towards Dorian then back at Fayden.

Fayden turned to Dorian as well, smiled, and then faced Wise Bright, still thoughtfully smiling, "She is amazing, Sire. Far more than we could ever have expected. We have gone through swimming, diving, climbing, with and without her armor, locations and regions, a bit of history, botanical remedies, and I told her of the willow trees."

Wise Bright nodded.

"Tonight I am going to show her how to fight with and against a variety of our own weapons." She added with a wink.

Wise Bright smirked, "Supper tonight will be some fun, I should think." He, too, threw in a little wink.

Supper came and unexpectedly, for Dorian at least, there were a few more Brights around the fire pit. Actually, there must have been an extra dozen that had joined! After all had finished eating, she discovered the reason for the additional crowd, and was ironically amused to find out they were an audience more than a simple dinner crowd. Fayden had risen first, from the pit, and disappeared for a while before returning, dressed in armor complete with helmet. She was also carrying a large bag hanging from her mouth.

"So, Dorian, how's about a little weapons practice? What'd you say?" She flashed a conniving grin.

Dorian shook her head, also grinning, "Think you can pull the curtain over my head, do you? Well, like I said earlier, I'm not going easy on you. And don't think our *audience* is going to deter me."

She pulled her Masamune katana from its scabbard and took a stance. Fayden nosed through the bag and pulled forth a chain. Not quite what Dorian was expecting but she was far from worried. Fayden gripped the chain in her teeth and started towards Dorian, jerking her head left and right, tossing the chain about. The so-called audience had formed a large circle around the fire pit, leaving a moat of grass for the two to fight upon. Dorian came forward, skillfully twirling and spinning her sword between hands, in front of her and over her head. Fayden leapt into the air and whipped the chain at Dorian. Dorian's katana swung and sliced off the very end of the chain. Some cheered. Some jokingly booed for good show. Fayden landed and turned quickly to face Dorian, who was coming at her. She dodged the blade and lunged at Dorian, striking her left side. Fayden *is* a tiger, a massive one at that, so when she was stricken, Dorian flew back a good ten feet but pulled off an impressive landing with a back-roll incorporated.

"Wow! This armor is great!" Dorian shouted to a few of the faeries watching while keeping her eyes on Fayden, who was now circling.

"Be grateful I'm holding back, dear." Fayden said.

Dorian was quick to shoot back, "Right. So are you going to prove that or just keep dancing around me?"

Fayden smiled, crouched down, and then pounced. Her chain swung over Dorian's head before she pummeled over the girl, bringing them both down. But Dorian stretched her legs out and managed to flip the tiger over and she rolled back then stood once more, facing Fayden who was twisting her body to attack again. This time the chain came low and Dorian brought her sword down. Fayden however jolted her head just at the precise time to jerk the chain in the opposite direction, causing it to wrap around Dorian's katana. She yanked her head right, pulling the sword from Dorian, and then dropped the chain from her mouth. She was swift in another pounce and brought Dorian down, pinning her to the ground. Cheers erupted from around the pit and Fayden laughed. She then bit down on Dorian's armor to pull her up. The two laughed as they took deep breaths and shook off the initial round.

"Now what?" Dorian asked.

Fayden smiled sarcastically, "I thought you weren't going to go easy on me. You must have been, seeing as how I beat you."

"Blah, blah, blah. I never said I would beat you. You're a tiger for crying out loud! A giant one, at that!" Dorian rolled her eyes but was not speaking in anger or frustration. It was all in good fun.

Fayden shook her head, grinning, as she walked over to the bag again, putting away the chain and bringing out a different weapon. It was a green serdie and something that resembled a nutcracker. It was made of metal, could be squeezed in one hand, like a nutcracker, but it had a clip, like a gun, attached and full to the brim with green serdies. Dorian didn't understand but Fayden explained what she was to do with the flower. Fayden turned her back to Dorian, stepping a few paces away then faced her, ready for another go. She let out a monumental roar then rushed at Dorian. Dorian stood, slightly frightened, seeing this enormous tiger charging at her without holding back. But when Fayden was only about ten or so feet from her, she clenched the handles of the dighsp, as it was called, squishing the flower. Doing this ruptured the flower causing it to release a heavy cloud and high-pitched tone 'round her body. She dove to the ground, rolled, noticing Fayden leaping above her to where she was just standing, and stood now facing the Commander's back. The tone and cloud vanished after only seconds and Fayden suddenly turned to find Dorian's katana under her chin with Dorian smiling at her in amusement. More cheers from around the circle.

"Haha. Good! One more." Once more, Fayden went over to the bag but instead of pulling another weapon out, she stopped, shook her head, and turned back to Dorian.

"What? No weapons?" Dorian asked a little confused.

"There will be times that you cannot fight an enemy with a weapon and you are forced to use personal strength and wit. You and I are going to combat one another, hand-to-hand. There's time to work with more weapons another day." Fayden was a little more serious now.

Dorian changed that, "Don't you mean hand-to-paw?" She smirked as a smart-ass kid would.

"This paw is going to end up in your little mouth, young lady!" Fayden smiled again.

"Let's go, Commander." Dorian took a defensive stance as Fayden did her circling routine again. Dorian had never understood the idea behind circling but just as she thought this, Fayden spoke.

"Do you know why I circle, Dorian?"

Dorian raised her brows, "Actually, I was just wondering that." Still holding her stance.

"I circle to cause anticipation. I circle to get your eyes and feet moving. If I were to attack you straight on, your stance would be planted and sturdy and you would have a firm focus on where you could either attack or block. Once you begin shifting and altering your focus, that sturdiness and preparedness decreases." She continued to circle, first clockwise, then counterclockwise, and back.

Dorian understood. She continued watching Fayden but pivoted only one foot now instead of shuffling both. Just then, Fayden made her move. She jolted to Dorian and raised a paw.

Dorian was alert and decided to dodge this one. She dove and rolled on her side, like a log, then picked herself up again. Fayden lunged again and this time brought her entire body up with her front paws falling upon Dorian. Dorian shocked everyone, though, by firmly planting her feet with one leg bent forward and the other stretched back with a slight bend actually embracing the attack. She put both her hands out, as Fayden had put her paws out, and ended up interlocking their fingers. Each was struggling to push the other, Fayden making more progress than Dorian. Arms and legs were trembling, feet were sliding, feminine grunts of exertion. For the first time since coming to the Core World, Dorian was actually instilled with fear as Fayden roared, then snarled, baring her enormous, sharp teeth. She was slowly bringing her jaw near to Dorian's neck. She knew Fayden wouldn't actually bite her or tear her apart, but still, she had an intuitive understanding that a tiger baring its teeth at you while going for your neck is scary! It gave her motivation and drive though and she glared right into Fayden's eyes. Dorian released the resistance in her legs to allow Fayden the advantage but as Fayden pushed forward with all her strength, Dorian unexpectedly twisted and swung her leg around, bringing it full force into Fayden's stomach. It must have caught the Commander off guard because she immediately released her grip and crumpled as she flew back a few feet in the air.

Dorian was hunched over, catching her breath and rubbing the leg she had kicked Fayden with. She looked up to where the tiger lay. Fayden was on her side, blinking her eyes, as though contemplating what just occurred. No cheers yet. All jaws were hanging in astonishment. Dorian went over to Fayden just as she was pulling herself to her feet. She stood on all fours, just staring at Dorian, while breathing roughly.

"Fayden, are you alright?" Dorian actually pat the Commander's head.

Fayden was not insulted by the gesture, "You truly are a remarkable entity, Dorian." Her voice rasped.

That's when the cheers erupted and everyone, feeling the entertaining combat had come to an end, stood and rushed to the Commander and warrior. Klum and Ostel had been watching, actually, all of the Council, a few faeries (including Kayfin), a

mongoose or two, a few Giants and Grostels, and dragonflies had been watching. They all congratulated the ladies, patting their backs and punching their shoulders. Dorian could see Fayden really was in a bit of pain. She stretched her arm over to stroke the tiger's back. Faintly, subtly, she heard and felt Fayden purring.
***

Waking the following morning was a painful chore for Fayden and Dorian. Both had strained muscles and aching joints. Fayden said her stomach was ok but Dorian couldn't help but still feel badly about it. They ate their breakfast slowly as Wise Bright and a couple others giggled away in amusement. Dorian commented that they should be grateful it wasn't them she and Fayden had battled. Their response was, "I am grateful. Doesn't mean I can't find it a little humorous!" Wise Bright was kind enough to have risen a little earlier to retrieve *chaipol* root – a root that relaxes muscles. He ground it and made it into a tea for Fayden and Dorian. They were very grateful because it set in really fast and they were quick to feel more inclined to move and twist again.

As they were finishing their breakfast, they heard a bit of commotion around the forest and turned to see what the cause was. Fayden stood, with an intense stare of horror mixed with joy. Without moving, she called for Wise Bright to come, then briskly walked forward to the injured creature. Dorian didn't understand what was happening or whom this could be but she followed Fayden to pull herself out of the dark. In low tones, not whispers, but speech under one's breath, she heard Fayden and the creature exchange words:

Fayden was low, crouching, to make herself equal, "Are you alright?"

The creature responded, "This can use some mending, I am in need of a good meal and long rest, but apart from that, I am alright. I am alive." Its voice was a bit shaky.

Then Wise Bright came from behind and Dorian became aware, "Lord Tukiund! My word. Come, Tukiund. Have a meal, let us repair your injuries, and get plenty of well needed rest. Please don't feel obligated to explain ANYTHING. Do so when you are well, friend."

A short, direct reply, closing his blood-shot and yellow tinged eyes in relief, "Thank you."

Chapter 6
Magik

Magik of the Core World is a wondrous thing. It is not an entity. It is not a deity. It does not hide within or boast without. It is the essence of Minaleth. The very breath, the heart of such a world entangled in our own. In the absence of this magik the Core World would become existentially debatable.

When the world was created, the new Plane of Existence formed at the will of the industrious Spirit, it was infused with the ability to *live*. Not so much as the creatures who populate the land but rather *live* in the sense of having the ability to perceive, endow - to act as desired by those that *will* the magik to exist. The magik responds to the deepest desires and hopes of those that desperately yearn for a world of real possibilities. One would be wise not to misunderstand the workings of the magik. It is not to be treated as a wishing well or a faith of sorts. Magik does not respond to prayers; it is not a deity. It does not take on any personas. It is an emulsifier between one's surroundings and the spirits of the land. One carries the magik within his or her self. So it is not necessarily a phenomenon only to be experienced outside the dimension of the Withering World but that world has become far too corrupt, polluted and enveloped by malice and ugliness for the magik to truly exist. These distasteful qualities prevent the connection between our souls and magik. Could the magik have the ability to manifest through the realm and above the surface, surely the vast majority of people would be no more than Shadows - depletions of their former selves to reveal what truly dwells within the depths of their souls.

Dorian had become aware of this. Every day, the glow of her being grew brighter and every day, she realized that much more how very unfortunate it was that her world could not exist as the Core World does. Despite her many sincere attempts, she could not bring herself to neglect the knowledge that the people she knew, her parents, Master Hakira, were all pieces of a distorted dream that she was losing the desire to return to. She missed her parents dearly but how could she leave Minaleth?

Even after all is said and done, regarding Nitris and this whole war, would Dorian remain in the Core World or would she part ways with her new friends to return to a feigning reality? With certainty, she felt no real desire to leave Minaleth. Even with the trepidation being stirred by Nitris, the world beneath our surface offered far more than Dorian could ever hope for or work toward. Although, she couldn't simply disregard the pain her parents must have felt. She knew they would understand her need to experience life and move as her heart directed but she also knew they desperately loved her. Soft emotions welled to the corners of her magnificent eyes whenever she thought of the bond she wished to feel once again with the two individuals that brought her into the world. She was perplexed to a degree that she could not hide from her emotions. This is where she felt she belonged. But can a foreigner truly belong to a world not their own? The deep, ocean-blue orbs that are her eyes were now forming rivers that broke free from their barrier to run down the contours of her delicate face.

***

Together, Wise Bright and Dorian one day strolled to the North Stream and silently sat side-by-side, watching the placid water seamlessly flow before their eyes. Gentle ripples every so often spread out in all directions from drops of dew no longer able to reside upon its leaf. Captivated by a Banyan overhanging the stream, Dorian was unable to contain her inquisitive wonder. A ballet of images danced in front of her eyes as she watched the colours of the tree reflect upon the water.

Dorian broke the silence, "Wise Bright," she began, "the Core World isn't actually in the *core* of the earth, right?" She spoke while still gazing upon the stream.

"Interesting you should phrase your question in such a way." Wise Bright replied with a funny little curl to his lips. "It is, in fact, not literally the core of your world. Rather, a collision has caused your world and ours to intertwine, mesh, with one another. The center of earth is as it should be. If it were not, the Core World would not manifest as it does. The climate, environment and even the way in which to reach this world are dictated in part by the traits of earth's *actual* core."

With a tilt of her head Dorian posed another question, "If the Core World isn't really the core of earth, why then is it called 'the Core World'?"

"A terrific question but one with a simple answer. The Council and I referred to our world as the *Core World* when we discovered our plane had come to rest on, not *in*, the center of the earth." A slight look of confusion set in on Dorian's face, driving Wise Bright to tell her the story of the Spirit responsible for the existence of worlds and planes.

Inspired, Dorian's eyes now sparkled with hope of possibilities, "So there are other worlds, apart from yours and mine?" She could hardly contain her ever-climbing intrigue.

Wise Bright was quite amused by Dorian's excitement and he hadn't the heart to steal from her such emotional elation by concealing the very answers she sought, "Dearest girl," he started gingerly, "there are, of course, other worlds. Many. Some of which to marvel at and others far worse than the nightmares dwelling in one's subconscious."

"Why would the Spirit form..." Dorian's question was cut short as Wise Bright knew precisely what she was asking.

"The Spirit was one of independence and desire. It was also one of great emotion, beyond what you or I can feel. Every world is a reflection of its momentary perception of life. Consider artists...works of art are created in the presence of emotion. This inspires the contours, colours, motion and other aspects of the piece."

Dorian nodded in understanding as she and the Cherry Tree of Old continued to watch the glistening beauty flow in unseen motion.

Dorian's thoughts started to seep from her lips, "If beings are able to reach the Core World, despite its co-existence with earth...should it not be possible to travel to the other worlds?" Dorian was now holding her head in the palms of her hands, sitting with her knees crunched in towards her body as she stared deep into the stream.

Wise Bright remained silent, allowing Dorian's thoughts to uncoil.

Dorian felt in her bones, in her soul, that there *must* be a way to reach the other worlds. How could there not be? The probability was just too great to ignore. But what could be the medium between worlds? She was correct in assuming Wise Bright did not know for certain. Though, it could have been a ruse to keep her from jumping to a dangerous plane. He had to have known, right? He had been living now for more than a millennium.

The conversation seemed to have come to its end. Dorian and Wise Bright returned to quietly enjoying the serene display of life. Wise Bright's eyes remained closed as he displayed a gentle smile, allowing his senses to absorb the world around him. Dorian was still lost in pondering the ability to travel between worlds not overlapping each other.

Chapter 7
A Silethin Proverb

Serian kindly opened his cabin to Lord Tukiund, taking the floor to allow Tukiund the pleasure of the hammock. Wise Bright had given him chaipol tea mixed with a bit of swellip along with his breakfast. And as he was eating, Flutter applied tynif moss to his torn wing and talon. He felt very much relaxed and decided to rest the remainder of the day. Serian, being a lion, had a very large hammock that stretched across most of his cabin, making Tukiund extremely comfortable. Hawks generally sleep perched but these circumstances called for a few luxuries.

The young Lord Tukiund possessed a type of royalty in his blood. At Minaleth's beginning, the Hawks that had come down evolved to become enormous in size, capable of speech, and even more powerful in flight. They chose not to participate in the Council but rather create a new order, the Order of Hawks. Their desire was to soar the Core World as patrol, ensuring its safety and peace was not compromised. Lord Undolnes was the Hawk responsible for the inception and continuation of the Order. He was considered the *king* of the Order though he was not referred to as such. He was humble and felt it unruly to declare power through a title. He gave all the members of the Order title of Lord, believing that was what they were. As it goes, Undolnes had a family, a son, whom he appointed successor and as time passed through generations, Lord Tukiund found himself appointed by his father to become head of the Order. The honour was passed to him only moments before a brutal attack by a Griffin and Nitris had stolen his father's life. It was not long after this that Nitris ordered the Griffins to destroy the Hawk nests and take the Hawks captive. Her purpose in doing this was to extract any helpful information they may have regarding any strategies the Brights may have conjured in the event of war. Of course they knew. The Order was not an enemy of the Council but a subsequent…branch, if you please. They knew all hope was lost if Nitris knew the Council had indeed summoned a warrior from the Withering World. Yes, it was true Nitris was a part of the Council when the law of a foreign warrior was written but, she was naïve to the Council's engagement of it. She thought it nothing more than junk; created to appease the ancients. Help them feel secure.

Now regarding Lord Tukiund – the Griffins guarding the captive Hawks had cleverly thought by releasing the young head of the Order, the others would feel less inclined to hold true to their honour and divulge the desired information. They soon found however that they were not clever enough. During the sinister interrogation of the Hawks, none gave in to succumbing to the temptation of life if they only gave up their secrets. This unfortunately grieved the Griffins and they eventually resorted to executing the Hawk Lords. They did not dispose of all the Hawks at once. They were structured in their evil. Each day they questioned a different Hawk, giving him or her, amidst torture, three days to divulge what he or she knew and if nothing had been accomplished after those three days, the Hawk was engorged by a cloud of the Griffins' sulfuric breath. When a Hawk took its final breath, those wretched griffins would have the creature strung up to dangle inverted from the ceiling. This was to break the spirits of the remaining Hawks. Tukiund had been so ravaged by the Griffins that he did not realize he had been followed to Redwood Wall. Innocently, unknowingly, Lord Tukiund brought the enemy right to the Brights' haven.
***

When Lord Tukiund awoke it was time for supper. Having been starved for weeks he was now very quick to indulge his newly returned appetite. Thanks had been given for his return and after the meal, he and the Council members met at the redwood in Easter Absent. Once again stepping down to accommodate their guest, Serian gave his stone seat to Tukiund, while he sat on the grass on Wise Bright's left.

"Lord Tukiund, young head of the Order of Hawks, descendent of Lord Undolnes, the founder of the Order, and son of the great Lord Ternious, we welcome your return with open hearts." Wise Bright proclaimed to the Council.

Fayden bowed her head to Tukiund, "Welcome, Lord. It is easing to know that you are well."

"Is your father well? Are the other Hawk Lords well?" Strike asked with a glint of fear in his voice.

Tukiund lowered his head, closing his eyes to hide the tears, and spoke in a low, tremulous voice, "They are not. The Griffins are torturing and murdering the Hawks as we speak. They are trying to discover what advantages the Brights have against Nitris." He paused momentarily to gather his words through his choked throat and tear-welled eyes, "She...and a Griffin...my father...they tortured him then...then..." Tukiund collapsed, tucking his small legs under his body and folding his wings back. In a whisper, "They took him from me. He is dead."

Silence fell all around as soft sorrow streamed from every set of eyes. Dorian could not suppress her instincts. She rose from where she was sitting, next to Fayden, walked to Tukiund and embraced him. She could feel his grievous drops fall onto her arms. She whispered gently in his ear so only he could catch her words, "We will not let this stand. I will not. Nitris, the Griffins, Shadows...not one will ever again breathe a single evil thought of delight in your father's death or of any Hawk."

She released her hold and caught the faintest whisper as she went back to where she had been sitting, "Thank you." Tukiund had raised his head and was wiping the tears away with his good wing.

Ostel spoke softly, "Is there any hope for the others, Tukiund?"

"I cannot say. It is my strongest desire but having experienced the Griffins' brutality, it is all but a guess to say they have been murdered by now."

Dreadful silence again.

Breaking the ambiance of death, Fayden asked, "How is your wing and talon?"

"Healing well, thank you. I am beginning to feel more like usual." His voice changed slightly, expressing a bit of ease.

"Tukiund, do you know the reason for their releasing you?" Wise Bright sounded concerned.

"No, Sire."

Wise Bright stared, "Curious."

"Before the Griffins had captured any of the Hawks, a few of us had discovered Nitris had gone missing. We thought it very strange and decided to find a reason for her disappearance." Lord Tukiund paused momentarily in thought, "It was not long before we spotted a small cluster of Shadows talking under their breaths. One of us left and came back, followed by two bats, and had the bats regurgitate what they could hear (our hearing is great, but a bat's is impeccable)." He paused again, "Through their conversing, we learned that Nitris had entered Dorian's dreams, hoping to deter her from engaging. They spoke of her cunning deception of vanishing from the Core World and returning in the same manner, without having been found out by either Shadow or Bright. After that they seemed to share worthless information so we thought it time to leave. But as I was turning, after the others and the bats had gone, my ears caught wind of one more bit of the puzzle. One of the Shadows mentioned his knowledge that Nitris had intentions of meddling with Dorian in more ways than one. That was all I could hear before I left."

Wise Bright knew all too well that Nitris was manipulating the magik of the world in a dangerous way. He knew it was only a matter of time before she would have the insight to alter all of Minaleth's magik to evil. Not only that but now there was confirmation that Nitris was indeed aware of the presence of a warrior from the Withering World.

The Council members stole glances from each other then all eyes were on Dorian. She was disturbed with fear and the sensation that her life was no longer her own. She was being *meddled* with by the malicious tyrant trying to claim a world. Definitely cause for panic but she did not allow the fear to consume her. She tried to untangle what she just learned, "My dreams?"

Fayden responded, "Yes. I thought there was a possibility she was intruding your dreams but now I am certain. You must not let them riddle you with doubt or terror."

"Fat chance of that! They just make me want to destroy her even more." Dorian's voice was raised.

Her response seemed to lighten the mood a bit. One could hear a few sighs and hidden giggles. *More ways than one.* Dorian tried to wrap her mind around the thought but could not decipher its meaning. "What do you think they meant when they said that Nitris was meddling in my life in 'more ways than one'?"

The others thought for a moment then Serian spoke, "I don't think we can answer that yet, dear. I think we must wait for Nitris' next move."

Fayden agreed.

"But won't it be too late by then? What if her next move compromises Dorian in some way?" Grenig directed the question to Wise Bright.

Wise Bright answered, "It is my understanding that…" he stopped and strained his self in thought, "…that Dorian is of special value to Nitris. I have yet to unravel just what that might be, but I trust she hasn't the intention to harm Dorian. At least not initially. I believe, as long as we are prepared, it is safe to leave Nitris free to act as she wishes. That is until the right moment for *us* to devastate her when our opponent arises."

Fayden continued his thought, "If we are prepared in all aspects, anything Nitris and her followers attempt will fail to be substantial. I believe we just need to give more focus to training – not just Dorian – all of us. We all have abilities and strengths. We must harness and improve them…I believe, Dorian, a book in your world speaks eloquently of knowing one's enemy."

"I know one thing," Klum interjected, "the Griffins may have sulfuric breath, frightfully long talons, and the ability to fly, but they are severely lacking in the wit department. They are dumb as doornails! I will admit this, we Giants are not the quickest of creatures, but we do have some supply of witty, logical theories and concepts that take precedent over the Griffins' quick acts of brute force."

"Well said, well said!" Grenig erupted along with a growl.

Dorian spoke, "I agree! Council members, Lord Tukiund, I know that we have the power to overcome Nitris. If not, I do not believe you would have succeeded in my summoning. We are equipped with not one army, but a hoard of armies – the faeries, Giants, Grostels, animals, and the humans willing to fight with us." She paused to look around the circle then started walking around it, "The markings on these stones depict courage and victory. Perhaps not always tangible victory but victory, nonetheless, of heart or mind. We are armed with wisdom, strength, and fear."

Flutter caught on to where Dorian was heading but Ostel didn't understand. He interrupted, "Fear? But..."

Dorian continued, *"Without fear, there can be no courage; without love, there can be no fear.* A Minaleth proverb bordering my doorway. The Griffins, Shadows, Nitris – they have no fear. They believe they are stronger, with more power, and will to conquer. We, friends, have abounding courage because we, unlike them, are wrapped in fear. Fear of losing ones we love. Fear of giving up the land we love. Fear of being strong when we feel weak. It is this very fear that drives us and gives us an unceasing surge of strength that, if unleashed, can overcome anything. I have not been here long but trust me when I say I have come to love you all and I have come to love Minaleth. I am ready to give my life here, to recover your land, recover the captive Hawks, and protect the Brights." Her words were powerful; invasive to the soul. Tears were shed. Then, in a moment of sheer brilliance to forever be remembered, Grenig stepped forth. Mighty, with bravery gleaming from his eyes, he stood, tears dissipating, proudly next to Dorian. Following was Serian, then Flutter, Strike, Ostel and Klum. Fayden and Wise Bright needn't move for they were already next to Dorian but, Fayden stepped from her stone with a smile and a single tear drop hanging in the crease of one eye.

"Depart, friends. Let us move with the words Dorian has magnificently spoken. Gather your kinds and encourage them to train in every way they can think of." Wise Bright's voice reverberated off the redwood, from the stone seats, and the surrounding meadow.
***

Flutter had the faeries work on their archery, enchantments, hand-to-hand combat, flight maneuvers, and weapons attacks. Ostel checked the progress of the younger Grostels in school and had the older Grostels, female as well as male, practice all aquatic basics, land tactics, speed, and a few special – talents – only Grostels could execute. Klum and the Giants fabricated a variety of clubs, bows, daggers, and a contraption capable of launching a Giant forward, in a tucked roll. They even fabricated armor, though they hardly needed it; their skin was tough as leather and their bones strong as steel. All

Brights were now training, improving, and perfecting their individual tactics of offensive and defensive strategies. The Council meeting had taken place after dinner but all the Brights of Minaleth were eager to get going, so most were up far into the night as they began preparing for victory. Grunts, clanging, and thuds could be heard all throughout the night over all of Redwood Wall, the meadows, Willow Plateau, the Lake, and Faerie Willows. Lord Tukiund slept soundly as a rock on Serian's hammock while Serian slept comfortably below. Fayden stayed with Dorian this night but Grenig and Wise Bright were asleep in each of their cabins.

Fayden and Dorian rose together and woke Serian and Grenig to join them for breakfast. Wise Bright was always up first having breakfast ready for the others. They all ate then retreated to the Rainfalls. Swimming and diving again, with everybody, then a climb to Willow Plateau. Everyone was fully armored and Grenig and Fayden were toting a bag each of weapons. Lord Tukiund remained resting in Redwood Wall to heal and regain his strength. When everyone made it up to Willow Plateau they began combating each other with their various weapons. The *sherzir* was a metal apparatus designed to send an electrical shock through a Shadow. It was comprised of two, three-foot poles which were pointed at one end and each pole had a soft ring around the center to act as a handle. The poles were hollow, making them extremely light, and were meant to be carried at the sides of an animal but used by another (preferably someone with hands and proper digits). One was to launch them towards an oncoming Shadow, trying to have them land some feet apart, and at the time a Shadow passed between the poles, a screen of static electricity would appear and shock whoever passed through. The sherzir was originally designed by the Giants but manufactured by the Faeries. The Giants found their hands were frightfully too large for the precision work. Another weapon was the *faulny*; a primitive devise created by the Giants and masterfully constructed and detailed. Made of pine, it was a small pulley-system, small enough to be carried on one's waist belt. With two 18 inch lengths of wood spaced approximately 12 inches apart and loosely connected with a rope, its purpose was to be thrown towards an enemy in order to snag a limb and lock it between the wooden

lengths. Whoever was using the weapon would still be holding the end of the rope, pulling the lengths together firmly, thus crushing the limb. This would allow another or the same individual to destroy the weakened enemy. Dorian had a bit of trouble getting the hang of the faulny. It took great aiming ability and a considerable amount of strength to fully bring the two pieces together – to cause any real damage, that is. The faulny Fayden brought along was the smallest in size. The Giants also constructed another more proportionate to their size of creatures. Each one was chiseled and decorated with designs and words native to Minaleth. And of course they made more than one of each size. The Giants were fully equipped with well-stocked artillery.
***

Hours went by on Willow Plateau as the group took turns practicing with the different weapons. Of course, no one was out to seriously hurt one another but, accidents happen. Grenig suffered the wrath of the sherzir when Dorian improperly aimed and ended up throwing one of the poles straight into one of his hind legs while he was turned away. Serian managed to walk away without any injuries however he was the culprit to crush Fayden's right ear with the faulny. Whipping it around his head to cast it really didn't prove to work anything but poorly. Dorian had scrapes and bruises absolutely everywhere from hand-to-paw combat, the sherzir and faulny, swords, clubs, and a few other weapons that were brought. It took twice the amount of time it took to get back to Redwood Wall than it took getting to Willow Plateau. Understandable, though. Aches and pains dominated Grenig and Dorian. Serian was absolutely fine, quite a ways ahead of the others, and Fayden was only slightly disheveled from her crushed ear but it did slow her pace a bit.

During the walk back, Dorian became curious as to the rest of Minaleth. She was now familiar with the regions occupied by the Brights but she was interested in viewing the other portions that were once theirs. Where were the other humans? Was it far to the Hawk Lords? What manner of beasts associated their selves with the Shadows and where was it they lived? So many questions of curiosity that Dorian was desperate to learn the answers to.

"Hey, Fayden. Do you think tomorrow morning you could take me around the rest of Minaleth? Or at least to areas where I can *see* the other parts?" Dorian asked.

Fayden answered over her shoulder, "I don't see why not but I must warn you now, Dorian, we will not be able to view the entirety of Minaleth. Don't forget, Nitris exiled us to the outskirts, so the Shadows, Griffins, and dark beasts are very territorial. If we were to mistakably trespass (as ironic as that is) into the wrong area, obsessively protected, we would find difficulty in returning home in one piece."

"Ooook. Well...sounds like fun, wouldn't you say?" Dorian joked.

"Hahaha. Dear girl, fun would not be the appropriate word, but adventurous, no doubt."

Serian joined the conversation, "Grenig and I will join the two of you tomorrow. It is not guaranteed that you will encounter trouble, depending on the care you take in where you travel, but it is guaranteed that should there be trouble, the two of you would simply be no match against an onslaught of Shadows."

"I appreciate that, Serian." Fayden said.

"And I as well. Don't worry; I know wandering around Minaleth isn't a joke. Sarcasm is just a ruse to cover my anxiety." One could see a hint of fright in Dorian's eyes. Not much, but, it was evident if sought.

Grenig came closer, "We will protect you. Actually, you managed to flip my sister just the other day! I think you will be protecting us!"

Everyone laughed. Dorian's increasing strength was undeniable now. Her power, for being an average-size, 20 year-old girl, was impressively beginning to equal that of her feline friends. Yes, she had been in martial arts since childhood, but her muscles were not the only factor in her developing abilities. Dorian trusted her body to flow with the momentum of energy she directed towards her opponent. She concentrated on the very moment at hand. She did not let her mind wander to the possibilities of what could happen in the moments to come or what occurred in the moments prior. She determined to overcome whomever or whatever stood in her way or threatened herself or her friends.

***

In a moment of terror, as the four were passing through the last bits of meadow before Redwood Wall, Flutter came to them in a rush of desperation and urgency. Beads of sweat could be seen rolling down the back of her tiny neck and her eyes were dilated with fear. Laughter was passing between the warriors when Fayden noticed the flustered faerie hurrying towards them. As the Commander raised her head, perking her ears, so did the others and all laughter immediately ceased.

"COMMANDER!!!! Come quickly!" She paused to catch her breath but the heaving continued, "Adalei and Dekel…out at the Lake…saw something…Griffins, three of them…just above the lake….going…Redwood Wall…"

Serian interrupted her, "Griffins are on their way to Redwood Wall?" He was calm, trying to decipher just what Flutter was trying to tell them.

She nodded her head, still breathing heavily.

Grenig speculated, "They must have followed Lord Tukiund. We need to get there now."

"Flutter, I want you to fly ahead. Gather 100 archers then go to the redwood in the Eastern Absent. It is the tallest tree and you will be able to see above everything. Position yourselves but wait until I'm there to signal the fire. Go, now." Fayden had abruptly transformed into the Commander she truly was, ready to protect her Brights.

Flutter nodded then turned. A flash of light through the meadow to Faerie Willows. She was there almost instantly. The others disregarded their pain and rushed back to Redwood Wall, shouting to all they passed to watch the sky and be on guard. Approaching the Council's cabins, Wise Bright was moving in their direction and before Fayden could relay what she knew, he raised an arm.

"I know, friend. The blue birds came to me as Flutter went to you. Unfortunately, the Griffins did in fact follow our friend, Tukiund. I have ensured his safety but there was a mistake. There are not just three on the attack. Redwood Wall is the target for a small militia of Shadows fast approaching the south side of the Wall." He spoke quickly.

Fayden wasted no time, "Grenig! Go to the Grostels immediately. Tell them to form a live barrier on the north side. Serian. The Giants. Go, now, and bring sherzirs. Go to the south of the Wall. Dorian and I will go to the faeries. Wise Bright, can you gather the animals and other creatures? Get them around the Wall's perimeter."

"Of course. And I have already instructed Strike to bring the dragonflies. Griffins are less forceful when blind." Wise Bright winked then left to do as the Commander ordered.

Grenig and Serian rushed off as well while Fayden and Dorian ran to the Eastern Absent. Just as Fayden had instructed, 100 faeries waited in the tree, bows prepared with far range arrows and Flutter hovering at the top, watching for the enemy. She came down when informed of Fayden's arrival and briefed the Commander of the faeries' preparations and the Griffins' positioning. Fayden told Dorian to wait while she climbed and clawed her way up the tree to the top for a better view. The Council new that in times like this, each member had the authority to give commands to their kind when Fayden was not present. That said, all others that were now at their posts waited for the very moment to give the word to attack. The Grostels were prepared to the north with their backs positioned in such a way to reflect the afternoon light. They hoped to blind their enemy with their shimmering undercoat. The Giants to the south were already loading their peculiar launching machine, aimed to fire west, with one of the smaller Giants. And throughout Redwood Wall Wise Bright and all the others were ready to battle. Now, despite Fayden's instructions to stay at the base of the tree, Dorian pulled herself branch to branch until she appeared from the leaves beside the Commander.

"I told you to stay down there!" She seemed – well – not pleased.

Dorian followed the flow of logic, "What good am I down there?! I am trained in this. This is what I do, Fayden. I can help."

"You are trained with humans of the Withering World. This is different. Do not assume possession of ease that does not exist."

Flutter's eyes were locked wide, looking from Fayden to Dorian, and back.

"I did not assume ease. I want to help. I know what I can do." She spoke directly. Dorian turned her gaze to the oncoming Griffins just shy now of the archers' range.

Fayden saw that she had upset Dorian but she was only concerned for the girl's safety. It would pain her to see her friend harmed in a preliminary attack by Griffins. She felt a responsibility, being larger, stronger, and older, to protect Dorian.

Flutter broke in, "Commander?"

The Griffins had flown within range now of the archers. Fayden nodded to Flutter then balanced herself at the top of the tree on her hind legs to sound the aggression within. Flutter shouted to all the faeries to fire and all at once a wave of arrows fired through the air towards the monsters. Agonizing, terrorizing screeches could be heard coming from the Griffins as they dodged the arrows. One was completely consumed by the wave and came tumbling to the ground, dead before the impact from an arrow that punctured his throat. Meanwhile, Serian and the Giants to the south were busy warding off the militia of Shadows. The first Giant launch brought down about five Shadows and another small group dropped after passing through a vine of sherzirs. Ostel had gotten wind of the attacks to the south and seeing as how the north was clear, he had all the Grostels follow him to the south to support the Giants. Strike and a hoard of dragonflies had flown to the scene, shooting their diamond-sharp bolts of breath towards the eyes of their foes. Blinded, a number of griffins were in turn killed for they could no longer see an eminent crash or attack. Back to Fayden, Dorian, and the faeries battling the Griffins. The first had been killed, another had dropped to the ground and survived but Fayden took no time in frantically leaping down the tree to charge the beast. Claws outstretch, teeth bared, she went at the Griffin with full force. One swap from her paw sent a large chunk of flesh flying from its back and Fayden managed to dig her K9's into its neck. The beast fought back in a fury, clawing Fayden's exposed stomach and lurching forward to breathe on her but she was biting directly where the valve, to release its sulfuric breath, was located. Tangled in fur and feathers, snarling and growling and screeching, the two tossed and wrestled with each other until the Commander pinned the beast down, one paw holding down a wing and the other gripping its throat, and savagely wrapped a portion of its head in her mouth and sunk her teeth into the flesh. The Griffin squealed and writhed but Fayden plunged her teeth as far as they could go, passing through its eyes, forehead, and left-side of its jaw. She jerked her head and like a stubborn branch, a bone snapped and cracked as a fountain of blood spurted from its mouth, leaving the beast motionless, limp. Fayden released her jaw and retracted her claws. Looking up to spot the last Griffin, she gasped and roared with the chill of a wild animal hungry to kill. Her mouth bloodied. At the very moment she looked up, the final Griffin had flown close enough to the tree that one could physically attack it. That's just what Dorian did. She had seen the fight down below, knowing she could do nothing from her standpoint and it would take her too long to get down, then she saw this Griffin fast approaching, already breathing sulfur. A number of faeries had suffered the effects and she was the only one actually doing nothing. When the Griffin was just at the right distance, Dorian drew her sword and *leapt* from the tree, landing on the beast's back. A cry of concern and upheaval sounded from every faerie as they watched their warrior grip the beast's ears as reins as she dug her heels into its sides. All jaws dropped in pure astonishment. Dorian was successfully controlling the Griffin. Fayden couldn't believe it. Controlled or not, her friend was still atop an evil creature over 100 feet in the air. She rushed to the tree and climbed it faster than a world champion squirrel. Tumbling through the air, the warrior and the beast struggled to gain the upper hand. Dorian's sword was still in her right hand as she pulled back on the Griffin's ears but now she released the creature's ear and, with a flick of her wrist to spin the sword about her fingers, brought the katana to the beast's face. She leaned in and pulled back the other ear in unison as the tip of the sword hovered at its right eye.

"You picked the wrong girl to piss off." She whispered in its free ear.

The beast screeched but Dorian already brought her sword back and plunged it right through its head, out the other side, then brought the bloodied sword back out. As the beast dropped from the sky, Dorian flung her sword to the ground, stood from the back of the creature with outstretched arms, and launched herself back towards the tree. A professional bungee jumper would have admired her form – legs together, arms out as a bird, back straight. She flew through the air, intentionally as it seemed, to a branch mid-way down. As her hands fell upon the bark, she gripped tightly and swung around a couple times in momentum before bringing her body to a halt. She straddled the branch, leaning forward with her arms holding on, and looked up with a smile to Fayden at the top. At first, no one could figure out if it was pure brilliance or stupidity. Perhaps it was a bit of both, but in either case, celebration and cheers erupted all around. Dorian looked down at her hands, skin torn from gripping the tree, blood smeared not only with her own. The battle here was over and Kayfin brought news that the south side of Redwood Wall had been successfully defended. Fayden looked down and met Dorian's eyes. A light smile swept across her face before she jumped to a lower branch that stretched far from the tree. She made her way to the end, clear of leaves, faced the south and triumphantly, growled then roared. The sky was fading to dusk (or the equivalent) and cast soft beams of mango from the west to the right side of Fayden's face. The green of her eyes was vibrant, threatening. From a distance, one could hear the returned roar of success from Grenig and Serian. The day – as it seemed – had come to its end.

Chapter 8
An Unexpected Friend

After the battle, when everyone was returning to their cabins and regions, Dorian had gone to her cabin to clean her katana and armor. She then chiseled away at one of the stones in the wall with a dagger one of the faeries had given her. As best she could, she engraved a depiction of a Griffin with a sword protruding from its head and mystical swirls swallowing the whole of its body.

The morning hours came with a stir. Had the previous afternoon truly occurred? Dorian – is it real? She jumped upon the back of a Griffin and drove her katana through its head? Everyone was completely bedazzled. Oddly enough, exhaustion was far from present. It seemed the immediacy for adrenaline the night prior had yet worn off. Fayden, Dorian, Flutter…all still felt the rush of battle rather than the muscle pain. Dorian had to defend herself once or twice before in the Withering World but without question she had never before leapt through the air to wrangle a Griffin and stab it through the face. She was still completely awestruck with herself. Something was troubling her, though. Fayden's lethality yesterday, disregarding the fact that she is a tiger, was exceptional. And she is the Commander. Dorian was curious as to how Fayden came to be the Commander. The beautiful, inspirational tiger that she was could not have simply been born with such capacity and in no way was she as old as Serian, whom was centuries younger in years than Wise Bright. And how did Fayden come into the Core World? There were so many questions going through Dorian's mind in the early morning hours that she knew would be invasive until later in the day.

Before joining the others for breakfast, Dorian went down to the Eastern Absent. She was interested in the engravings on Fayden's stone – interested in learning a little more about the Commander's journey. She wasn't surprised at all to see numerous depictions of the great tiger atop a recurring enemy. The "enemy" wasn't a Shadow or Griffin or anything tangible, really. It was a Silethin word, deleneb, which Dorian hadn't learned, so she had no idea what it meant. There was also a chronological line, it seemed, of images of Fayden (Dorian presumed) growing from youth to the marvelous tiger she is now. It was fascinating. Starting with a small tiger cub, something one could imagine in a children's' movie with cave drawings, content and playful – moving to a slightly older cub, only slightly, now appearing despondent. Moving along the line, the pictures conveyed searching, seclusion, and defeat before displaying the Fayden that Dorian had met; overpowering, majestic, and unwilling to allow anything get in her way. Not all of the engravings were completely interpretable. Hopefully, Dorian thought, Fayden would have enough trust in her to share.

After breakfast and a wash at the Rainfalls, Fayden, Serian, Grenig, and Dorian headed west so Dorian could see the parts of Minaleth the Shadows had claimed. The walk would end up consuming just about two days in total, if they crossed north over the mountains rather than traveling the distance around. They started off through the meadows, nothing that Dorian wasn't accustomed to then they entered into the forests between the meadows and mountains. Not too dense, but pleasantly open, filtering through bits and beams of light that brought the colors of the leaves, grass, and flowers to life. Even the soil seemed to dance and slither in the magikal skyshine. The colors and textures and aromas were all intensified in the covered landscape, saturated by the delicious shades of red, orange, fuchsia and yellow. Fayden and Dorian walked ahead a few yards of Serian and Grenig as the buzzing of bees (rather, bee-like creatures), songs of birds, and playful banter of young critters permeated the air between trees and plant life. From behind, Serian explained to Dorian that presently, they were heading west through the Bridge, the forested region between the meadows and heart of Minaleth. The Bridge continued west and eventually spread southwest and northwest into the mountains, forming a type of valley in which Minaleth's core was located. Percentages of the Bridge and mountains had been destroyed by the Griffins as well as the Valley (Dorian learned then that the "Valley" was the proper name for the heart of Minaleth…it was equivalent to "downtown"). Serian further explained that the plan was to move northwest across the mountains and into the valley before returning home.

Fayden opened herself to Dorian as they walked. All the questions Dorian had before wondered about were coming to light as Fayden gave an account of all the years she had thus far been privileged to live. When she was just a small cub, she woke one morning to the horror of being alone. Her family was not with her and searching proved to be futile. Being a cub, wandering through the jungle and open terrain unprotected was a hazardous endeavor she had no choice but to risk. She had yet to discover where she was going to but she felt a pull in her heart and was henceforth determined to reach whatever mysterious destination lie ahead. Numerously she was stalked and attacked by predators much larger and stronger than she. Being only a cub it was difficult defending herself. But having such threatening situations ensnare her life, she was forced to pull from her soul all the strength and fury a tiger cub could hope to muster. Time after time, Fayden proudly stood upon her defeated foe, victor of yet another enemy. It became a game to her. In the safety of the day she would role play; climbing and jumping through trees to avoid capture, crawling as a worm along the ground with not a sound, to pounce an enemy. On her journey, the jungles and forests were her playground – her boot camp. For years she walked the land in search of the destination she intrinsically knew existed somewhere beyond her sight. Her beautiful, young coat had become a tapestry of wounds, scars, and gouged skin as time went by. Her eyes grew intense. Her muscles rippled, accentuating her natural-born chiseled features. The furrows of her brow became a deepened framework of the intimidation that had permanently taken up residence within her facial features. The time came when she came to the very mountain that Dorian had been drawn to. The dormant volcano whispered with the breeze through Fayden's young soul. The call was too strong for her to resist. The extremities of the mountain pushed hesitation through her nerves but she was unwilling to allow steep inclines, narrow edges, and loose surface rock to dissuade her from continuing on the path she knew was hers to conquer. She had nothing else. Nowhere else. Just as all others that made the climb to the peak of the mysteriously harnessed volcano, she crept to the edge of the opening and peered into the blackness. How far was the plunge and where would it take her? Those were the questions that swam through her mind. Hesitating, wishing desperately to have by her side her family that had mysteriously vanished, Fayden turned away; not to forfeit to the destination she felt so strongly pulled to but rather to give distance, in order for her to get a running leap. Like a lunatic, sick with dementia from loneliness and trials and having nothing but her own existence to lose, the future Commander rushed to the edge and sprang forth into the air. A misshapen swan, she soared with outstretched limbs, whiskers and ears pulled in momentum, until gravity subtly drew her body from its levitation. Gently into the blackness she fell. Thoughts only of hope flooding her mind as she went further and deeper. Blind, silent – absolute desolation until finally her nerves warned of the oncoming end. Her eyes were not glued shut in fear but wide open in anticipation and just as expected, she poured through the rocky ending and entered into her new home.

"I apologize for interrupting the story, ladies, but Dorian, we're now at the end of the Bridge and heading into the mountains. You see this path? This leads across all of the northwest range and eventually bends to connect to a path through the southwest." Serian lifted a paw to point as he commented.

Dorian asked, "Are there not any Shadows or Griffins in these mountains?"

"There are not many and the few that do reside in this region are generally uninterested in Brights. They should not cause trouble but the humans in the mountains could pose a threat, as well as the occasional Griffin. Some of the humans that sided with Nitris chose to abide in the mountain ranges because the sulfuric-desert atmosphere of the Valley was too much to handle. We do need to be on our guard." Serian moved his eyes from Grenig to Fayden and both looked back in acknowledgement.

"Fayden, keep going! What happened when you got here – to Minaleth?" Dorian was enthralled.

Fayden continued her account. Now when she had landed in Minaleth, it had yet been parted by Nitris, so Brights were still occupying the Valley, Bridge, and meadows without persecution. She was completely captivated with the extraordinary landscape and sky. Despite her travels, the vibrancy of aromas, textures, and colors were unlike anything she had ever before encountered. And though she had gained a great deal of maturity along her journey, she was guilty of being irresistibly submissive to her youthful resonance. But of course pouncing and chasing the insects and smaller animals of Minaleth quickly demonstrated the magik that saturated the new World. Rabbits, butterflies, and birds all shocked her with speech that she too was capable of but not yet aware. She understood the words they playfully screeched but couldn't trust herself to create the right sounds for the words she wanted to drain from her lips. That is when she met Serian. He was an adolescent lion, some years ahead of Fayden, and he realized Fayden's new arrival and desire to speak as the others. He helped her understand how to form the words that already lay waiting to be released. He befriended her completely, introducing her to his friends, Wise Bright, and the Council. He took her throughout Minaleth showing her the regions and introducing her to the various creatures that inhabited the land. She quickly fell under the careful guidance of Wise Bright, who learned of her journey of turmoil and loss. He saw the strength and power she had and decided to have her and Serian grow in battle together. The combination of a male lion and a younger, female tiger was certainly the best way to give both the necessary challenge needed to progress. With Fayden's ferocious, female agility and Serian's brute, male force, each taught the other how to anticipate and utilize the other's advantages. Fayden looked back to Serian as she recalled this. A glint of appreciation glazed over her eyes as she thought of irrevocable love she felt for Serian whom had become an older brother to her.

She went on to explain that it wasn't long in years before Wise Bright initiated her and Serian into the Council. They had both demonstrated wisdom and strength beyond their years and each had a love for Minaleth that gave them motivation to lead with integrity. It was around that time that Nitris decided it was time for change. Upon the upheaval against the Council and Brights, Fayden made the mistake of following Nitris' coalition of Shadows and Griffins to voice her opinion of the absurdity of exiling the Brights from the land of which they shared every right as she to inhabit. Minaleth was Fayden's home. She had none other and was unwilling to relinquish the land she loved just because a rogue Bright chose to oppose the Council. She went as a phantom at first but was soon discovered by a group of Griffins interested in proving their dominance. An ill-mannered brawl ensued, leaving two Griffins dead of blood loss, and Fayden's belly wounded of a fatal blow from one of the beast's dreadful kicks. They knew Fayden was severely injured but her ability to kill frightened them to retreat and leave her to fade away. Struggling for breath as the pain of her ruptured stomach diminished her capacity to inhale, Fayden lie weak and alone on the accepting, multi-shaded blades. Memories of this very same pain and seclusion crept into her mind and the tears overwhelmed her bloody, dirt-covered face. Drifting into unconsciousness was when she heard the purr and cry of an oddly familiar creature. The young male hopped to her side, nudging her with his head, caressing her with his tongue, desperately trying to ensure her awareness of the life she still possessed. Meeting eyes, both stranger and injured warrior gasped then broke into silent, uncontrollable tears, as they realized the kinship they shared with one another. Dorian was now damp in tears as Fayden said with extreme, heart-felt gratitude that the tiger was her cousin, Grenig, who had travelled just as she to this very land. From this point of the story, Fayden explained that she and Grenig made it back to Redwood Wall safely, where both were cared for and celebrated. Upon their return, the Council decided to appoint Fayden as Commander of the Brights. She had gone from daughter, to orphaned traveler, to warrior, and finally Commander of an army in a world she now considered herself native to. Having her beloved younger cousin returned to her brought abounding joy deep into her heart as well.

The time came when the Hawk Lords were forced into captivity and though Fayden did all she could, relinquishing their freedom was far more challenging, physically and politically, than what she expected. The rest of her story was history – events Dorian had already been told of or personally witnessed.

"Quite the Commander we have, eh Dorian?" Grenig was now walking alongside the ladies looking over towards Fayden with a smile.

Dorian was still slightly emotional from the story. She loved and respected Fayden greatly from the beginning but knowing her trials, perseverance, and will moved Dorian to even greater love and respect. She wished more than anything that she could have been there for the great tiger. Been there as a companion. Been there to protect her in some way…even if she was younger, smaller, and of a completely different species. Dorian now understood her perception of indifference in the Commander. It wasn't that Fayden was heartless or completely cold to the world but she had tasted loss, experienced segregation, and fought for her very existence. With the exception of Dorian's progress in becoming familiar with Minaleth, not much fazed Fayden; she was resolved in knowing and understanding that not all that occurs is good and the inevitable demise of existence could not be chased away. She accepted that which took place in her life, appreciated the time, and either learned from or praised the experience. She knew she would one day die as all do, so she did not concern herself with a clutch to life when desperate situations arose. This is what made her such an exceptional Commander. Her ability to draw from her wisdom and act only in the times that truly called for action.

Thus is the story of Fayden.

***

During the course of Fayden's tale, Serian and Grenig had interrupted on numerous occasions to give explanations regarding historical context of the various regions they entered as they travelled over and along the northwest mountains. When Fayden had finished her story they were just at the river-crossing into the Valley and Serian was describing how the layout was not much different from Redwood Wall. Cabins of stone, tynif moss or even a shimmering, clay from beneath the surface scattered the barren landscape. Dust, patches of grass, dead or dying trees…that was all that was left since the Griffins wreaked sulfuric havoc in the Valley. Nevertheless, it was still delightful for Dorian. The expanse carried within it dusty particles of magikal history scarcely remnant. How breath-taking it would have been to see the Valley before the exile of Brights. To catch the deep rouge rays peaking through the full-bodied trees, dancing upon the luscious grass that stretched abroad. To witness a creature lured into the Core World step upon the turf for the first time; breathe in the delicious air and slowly begin to cast a radiance as the Brights do. How amazing that would be, indeed.

Cautiously they made their way around the fringe of the Valley – knowing that was the best route to avoid confrontations with particularly anal Shadows and Griffins. As they walked, Dorian noticed an increasing amount of movement through the bare trees and burnt bushes. For the first time in…well…she couldn't actually remember how long it had been…she saw people. Not hoards of people as in a large city or even a marketplace but a casual flow of mostly men and women; not too many that were much younger than about 22 years of age. Each was dressed as she – linen-like tunics and trousers of earthen colors. Many of them looked as anyone would – without luster or magikal expressions but every so often Dorian caught a dim aura coming from an individual that passed by. Do not be misled to believe the only human habitants of Minaleth were of Western decent. All manner of heritage and nationality had over the years found his or her way to the Core World. It was actually very refreshing to see so much diversity even in a mystical world beneath the Earth's surface. It caused Dorian to ponder for a small moment of the reality of natural, absolute differences in the human race. As she weaved through the shallow crowd of people with her friends she noticed they were heading towards a small village of sorts. Most of the people around were either coming from or going to a quaint market in the center of the village, with bundles of individuals surrounding various stands and kiosks trading the goods they had for the goods they needed (currency was pleasantly non-existent). Of course there were animals, insects and other creatures going to and fro but Dorian, understandably, was somewhat fixated on the presence of *her kind*.

Continuing along the path that led back up through the forest and into the southwest mountains, though the group was now heading east, Dorian, Fayden, Grenig, and Serian made their way around the outlandish region and came to a stop where a hoard of young individuals stood gathered in a circle. Smiling and excusing their selves, the group weaved through but Dorian abruptly stopped and suddenly gasped in astonishment. Fayden turned to tell Dorian to keep moving but noticed the stunned and perplexed expression on Dorian's pale face.

"What is it, Dorian?" Fayden asked quietly. By this time Serian and Grenig had turned around as well.

Entranced, Dorian didn't even realize Fayden had asked her anything. She moved forward slightly then called out inquisitively, "Reilly?"

The young girl looked up. She seemed different, though Dorian was unable to figure out just how. *Something in her eyes, perhaps.* "Dorian! What the hell?"

"Why…how…what are you doing here?!" Dorian was flustered and confused for so many reasons. Not only had she no idea why or how Reilly had come to the Core World but she was also a little bitter towards her young friend who had left in such an abrupt, mysterious state.

Reilly seemed to speak as though she had practiced the very response she intended to give Dorian, "When we moved, I ran away to nowhere in particular. I just kept going when I found myself at the bottom of Mt. Solace then when I reached the top I thought, 'what the hell…what have I got to lose'. I couldn't tell you how long ago that was but since then I have been here in Minaleth."

Dorian raised an inquisitive brow and stepped back, oddly, "That – that doesn't really make any sense, Reilly. What would have caused you to head towards the mountain then jump down the volcanic spout?"

"I might ask you the same question." Reilly was defensive now.

Something inside Dorian told her not to disclose exactly what brought her to the Core World, "I just – felt I was supposed to be down here." She dared not look directly into the girl's eyes, knowing Reilly would surely pick up on the information she omitted.

Reilly then muttered something under her breath but Dorian caught a few words of it, "Ihe…noku wydos san…menid." Fayden had continued to give Dorian little lessons in Silethin during their journey, so Dorian had just enough understanding to interpret the few words she caught, *"You…not as wise…think."* *What does she mean by that?*

Serian sensed the potential quarrel ready to ensue so he acted quickly in pulling Dorian away from the situation, "We best keep moving, Dorian."

Dorian kept her eyes curiously on Reilly's as she started to turn to follow Grenig, Serian, and Fayden. Reilly only returned a menacing glare with a disturbing smirk which caused Dorian to experience a jolt of discomfort. And at that the odd encounter dissipated as Serian led the group further along the path to the southwest mountains. The others travelled along in serene delight of treading the ground they knew as home. The land may not have been as beautiful as a Tuscan field but the warmth, sky, and heritage of it deeply penetrated the core of the Brights' souls. Despite her intentions, Dorian seemed, however, unable to pull her mind from the thought of Reilly living in Minaleth. Confusion and curiosity plagued her mind, consuming every free space, and short circuiting all other thought patterns.

Fayden turned to see her young friend distressed in thought and decided it would be best to perhaps help guide the process a little, "Dorian, were not your dreams of that very girl?"

Dorian hadn't even contemplated that! She couldn't believe it. *Good god. Are my dreams...prophesies? Or premonitions? Holy shit!* "Fayden! Do you think it's possible for my dreams to become reality? Do you think if I dreamt of Reilly causing me so much grief, only to discover that she *is* in Minaleth with us, that she is capable of what she did in my dreams?"

Serian and Grenig had now turned as well, for Dorian's voice had begun shaking in high-pitched tones, "Dear," Fayden said softly as she moved in to allow her fur to engulf Dorian, "that girl is puny, insignificant, and surely incapable of procuring any manner of dominance over you. You may say she possesses strength but that is only of surface physicality. She lacks in the strength you own within your heart and mind. There is not one creature I have before had the privilege of knowing that has had such a mastery over her psychological tapestry of woes, wonders, and wisdom. *You*, Dorian, Warrior for the true Minaleth, are a prodigy of battle."

Dorian's arms had been wrapped around the tiger's neck and were now squeezing intently, as if to absorb whatever affection, courage, or peace that lied within the Commander. "Thanks, Fayden" she looked directly into those piercing, enchanting green eyes, "I'm glad I came down here – to the Core World." She smiled.

Fayden returned the smile with a gentle purr.

***

East through the southwest mountains, Fayden, Dorian, Grenig, and Serian made their way back to Redwood Wall. Dorian was interested in detouring towards the remnants of the Hawk Lords but the idea was rejected. Serian assured her it would be far too dangerous. Griffins and Shadows would have the area completely swarmed and an encounter between three Brights, one human warrior, and an unknown number of Shadows was a risky endeavor to pursue; especially considering the recent events that occurred at Redwood Wall. Despite the lion's warning and disproval, Dorian took it upon herself to make her way to the Hawk Lords. She was armed. She was trained and capable of battle. Why couldn't she go? Maybe she could rescue those that were captive and surely being tortured. *Right*?

Come nightfall, they found a safe place to rest and rejuvenate before the long stretch east to Redwood Wall in the morning. They made a fire and Dorian (being the only one with fingers) cooked up a bit of grub they had brought along on their journey. Once they ate, Fayden spent a bit of time teaching Dorian more of the Silethin language. In the time Fayden had lived in the Core World, she had learned from the faeries a handful of Silethin words and phrases that could be used as enchantments. There had yet come a time for her to utilize her knowledge of these but she was grateful she had learned them and trusted wholeheartedly they would one day prove to be a great asset. Fayden thought it might be useful to teach a few such enchantments to Dorian.

"Griffins have a fierce attack with their talons. Yes, the sulfuric dust they breathe is lethal and by far the worst of their tactics, but if you are gouged by a talon, you will not die (unless struck in appropriate places on your body) but the transfer of their DNA onto your skin will produce a most excruciating welt that will cause immobility to the injured limb. Worse yet, the wound will slowly erode the tissue until it is completely disintegrated. You will thus be left no longer having an arm, leg, or wherever you are struck…the surrounding tissue will diminish." Said Fayden.

Dorian was busying herself with a handful of grass, "So I'm assuming there is an enchantment against this?"

"Yes. If this devastation should ever occur to you, find any manner of plant life nearest to you. Place it where the Griffin penetrated you and speak the words, duhlanis metip, and surely within a few moments there will be a suppression of blood loss and numbing of the pain. In an hour's time the wound will have ceased its deterioration."

"'Duhlanis metip'", Dorian asked, "means?"

Fayden answered, "World's power."

Dorian continued with her insightful query, "So the enchantment calls upon the power of the Core World to heal? But, how would," she caught herself as she began to piece together just how such an enchantment worked. Fayden followed Dorian's gaze…studying the fascination swimming through the young girl's mind, "It's the same reason one begins to glow after having inhabited Minaleth. The power, the magik, of the Core World takes effect and the faeries must have discovered the use of words in summoning the power. How fantastic. It's as if – as if one is able to *speak* to the World and in doing so, it responds. " Her eyes glistened with discovery and excitement.

"Such wisdom is not often found so quickly. Well done. Take care not to discard the insight that falls upon you. Too many individuals of intellect gain exceptional knowledge and depth but fail to apply it, thus causing the consequential wisdom to lie dormant and forgotten within the soul." Fayden kept her eyes intently on Dorian as she spoke.

"I know." Dorian said simply.

The Commander squinted slightly, turning her head in doubt, but smiled to conceal it. The night had well descended upon the group and Serian thought it best for everyone to retire. The three felines cozied their selves around each other near the fire while Dorian slipped under her pup-tent. It did not take long for the others to drift into slumber, resting their worn minds and muscles. The night was soft – soft in ambiance, soft in aroma and in sound – soft. As the sand carpets the ocean's deep, so the night masked the sky and gently crept through all space, leaving nothing untouched. Dorian played out her plan in her mind as she lay staring up into the vast expanse that was not truly a sky. *If I follow this route back north a short distance then continue slightly west, I know that would put me in the general area of where the Hawk Lords are held captive. As long as I can free one I should be Ok because whomever I free can, in turn, help me to release the others and retreat. All I need to do is beware of the Griffins, really. Take care to avoid their talons and suppress them in any way before they have the chance to douse myself or any others in a sulfuric cloud.* To Dorian, the plan seemed plausible and likely to be successful. She was so desperate to put things right, to rescue her allies, that the logic of her mind hadn't the ability to dissuade the determination of her heart.

Under the shade of night, Dorian silently crept from the others, suited in her armor and equipped with her katana, as she made her way back up the path she had earlier travelled. Heading north, northwest as planned, Dorian allowed her boots to meld to the ground beneath her in order to absorb the noise of her footsteps. Slowly Dorian put an increasing amount of distance between her and the others. She was careful to avoid loose debris that could potentially give away her presence and as she walked she allowed her senses to capture every sound, movement, aroma – all momentary changes. The wind that swept past her face, over her hands, through her hair, carried in it the essence of the mountains. More than once the hair on the back of her neck stood on end as she heard the distant rustling of a potential enemy. She was swift to crouch then lie completely flat on her belly as a snake. Slithering over the soil, she would make her way to the nearest covering and wait for the phantom entity to dissipate beyond her awareness. Once under the impression that all was clear and safe, she would emerge and continue her quest to the Hawk Lords. *We have the ability to rescue the Hawks and I can't let that pass. I think the others underestimate our strength…we're this close; we must be capable of some good.*

Little did Dorian know her mind was being clouded by naivety and ignorance. Her thoughts were being manipulated by bitterness, power, false confidence and confusion. She was unknowingly allowing an inevitable trepidation to consume her life.

In no way was Dorian's nightscape easy. She was smart to understand this was not actually her world and there was a plethora she knew nothing of. For all she knew, a granule of dirt could suddenly sprout up against her with a pitch-fork. Yes, that is absurd, but she didn't want to find out the hard way so though she *knew* the sounds tormenting her were only resonance of wind and animals, she took extra precaution and stayed mainly to the ground, crawling. The first little while, she quite enjoyed herself. She felt like a soldier - crawling along the soil to avoid enemy capture – the child in her was too much to resist. After a couple hours of it however, and being covered in muck, one rethinks the joy of such a situation. The areas of skin not protected by her armor were blistered and bloody with scratches as she was forced numerous times to climb over and through hazardous, inanimate life. Thorns, bark, rocks, and the like manipulated and abused the vulnerable bits of the young girl. Near dawn, or the equivalent thereof, Dorian had far gone from the path, through brush and overgrowth, and had found her way to the forest of trees the Hawk Lords once possessed though now were held captive within. Her persistence was great but Dorian knew before engaging in anything she would need to rest and restore her energy. She scanned her surroundings for a haven and was lucky enough to notice a decaying log, completely overgrown in moss, topped with leaves, perfect for a little needed self-restoration. She crawled in, had a bite to eat and guzzled as much water as she could, then without worry or hesitation fell fast asleep, curled in a ball.

Chapter 9
Admirable   Confidence   or Foolishness?

"Dorian is gone!" Grenig shouted in great desperation. He had woken first and when he could see Dorian was not near their site, he went looking for her and knew she had either left or been taken when, after an hour, he was unable to find the girl.

Fayden was quick to understand where their warrior had gone, "She has gone back to the Hawk Lords. Damn that girl's persistence." She said, shaking her head. The Commander was disappointed. Dorian led them to believe she would not attempt to rescue the Hawks. A noble endeavor, yes, but Dorian was aware of the danger and hazards liable to fall upon her as well as the others and perhaps even Redwood Wall. Fayden understood the warrior's earnest desire to free their comrades but far be it from the Commander to overlook foolishness.

Serian could see the frustration upon his friend's face, "Commander, dear Fayden, the girl's move was foolish indeed but with noble intent. We cannot scold our warrior for doing that which she intrinsically cannot ignore. She *is* a *Warrior* in every respect." Serian's words were true and with good intentions but Fayden could not shake the fear and frustration she had for Dorian. She knew what dangers lay in the region the young girl was heading towards.

***

When she awoke, the sky was radiant in its other-worldly display while the unfortunate landscape conveyed sorrow, desolation. The green of trees and the colors of occasional flowers were still there but the eminent beauty had been lost. Dorian stretched as best she could in her log haven before crawling out to reach full, satisfying extension. It was then that she began calculating the safest and most efficient tactic for infiltrating the nests that were once home to the Hawk Lords. The nests that were now torture chambers to noble, powerful creatures of beauty. Without warning, not even so much as a twig snapping,

Dorian was pierced with a spell-bounding pain that sent quivers up her spine and numbness to all her limbs. She did not dare shriek but with her eyes searched for the cause of such an attack.

"You will not see me, as best you try. Do not attempt to overpower me, for I, who without question, hold you at dire disadvantage." The voice was raspy, deep and distinctive in pitch. Dorian's tiny neck hairs stood on end at the sound of the creature.

"Who are you?" She inquired, convincingly disguising the concern in her voice.

"I wonder, how is it that you first ask 'who' rather than 'what'?" The voice spoke.

Was this a trick? "I have seen many unique creatures in Minaleth in my time here thus far. What reason would I have to question one's structure when it is not the structure with which I am interested?"

Dorian's response seemed to impress the being, "You speak well for a youth. The wisdom spoken of you proves true." The numbing sensation ceased as the creature continued, "You are the warrior that has been spoken of. Words of your skill have travelled through Minaleth. I urge you once more, for I sense your courage – do not attempt an offense against me. Understand that you can neither see me nor fathom the advantage I have against you."

Still without full comprehension, Dorian submitted to that which had her control, "I only wish to know who you are,"…under her breath she added, "…and I'm not *that* young."

"Warrior of the Withering World, child of Man, you speak now with Loreuhnd. A drisolek." He, named Loreuhnd, spoke very directly in a nerve-rattling way.

With that said, Dorian was quickly relieved of the mysterious spell that had concealed the drisolek and was now looking down at a kneeling being who appeared human but possessed visible differences. He had taken position just to the right of the log where the scarcely moss-covered ground dipped slightly.

"I am not dense, young warrior. I see by your eyes that you are curious as to my origin." Dorian couldn't argue that. It was true. "I – as I said – am a drisolek. In centuries past when the first humans made the descent to the Core World, only the following generation were human borne to a new world. Every generation henceforth of human heritage was pure from Minaleth soil. Pure to our blood of Core World magik, though resembling with reason the image of our Withering World cousins, we became known as drisoleks. A term derived of the Silethin language aptly meaning 'human of below'."

Dorian nodded and gazed in fascination. The tale made sense and from Loreuhnd's appearance, seemed legitimate. Pulling his self up, he stood comfortably around eight feet in height, emanating a dark, bronze sheen and eyes reflecting the shadowed greens of a forest. His arms, legs, and torso were protected in a light weight, black armor, undecorated yet in some way omnipotent. Beneath this was a predictable earthen-colored tunic and knee-high boots having no heel and made of a leather-like material. These laced up under his tunic, attaching to an unseen waistband. Weaved in the laces on each leg hid a small hilken dagger, neither straight nor curved but extending shortly from the handle in a sideways 'V'. It reminded Dorian of a jagged question mark. Around his chiseled neck, Loreuhnd wore a tightly fitting necklace forged of blunted pieces taken from the iron riverbed. Similar to what hung 'round the faeries' necks. These – he explained later on – gave the drisoleks cognitive power of Core World magik. From the direct and constant connection to the riverbed, drisoleks had the ability to discern and anticipate through concentration the location and intentions of foes. The difference between what Loreuhnd wore and what the faeries fashioned was the manner in which the pieces were forged. The medallion that faeries wore was a sign of allegiance to the Brights. A symbol of alliance to all that is good and right. While faeries worked iron that had chipped from the river, drisoleks worked the iron directly from the river. His hair -- as all male drisoleks – was ebony in color and course in texture – perfect for the wild yet controlled hair-do; a style the male drisoleks fashioned. Stiff spikes of about four inches in length stood from all 'round his head. Intimidating, rather than ridiculous, they were strategically placed and appeared pointed for the intent of inflicting harm.
"What is it you intend of me?" Dorian finally inquired.
Loreuhnd responded calmly, "I'm sure you have been told of the 'human' beings that dwell in the Core World and of our neutral

stance. It is true we are neutral to battles though we very much find no appreciation in the common and unchanged mistake in the description of us as 'human'. We are more than human. More powerful and with many advantages. For this we hold bitterness to the Brights. But we are given no respect from the Shadows, Griffins, and other creatures of Minaleth and thus side not with them either." Dorian nodded in understanding and the drisolek continued, "We do however find need to be active and so agreed to aid the Griffins when they asked of us to guard the region we now speak within."

"What is it you were told do with those you caught?" Dorian was curious.

Loreuhnd could comprehend the girl's concern for her welfare, "The Griffins merely instructed us to bring any unwanted creatures to the cluster of trees not far from here."

"You are aware that they are holding captive the Hawk Lords? Inflicting brutality and degradation upon such noble beings?" Dorian's heroism began to flare.

What she said appeared to strike the drisolek with shock and interest. He paused momentarily in thought, "I was unaware but it is not in my nature to inquire of details such as these." Loreuhnd was evidently processing with some stress the new information he had been given. Drisoleks were not eager to join any particular side but the Hawk Lords had provided relief to the drisoleks many ages ago when Nitris had cruelly decided to set her sulfur-breathing Griffins to the homes of the humans of below. Many young drisoleks had been caught in the unconstituted attack, along with a number of elders and well-fitted men and women. In their wisdom, the Hawks had anticipated Nitris' foolish antics and were to the drisoleks' rescue within moments of the initial onslaught.

"Lord Tukiund was responsible for the salvation of my daughter, Oreighnthia, who had been caught in a sulfur cloud made by Griffins. I had been elsewhere on the offensive when I heard of her predicament. Tukiund however braved the sulfuric burns and brought my daughter from the devastation." Loreuhnd expressed emotion as he continued, "My dear friend was not so fortunate to escape the Griffins. In his attempt to aid Tukiund and my daughter, he became ensnared within the grip of those treacherous talons of one of the beasts. His battle distracted the others from the Hawk and my daughter, luring them to assist in his destruction. Those dark creatures tore him not simply from his limbs but from every joint and muscle in his powerful body."

Dorian could see the pain in Loreuhnd's eyes and understood with great sympathy what he was leading to, "I'm sorry, Loreuhnd." She said with earnest sincerity. She felt hesitant however to describe Tukiund's deceptive freedom to Redwood Wall.

"I will assist you, young warrior," he looked down to Dorian's eyes, "to avenge my comrade and cease the Griffins from inflicting such horrors on you or your friends." His enchanting, dark green eyes burned with hellfire as he said the words. "I cannot simply disregard the task the Shadows have given me, however. If so, they will inquire of me and surely I will be executed." Loreuhnd moved his eyes in thought before motioning for Dorian to draw nearer.

***

Mid-day, Fayden and the others were continuing to follow Dorian's scent. They were cautious, however, being sure to press on slowly and without displaying any real intent of search. If they were to be ambushed or scouted by any Shadow they certainly did not want to divulge the truth of Dorian's presence. Many a moment, one of the dear creatures caught on to her trail but was given only the slight hope of her direction, for without expectation, her scent would dissipate. They could not conjure an explanation between each other for their phantom warrior. Nevertheless they trekked on, determined to find the precious girl.

As the group of three marched on, Serian and Grenig could not understand why their great Commander was sorely cursing the path Dorian had chosen. Her words, spoken in true Silethin, were barely distinguishable to the other two, but Serian was able to discern an unanticipated anger in her voice. It was especially brow-raising, considering the level of affection and joy Fayden and Dorian had shared in the weeks leading to now. He watched ahead, observing the Commander as she brushed her nose vigorously through the dirt and among the flora. Why was she so irate? Why did she seem to be losing control? He dared not ask but decided to allow his concerns to linger in his thoughts.

***

"Young warrior, are you ready?" Loreuhnd asked, if not slightly worriedly.

Dorian looked to the concerned Drisolek. Speaking softly with great authority she said in a nearly perfect Silethin accent, "Nokun terr reyh yevir kuna vodan; nokun corris reyh yevir kuna terr. Kelden reyla bej ihn rol wilrev." She did not have to wonder if Loreuhnd understood the proverb. A glaze of emotion and confidence welled in his eyes as he smiled, ready to defend and defeat.

The drisolek knew full well that as close as Dorian had travelled to the Hawk Lords there were sure to be a few Shadows lurking around the woods. He instructed Dorian to gather her things and begin climbing a nearby tree so she could have a bird's-eye-view of the surroundings and her destination. This was a ploy to fool any Shadow that had been aware of Dorian but it was also a tool Loreuhnd wanted the girl to have. With such a view, and a warrior's memory, she would be able to navigate the region. After slinging her katana over her back, Dorian threw her blanket around the trunk and shimmied up the tree with ease. Atop the tree on the highest branches she took a secure stance and gazed out upon the western mountains stretching across a vast, dreary landscape with only pockets of remaining beauty. Just north of her current position, Dorian could see a cluster of enormous, thick trees. *The Hawk Lords. That must be where they are. I can save you...I can.* Immediately, everything disappeared from her sight. She was blind. Calling for Loreuhnd, she noticed one other ailment...her voice had been taken. Putting her training to action, Dorian crouched for secure balance, slowed her breathing and trusted her remaining senses to guide her. *Perfect,* she thought. *I try to rescue great beings but end up blind and mute at the top of an enormous tree.*

Resenting her current predicament, Dorian wondered the whereabouts of her new-found friend, Loreuhnd. She reached slowly for her weapon as she heard the faintest rustling of leaves. But with her fingers grazing the handle of her katana, she suddenly found herself smothered and forced into a sack. She did not struggle, for it would have been futile...she was blind and mute...what would she do, even if she was able to break free? As Dorian considered who had captured her and where she was being

taken, she slowly felt heavy disorientation take hold of her. *Oh wonderful! A poisoned sack...let's just see how lon.....* Her thought faded as did her consciousness.
***

The enormous, mystical cats instinctively crouched all at once. Each had caught the fowl scent and knew they were being followed. They glanced at each other, understanding the meaning conveyed with each set of narrowed eyes. Fayden drew her thoughts from Dorian and now focused on the potential danger at hand. She moved back to Serian and Grenig in order to form a circle, each cat facing a different direction. Their ears flickered and flattened as they listened for trouble. Their pupils were at their widest as they scanned the woods. Nothing seen. Nothing heard. But the stench permeating the area was proof of something or someone approaching.

"What do you suppose is going on?" Grenig whispered to Serian, in a barely audible voice below his breath.

Serian did not even turn his head. Still intently scanning, he whispered in return, "Something ominous."

PART TWO
FRIEND OR FOE?

Chapter 10
So Much for Trust

Dorian awoke coughing and hacking; *sulfur*, she thought to herself as she noticed the foul taste in her mouth. Her eyes had crusted over from whatever magik that caused her to be blind but without even seeing she could discern that griffins were involved with her current predicament. She wondered if Loreuhnd had anything to do with this. Or perhaps he, too, had been captured. If he had been captured, he certainly would be dead by now, as he would have been considered a traitor to the Shadows. Dorian began mentally beating herself up, thinking her irrational behavior now resulted in her capture and the possible death of a drisolek.

No. You can't think like that. Breathe. Focus. Dorian began relaxing her tense muscles, giving pace to her breaths, and pushing out the instabilities of her mind. *Calm*, she thought to herself. Meditation set in. Dorian had yet opened her eyes. Not knowing where she was or exactly what kind of disadvantageous position she was in, she emptied her mind of all matter surrounding her. She completely let go of all thoughts, emotions and fears that were clouding her mind and sank into a deep meditation. Dorian knew that if she allowed her emotions and self-criticism to alter her perceptions and focus, she would never find a way out of the situation.

Without fear, there can be no courage; without love, there can be no fear. Dorian used the beautiful proverb as a mantra. As she sat reclaiming her warrior mindset, she heard the sounds of someone, or something, entering the room.

"Look at that stupid human. Look how she's sitting!" She could discern from the raspy, course words that this particular individual was a griffin. He spoke in a menacing, mocking tone, "Tryin' to forget how pathetic you are? Preparing for your much anticipated death, little girl!? Ha!"

Another voice broke in, one she recognized, "What is it you plan on doing with her?" Loreuhnd spoke, but with a slight tremble in his voice.

"What's it to you, maggot!" Dorian peeked with one eye to see a power-hungry griffin standing in front of Loreuhnd, who was locked in the arms of a Shadow. He angrily glared deep into Loreuhnd's eyes, taunting him with delicate spurts of deadly breaths. "You filthy drisolek! Helping this sad excuse you and the Brights call a *warrior*! Do you not realize that you will surely be terminated for your insolence?"

Loreuhnd rebutted in a calm, democratic manner, "My insolence? Why, I believe I did as I was asked. I brought this foe to your attention, ceasing her strategy to infiltrate this very place." Dorian's ears perked as she quickly made the connection and knew she was somewhere in the cluster of trees where the Hawk Lords were being held. She decided to listen in a little more intently to the commotion ensuing through the opened door in the next room.

The creature holding Loreuhnd gripped tighter as she scolded, "You filthy, human descendent! Do you think us incompetent? We know you had intentions to aid her plight." The Shadow struck Loreuhnd across the face with such viciousness to leave a bloody gash beneath his right eye. The drisolek just stood silent.

Ummm, this guy is down-right confusing. I need to figure out if Loreuhnd is trustworthy or just a wolf in sheep's clothing.

The Shadow holding on to Loreuhnd was something Dorian could hardly describe. The wings of a bat, though a deep red in colour. She, discernible by her voice, stood with unnatural dimension…standing on her hind legs that bent opposite to the natural way while grasping the drisolek with her front legs (or arms). Bird-like feet with powerful looking claws, all a midnight black, clasped and pierced Loreuhnd's body. Her eyes, narrow and malicious, burned with the same deep, blood-red of her wings. Neither beak nor lips, she spoke through a frightening maw much like a lizard's, but with far more and much bigger teeth.

What a disgusting creature. She's going to be a problem.

Just as Dorian thought this, as if it had heard her thoughts, the Shadow cast a petrifying glare Dorian's way. Noticing the subtle movement when Dorian shut her open eye, the Shadow motioned for the Griffin to check on the girl.

"Get up, *warrior*!" The Shadow teased, "Don't you have Hawks to save? You pathetic human! Your precious Wise Bright has no chance against Nitris and her followers! You should try getting that through your head!"

Dorian confidently replied, "Well, if you put it that way then that thought has already gone through my head...it just went in one ear and out the other." She smirked. Immediately the Shadow shoved Loreuhnd from her arms and into the arms of the Griffin as she dashed across the room towards Dorian, murder burning in her eyes. It approached Dorian with an outstretched arm and pulled the girl to her feet as she dug into Dorian's neck with her claws. Dorian couldn't help wincing in agony as she felt the sting of the creature's claws penetrating her flesh. Steadfast in heart, confident in mind, Dorian went with the flow of actions.

"So, I'm Dorian. Now you know me, what's your name?" Dorian was calm and spoke mordantly as she looked the Shadow in the eyes without fear.

The now perturbed, sadistic Shadow leaned in closer, so as to intimidate the young girl. She tightened her grip on Dorian and forced her against a wall, "You are in the clutches of Atorik and if you wish to sustain your impudent life, I suggest you cease the mockery and shut your mouth!"

Dorian wanted so badly to respond with sarcasm but she could feel blood trickling down her back from the voraciously given wound on her neck and knew it was time to stop. She said nothing in return but did not pull her gaze from Atorik's smoldering eyes. Dorian held her ground, now very aware that she and the beast were equally threatened by one another. Dorian was well trained in the ever vast arts of the mind and its systems of branches and rivers and orchestrated lightning strikes all 'round. She knew the beast was aware they were now on level playing ground.

"You are lucky my orders are to keep you alive, otherwise..." Atorik made a motion to indicate her desire to kill Dorian. With an evil grin and hard stare down, she finally loosened her grip of Dorian to allow the girl to drop to the floor.

"Now what do we do"? asked the griffin while continuing to hold the drisolek. Atorik said quickly as she began to storm out, "Give me this fool," she was referring to Loreuhnd, "and you go chain up that impudent pest." Finishing her sentence, she led

Loreuhnd out the door while Dorian was fastened into a pillory by the griffin. There were many words Dorian wanted to say to him but she eerily grinned and did not attempt to fight back or escape. Once secure, the griffin left the room, leaving Dorian in solitude. Finally.

***

Alert, standing prepared for battle, the three magikal cats were relieved when instead of a troublesome diversion from their mission, they were greeted by Dekel. However, the exhausted blue bird was struggling to catch her breath as she frantically arrived and perched herself on a rock next to Fayden. When she was calm, she informed the small pack of a group of griffins not far from their current position but she was fortunate enough to hear them discussing matters regarding Dorian's whereabouts.

"...as helpful as your message is, I cannot forfeit my curiosity of why you are here in the first place." Fayden was not angry but Serian detected a hint of contempt in the way she spoke to Deki. Serian's thoughts on the matter drifted in his mind as he decided to focus on the important information of Dorian's location.

Deki did not hesitate to answer, "Wise Bright asked of me to seek you. He knew. He could feel the hardships confronting you."

"Where is your other half?" Grenig asked with a smile, unknowing of the intricacy of the simple question.

With a sullen expression, Dekel answered, "Adalei? Something has poisoned her heart, her mind. She is gone; a Shadow to become. Kind-hearted as she may be, righteousness of such has clouded her mind..."

Serian spoke, quick to change the subject to get to the pertinent matter at hand, "Our gratitude is immeasurable, sweet Deki! Please, do not wait any longer and tell us where our warrior is!"

"I'm sorry, Serian, I do not know,"...Deki appeared petrified. Perhaps she felt the intrinsic fear birds have towards cats of all kinds... "I only heard the beasts speaking her name and the torture she has been suffering not far north of here."

Grenig caught the faintest hint of a growl released from Fayden, "Commander..." He gave Fayden an assertive glare before she shook away what Grenig was sensing. Serian then broke in once more to get down to business, "Dekel, lead us to the griffins."

***

The griffins Dekel had spoken of were surely in the place she led them to. Standing as a group of three, they were exchanging vulgar gestures of what they believed was happening to Dorian. They were unguarded and mentally absent from the danger now circling their position. Dekel had once again perched herself out of harm's way, slightly hidden by the leaves on the branch of a nearby tree. Her given task was to distract the beasts – pull them from their current position so Fayden and the other two would have the chance to gain the advantage of first strike. Serian and Grenig flanked either side of Fayden as each inched closer in their phantom cat-like way, making not a sound as Deki gave intermittent chirps. It was crucial for the strategy to be executed with extreme precision. Serian and Grenig each needed to attack a beast while Fayden was to control the third. Targeting the jugulars was imminent to succeed.

Dekel was clever and drew the griffins from the small clearing they had been in to a maze of trees. The cats used this and took position within the trees, with the exception of Fayden. She boldly yet cautiously walked in full view towards her target. It was a cause for concern, particularly for Serian, but she seemed to know what she was doing and was, after all, the Commander, so Serian let his doubts evaporate. The three cats were attuned to one another's unspoken language…such as the communication with their eyes, body language, and the like. Understanding the moment of attack was at hand – paw, that is – Dekel gave a final chirp as Serian and Grenig each pounced a griffin with ready bared teeth and outstretched claws. Serian's attack was strategic, waiting as his target's attention was pulled toward Grenig, then leaping with a fatal swipe of his massive paw. The thing screamed in a retched gargle as muscle and flesh were exposed and torn from its body. Serian did not hesitate to finish the kill. After landing, he swiftly turned, jowls wide with respite, teeth bared, and ripped the remainder of the griffin's vital arteries from its throat. Grenig was a little more direct in his attack. He aimed for his target's vulnerable throat as Serian had, but was interested in a more immediate kill. He jumped to his opponent and in a matter of seconds the beast was down, Grenig on top of it, its neck broken and throat torn to shreds by Grenig's powerful jaw. Still, Fayden was not ceasing her determined strides towards the final griffin.

As well, the griffin seemed frozen in time. It did not flinch, shift, even blink. Why and how would Fayden and this particular griffin put on such a synchronized demonstration, thought Serian. When the two creatures were a mere ten feet from one another, Fayden came to a halt without taking her powerful glare from the beast's own eyes. Grenig, too, was now watching the spectacle, utterly lost as to what to think. Serian could no longer passively observe while his Commander stood so fatally close to such an unorthodox griffin. He made a move towards them but only managed a couple of steps before he noticed the subtle shift in the petrified griffin's eyes, as if it was silently telling Fayden where something, or someone, was. With no hesitation, the beast then lowered its head in a sort of ritualistic way as Fayden, on cue, placed a paw on its head, wrapped her mouth around its neck and jerked her head to twist its neck. The thing lay dead at her feet. She turned to see Grenig and Serian dubiously watching her, utterly perplexed at what they just witnessed, waiting for instruction. They knew not to inquire about her odd interaction with the dead griffin as it would undoubtedly procure disastrous results. Finding Dorian was the first and foremost priority.

"And now?" Serian asked in a rather grave tone.

Fayden replied blankly, "We move on." Nothing more. No explanation. No direction. She simply turned and began walking in the direction the griffin's eyes had glanced towards in its final moments.

***

When Dorian had been left in captive solitude, she did not immediately struggle and try to escape from the pillory-like contraption she was in. She did not call out for help or shed a tear. Rather, being the warrior that she was, Dorian's first response to her segregation was meditation. She let her body fall limp, easing the tension in her muscles and allowed her mind to deviate from the current situation. Methodically she inhaled, then exhaled…slowly inhaling through her nose and exhaling through her mouth. Inhale. Exhale. She relaxed her mind to concentrate only on her breathing. Pushing her stomach out rather than her chest, she brought oxygen into her body. Feeling it inhabit every muscle, each cell…inhale. Exhale. She focused on the ever useful oxygen now enveloping her sweet brain and swarming her lungs.

With her eyes gently closed she continued this, directing her focus after reasonable time to different parts of her body until she felt an all-around calm. Her mind gradually sauntered away from the focus of breathing to yield an inner calm and stretched its boundaries to include thoughts of her journey thus far. She opened her mind to Minaleth, to all she learned, heard, saw, felt. Scrupulously Dorian fished through the ripple of thoughts for anything hinting of a favorable solution. Before long she remembered something Wise Bright said, though not to her. It seemed, somehow, Dorian's mind passed through some sort of channel because what Dorian was remembering was what Wise Bright had spoken to the Council when he announced Nitris was after war. With her eyes still closed and rapidly moving beneath her eyelids as she recalled the event she hadn't actually been present for, Dorian slowly raised her left leg. Gracefully, as she was quite limber, Dorian's leg drew near enough to her right hand for her to touch her boot. She manipulated and stretched her fingers as she reached inside and pulled out a small quantity of dirt. She then allowed her leg to drop freely once more, while she clasped the bit of dirt in her palm. The entranced warrior delicately fiddled with the granules as details of her current predicament fled her myriad of thoughts and entered the small particles of Minalethin soil tumbling between her fingertips.

In the beautiful skyshine of violets, pinks and oranges, Wise Bright suddenly felt a shiver that ran up his small trunk and through his blossoms. He was familiar with such a feeling but it caught him off guard. Wise Bright had been serenely still, watching the magikal sky in solitude in the Eastern Absent. In the moment Wise Bright felt the shiver through his body, he immediately directed his thoughts to his small yet mighty roots that stretched below. As electricity travels through conductive materials Wise Bright's thoughts rushed down his roots to meet with the fragments of magik sent by Dorian. The Cherry Tree's consciousness travelled, passing by fierce currents of magik, skyshine and rock. A kaleidoscope of colours, textures and sounds all intertwining but not becoming tangled in the voyage. A collision of desires finally occurred with a blinding flash of white light and Wise Bright was filled with the torment his dear Dorian was now experiencing. Again his consciousness travelled through the intangible and with a single breath, Wise Bright opened his eyes.

Chapter 11
Unnerving Revelations

Two nights had passed since she first wandered away from her three Bright friends. Dorian still dangled from the pillory like a suit up to dry. She had been beaten and bruised for no other reason than to satisfy the sick nature of Atorik and the other beasts holding her captive. Dorian could even hear the groans of the Hawks that had been tortured in a nearby room far worse than she. It made her cringe to think of the cruelty. As well, Dorian was forced to eat the second day and she dared not ask what she was consuming. She knew. Something in the texture maybe. Or the flavor. But she knew.

While Dorian was not doubting the probability that her friends would find her, she was beginning to feel somewhat anxious for various reasons. 1. Her arms and neck were now extremely uncomfortable from being held and locked up for so long 2. She had yet been allowed to satisfy her biological needs to expend the waste building up in her body and it was causing her a completely different kind of discomfort 3. She was worried something may have happened to her friends. It caused her grief knowing that if she had obeyed Fayden and not gone off on her own, they may not now be facing great dangers. She was more than aware that her overzealousness was the reason she was in this mess but she could not bring herself to discredit her choice. While Fayden was the Commander of the true Minalethin armada, it did not sit right with her leaving to return to Redwood Wall while precious comrades remained captive. Dorian did not hope but trusted wholeheartedly that Wise Bright, despite certain troublesome obstacles, would cross worlds to rescue Dorian if need be. The relationship between him and Dorian was intrinsic. They had not yet spent years with each other but it was the way they communicated, verbally and nonverbally, that made her feel connected with him in an intimate way. As if she had known him since the beginning. Though she was unable to pinpoint of what beginning she felt.

"It is a shame your friends could not accompany you," Atorik said wryly as she came abruptly through the door. "But I'm sure you are anticipating their arrival."

Dorian did not respond.

Atorik grimaced and started to wander the room as she spoke, "You know, young warrior, I understand that you are not the only human currently gracing us with her presence." She paused to read Dorian's reaction.

The young girl was not so daft though and concealed her displeasure with the reference to Reilly, again saying nothing.

"Speak you insolent child!" Atorik was obviously becoming aggravated with Dorian's silence. Clearly she was hoping to draw reactions of contempt from the girl but Dorian was not going to give her captor the pleasure.

As Dorian simply looked at Atorik with a blank expression, Atorik came in with a hard slap across Dorian's already tender face. A claw intentionally pulled skin and muscle from a part of Dorian's cheek. Finally, Atorik's attempts to elicit any kind of response from the girl succeeded.

Blood dripped from Dorian's ever sweet, blood-caked face and she slowly spoke, "Your name...is Atorik...is it not?" Between words Dorian paused for breaths but also to build suspense to her intent.

"Yes, that is my name! What has this to do with anything?" The prominent anger could not completely mask the confusion and uncertainty in the creature's voice.

Dorian allowed her words to seep out as molasses, "Atorik...what, pray tell, do you know...of this other human?"

The beast narrowed her raging, inferno eyes, "There is a discord between the two of you..."

"You are quick to assume our acquaintance." Dorian said.

Atorik replied, "It is not an assumption, child."

"Then tell me...what great insight...has this human divulged to you?"

Something about this line of questioning did not sit right with the beast and she decided to expedite the annoying process, "The doings of the girl are of no importance to you. Cease this pointless game you are playing for I am not so easily fooled." At that,

Atorik made her way towards the door to once again leave Dorian to herself.

But Dorian had one more thought to send Atorik's way, "Curious, is it not, that in the time your leader...Nitris...went unseen...this other human happened to find her way to your World?"

Atorik's blank expression told Dorian that the thought had failed to cross the Shadow's mind. Without any further banter, Atorik left the room but Dorian had gotten what she wanted. Completely unaware, Atorik had indirectly hinted that she and Reilly were cohorts. That knowledge was if nothing else, a step in the right direction.

***

Despite their innate tracking abilities, Serian and the other two felt they had been travelling in circles over the past couple of days. The wise lion knew it was taking far too long to get absolutely nowhere. With every word and every step, he grew more cautious, if not suspicious, of his Commander. Her actions were appearing increasingly confused...as if her mind was being consumed by a thicket of rose vines. Often Serian would catch the faint mutterings and darting eyes Fayden tried to conceal as she shuffled back and forth.

"Commander..." he gently began.

"Please, friend" she started in a calm tone, "I know the words you wish to speak to me. Do not worry for me and do not lose hope. We will reach our warrior."

Serian did not wish to disrespect or rebut his dear friend and Commander. He bowed his head slightly and left her to her to return to her inner sanctum. It was the time of dawn, now. Still the sky displayed deep, dull shades of royal colors. A reaction from the Core World itself to the ensuing battle between those sharing the very same grace of life. To the world, it was a time of melancholy. Serian gazed up to the approaching skyshine of what he thought to be a beautiful dance of unfortunate emotion. The powerful lion was doused in a flood of the deepest of a gem-like purple shine emanating in waves from the Eastern Absent. It softly highlighted his majestic face, prominently the left side, climbing up over his eye from where his whiskers protruded. His sweet lashes sparkled as the dew upon them caught bits of light. Continuing over most of his magnificent mane and following sweetly along his thick, toned back the unique orange of his coat appeared deeper as the aged and brittle leaves that fall in the autumn of the Withering World above. Somehow reaching out too, from below, the fur of Serian's underbelly breathed quietly in the low undertones of shine. To Grenig he trotted, seeing the colossal tiger resting beneath a nearby tree looking as a tear-worthy work of art. The bulk of the tiger shone with the tones as Serian because of the orange hue but the black of Grenig's stripes magikally absorbed the high tones of shine and cast them again, causing beams of light to burst from them. Opposite of the usual attributes of such an absorbent dark color. Then again, nothing was usual in this magikal land. To lay one's eyes upon such a sight of beauty would steal one's breath. The greatest artists could not capture the awe.

Grenig was not in a slumber, merely resting his head on his outstretched arms, allowing his eyes to rest as well. Serian walked to his cousin and gently lowered his body adjacent to the tiger, tucking his hind legs and straightening his front, to sit as the mythical Sphinx of Egypt. He let out a great yawn that incidentally turned into a small roar, causing Grenig to casually open his eyes, acknowledging his friend's presence.

"You too have heavy shoulders, friend." Grenig commented.

Serian shared his troubles, knowing and understanding that two of equal strength is better than one with strength not to spare, "I fear for our Commander. She is acting in a way I have not had the misfortune of previously experiencing." The lion's sweet eyes looked morose.

"Friend, have you yet considered she could be chained to secrecy of what darkness she is suffering?

"How do you mean?" Asked Serian.

The usually quiet Grenig explained, "Perhaps we are unable to see all that is at play here. Considering the recent events that have taken place, the changes of attitude and the very fact that Nitris seeks war, is it not plausible that our Fayden has fallen under obligation to the very enemy that has taken hostage our maiden warrior?"

Serian allowed the thought to sink in. Such a scenario had not crossed his mind before this encounter. His eyes went wide with realization as he mentally connected the course of their journey.

It was not until the group's passing by Dorian's so-called friend that matters turned sour. He abruptly dropped his jaw and firmly spoke his thoughts, "That girl. That child that caused Dorian grief!"

Grenig was quick to follow, "Reilly. But of what consequence is her junction in the matter, do you suppose?"

Serian did not know but he was certain that the girl was playing a key role in what was now appearing to be a treacherous game. Just then both tiger and lion pricked up their furry ears and started flicking them this way and that. Their large pupils grew even larger as they became intensely aware of an approaching presence. They stood from their positions of rest, grazing alternate hips as they took ready positions facing opposite directions. Without warning both Serian and Grenig felt a tap on their spine and each of their rear ends went up in surprise, with their tails raised and the fur along each of their backs now fluffy. Alert and tense, their claws gripped the dirt as they raised their shoulders and lowered their turning heads to see what caught them off guard. They blankly stared at each other, exchanging head shakes of confusion. Again the cats were surprised when they each felt something brush the fur of his belly. Their ears flattened and their tails lowered. Looking in opposite directions once again, Grenig did not have the pleasure of witnessing what was about to occur. Without a sound, without any visible sign, Serian felt a slight tickle by one of his ears and unexpectedly heard a low, slow whisper of a small voice,

"Helloooo Serian".

Grenig swiftly turned his attention as the wondrous lion let out a blood-curdling roar as he literally jumped straight off the ground with all four legs and landed with his entire body fluffy in shock. His pupils now consumed the whole of his irises and his ears were now embedded to his skull. When he turned to face Grenig, the tiger was keeled over, pawing at the air with his legs as he rolled around in hysterics at what just happened.

"What do you laugh at, you cub!?" Serian thundered, completely confused and flustered.

Continuing to laugh uncontrollably, Grenig simply pointed towards Serian with a paw and it was then that Serian was enlightened. Ralkan, a young but powerful male of the faerie regime, slowly descended and came to rest atop the lion's humorously fluffy head. With a hand over the hilt of the sword at his side, Ralkan bent over with a smirk and waved his other hand as his eyes met Serian's. Serian simply glared back at the menacing faerie, ears still flat, a low growl coming from deep in his belly. Grenig was still out of control on the ground, enjoying the spectacle while Serian's paws went up to scoop Ralkan from above his head and sweep him to the ground. While Grenig was gathering his composure, Ralkan brushed himself off and stood respectfully before Serian. He was a strong faerie with powerful legs and a relentless passion for the art of sword fighting equal to that of Dorian. As all faeries, Ralkan carried the traditional dagger but holstered next to that was a katana fashioned by the hands of a magnificent faerie craftsman. The fighter's wild hair shone a brilliant cobalt blue, along with his wings. The tone of his skin was slightly darker than that of his kin. It was because Ralkan spent much time observing and understanding shadows. Still a Bright, his magikal luster was simply a different hue. The katana at his side was proportional to his small stature but completely undiminished in ability. Engraved along the edge of the blade was the phrase, *"Regret not, for everything you have has made you who you are."*

"I apologize for such an informal greeting, Sires," Ralkan began, bowing slightly as he spoke, "I do, in fact, come with a message. I have been sent by Flutter to have you return to Redwood Wall." *Why in the world would Flutter summon our return?* Thought Serian.

Ralkan explained further, "Wise Bright has sensed a direct disturbance from Dorian." The faerie knew very well the fragility regarding Dorian's well-being. He was careful with his following words, "Wise Bright fears for the continuation of habitation in Minaleth. He wishes the three of you return immediately to be ready for battle as well as form a rescue coalition to retrieve Dorian." Ralkan paused to allow necessary processing.

"So, why…" Grenig began but Ralkan interrupted, knowing what the tiger was going to inquire, "Wise Bright needed Flutter, so Flutter sent me." Grenig and Serian nodded in understanding.

"But where is the Commander?" Asked the faerie.

Serian turned his head in the direction Fayden wandered, "She is taking a moment."

Ralkan did not push the subject. He knew it would be unwise to express his opinion about Fayden stepping away in such a time. His head nodded in acknowledgement of the silent communication between him and Serian. His wings gracefully flapped as his body lifted from the ground to hover at eye level with the lion. With a subtle exchange of bowed heads Ralkan was off, swiftly heading east to Redwood Wall.

Serian and Grenig watched as the faerie flew out of sight. An ominous breeze of cold swept through the trees all about them, breaking the calm of the World at that moment. The deep rouges and violets of the morning skyshine had dissipated and swirled with reflections of the emerald ground, creating a magnificent display much like that of Aurora Borealis in the North of the Withering World. The large cats watched as the colors seemed to manipulate the leaves and even the dust and soil at their paws. As the two slowly turned their bodies to make their way to Fayden, the Commander happened to be sauntering towards them, also observing the spectacle of magik. That breeze now danced along the ground towards Fayden and engulfed her being in a tornado of colour, energy and magik. After a moment, Fayden, Serian and Grenig made eye contact with one another. Each, including Fayden, understanding the precarious situation they were now faced with.

In a brisk, determined pace, the group of one less finally made their way back over the mountains to Redwood Wall.

Chapter 12
Ensumei

Dorian awoke abruptly from her painful slumber as she still hung in the pillory. Dripping in a cold sweat she swiftly searched her mind to remember the dream that was overwhelmingly profound. She closed her eyes softly and tried to rekindle the sensations, what she observed, what she felt. Slowly and vaguely the scene came back to her memory. She could feel a breeze, powerful and exuberant, displacing the plush soil beneath her feet and softly breathing amidst the tender grass. She was standing in the meadow, at the bank of the North Stream. Her eyes were yet opened but she felt the misty sensation of the comfortable water being lifted through the air as the breeze waltzed in her presence. A whimper of pleasure seeped from her being as a tropical-like warmth enveloped her body and cast upon her rays of glorious joy. Gazing across the brilliant turquoise stream, glinting with wisps of an enchanting gem-like shade of Bleeding Hearts. The sight of clear blue waters in a tropical escape is unsurpassable to the hypnotic, mesmerizing display of such a magikally inclined stream. Recalling such a magnificent vision to behold quieted Dorian's spirit. Is was as if she was actually back in her dream and experiencing it for a second time. It felt all too real. Her extremities were tingling with anticipation as goose-bumps appeared upon her creamy skin. Just as the magik of the Core World had enveloped Fayden just prior to her, Serian's and Grenig's return to Redwood Wall, so the magik once again began to dance and move in sync with the breeze until it had fully engulfed the Banyan resting peacefully within the water. It was a captivating sight! The tree was now aglow with a white light cast as from magnesium flares. Still, yet, were the colors effervescent in the permeating cloud of magik. Still pulling the scene from within her subconscious, Dorian caught a brief glimpse of another entity. She was unsure as to its origin but felt a breath of familiarity. Squinting now, both in her dream world and as she hung captive, she was able to faintly make out the features and size associated with faeries. Though she could not determine the particular faerie. With a thunderous clash of magikal impact, Dorian woke from the recollected dream world and felt in her soul the fiery coals of emancipation!

"Kayfin!" She exclaimed under her breath, eyes wide in one thousand fathoms of confidence and understanding. Dorian was now dangling in the contraption holding her to the wall with a wry smile and twitch of her head. It was time.

***

"Ralkan!" Wise Bright opened his arms with welcome and gratitude as the group made their way to Council's cabin quarters. "Thank you, Sir Ralkan, for returning to us these precious warriors." The Cherry Tree of Old then lowered is head in a bow to each of the returning Brights but wasted no time in getting to business.

He began, "Intelligence has discovered the Shadows have made massive headway in their excavation to the riverbed. It is their purpose to seize my connection to the riverbed, as well as any other connections, in order to minimize our options and advantages. Disconnection of any sort disables our cognitive intuition derived from the magik of our world. The situation would become desperate."

"What are your orders, sire?" Fayden asked, still somewhat displaced from earlier.

Drawing reactions of shock, Wise Bright replied, "Let your mind not be perplexed with how to aid Dorian. She must now learn her own strengths, weaknesses and draw from her wisdom to alter her predicament. Fear not, she will return to us in time."

Every creature that heard the words spoken from Wise Bright could not believe it. Only one dared challenge him, "We cannot just…" Fayden had began in frustration but was cut short by Wise Bright, "We can and must. She is in her own battle now." He said with pronounced fervency and sternness.

***

All along, without the knowledge of any creature in Minaleth, not even Wise Bright, Kayfin had ever so diligently continued to keep watch over Dorian on her quest. When Dorian had slipped from the watch of her Bright friends, Kayfin did not falter by leaving the warrior to traverse the dangers of Minaleth without any semblance of assistance. No, Kayfin silently took wing, high out of Dorian's ever watchful eyes and discerning ears, the young faerie remained a phantom in Dorian's presence, within the tree tops. It so happened that as Dorian had climbed skyward to get that bird's-eye-view before Loreuhnd captured her, Kayfin had scrambled to use the magik of faeries to cloak her presence as a leaf, for she had been patiently waiting within the very same tree. So of course Kayfin was sure to follow the drisolek, with his sack o' warrior, right to the cluster of trees wherein Dorian was to be held as captive, along with the Hawk Lords. Discovering such a tumultuous situation was far beyond the abilities of the young faerie and she knew well of it. With her icy faerie eyes, she imprinted the location in her memory and flew off with mach speed to deliver the news of the warrior's capture and return to her rescue with aid.

When Dekel had shown Fayden, Serian and Grenig where to find the small group of griffins and played her role in their demise, she had separated from the cats to return home but as she flapped her wings she was caught in a melodious whirlwind that sent through her being the irrefutable desire to turn 'round. To fly back in search of a faerie in dire need of assistance. The sensation was overwhelming and frightening to the blue bird that now soared in solitude. She dared not overlook the magik of her world so she immediately altered her course and as she made haste, following only the guide of magik in the air, a great collision ensued in the forest. As it happened, in Deki's haste she was unable to discern the oncoming force of life, who was none other than Kayfin, also distracted in her haste and unable to see the bird's flight path was that of her own. Shaking the stars of the crash away, they recovered to stare blankly at one another, not in confusion or disillusionment, but in glorious understanding of the immediate need for the other. Without speaking Kayfin regained her composure and helped Deki resume her balance as well. Then, as though spoken with unheard words cast upon the world, Dekel knew she was to follow Kayfin, and off they flew. To blink would be to miss the two as they travelled with such speed, the blue of Dekel offsetting the brilliant pink of Kayfin's hair and wings. They started in the direction of Redwood Wall as Kayfin explained to Dekel what she had witnessed and the urgency of the situation. Deki suddenly broke the soft wake of their flight as she realized the profound importance of the faerie had just divulged.

"What matter has you so abruptly altered in course, dear blue bird?" Kayfin asked, winded from the sudden halt.

Deki hurriedly spoke her thoughts, "Kayfin! You said the drisolek who carried Dorian off went by the name Loreuhnd, did you not?" The bird was quite ecstatic and slightly incomprehensible.

Kayfin replied, "Yes, his name was such."

Excitedly Deki explained, "Oreighnthia, dear faerie! Oreighnthia is the very daughter of the drisolek that stole our warrior! Do you not see?"

Kayfin's eyes grew wide in confusion.

"I know the home of the drisolek's daughter! We reach her and tell her of the woes befallen our great warrior and the inclusion of her father and she is sure to accompany us on our quest!" Dekel was tripping in her excitement as the epiphany fled from her beak. Kayfin needn't further details as she was now wholly aware of their newly developed plan. With a smile and wink of cohesion, Kayfin bid Dekel to lead the two to Oreighnthia, daughter of the drisolek of whom Dorian was tricked.

***

Upon Wise Bright's orders, Ralkan and Flutter made haste to Faerie Willows and the Willow Plateau to gather the troops and prepare battle formations. Flutter bequeathed to the younger faerie a detachment of his own to lead. Ralkan's regime of fighters was comprised of a gruff bunch of lads eager to dive into the situation in any way to help the warrior; a group, Flutter knew, would be all too ready to pursue Dorian's transgressors, as their noble hearts could not accept a damsel in distress. The detachment was of approximately two hundred warriors, likely to split into further ranks in the midst of ensuing battle. With these faerie warriors travelled two great nirfens and a dighsp for every fighter. As well, Ralkan gave a small group of boys charge of four sherzirs; two large and two smaller. Meanwhile, Flutter arranged for the weaker elderly and younger faeries to remain hidden in the caverns beneath Faerie Willows. She then went about gathering the remaining faeries capable and willing to go to battle for their lost warrior and homeland. Upon Willow Plateau did they all gather and arrange battle formations, ranks, weapons carriers and the like. In the time all of this took place, Fayden had given Serian the task of assembling the giants and grostels, while Grenig was in charge of assembling the remaining Brights devoted to protecting Minaleth. Upon encountering Ostel and Klum, Serian's task became exponentially easier, as the two council members took to calling together their kinds to meet on the south bank of the Lake as one large assembly in order to receive the Commander's orders as spoken through the wise and gentle lion. Not one grostel or giant desired to forfeit the opportunity to take up arms. Knowing the youngsters would be disappointed to learn the situation was beyond danger they could handle, Serian, Ostel and Klum were able to devise and procure a strategy specifically to appease the zealous youth. Upon hearing the plan, the school of grostels along with the ever growing giants yet to reach adulthood, felt a great confidence surged through their young Bright spirits, for the plan would only be successful if executed by this particular regimen. They were all so honored to be given such an opportunity to engage in battle that the strategy's execution was immediately commenced and as discussed, they made their ways down to the Rainfalls.

Wise Bright and Fayden, in their solitude at the giant redwood in the Eastern Absent, gravely discussed the current predicaments, obstacles and possibilities.

"Sire, what of Dorian?" Fayden asked in low discourse.

Wise Bright leaned his small tree-self over the map of Minaleth that was laid out upon one of the stone seats. With a shake of his head, hung low in uncertainty, he responded, "Sweet Commander, I do not know what waits for our warrior on the path she has taken. I trust you have shown her great insight into our world?"

"Yes, sire."

"Then the choices she must make will surely reproduce providence for her as well as us." Wise Bright was distraught but the trust in his voice, that Dorian would discover a way to return to her new family, emanated serenity. The tiny tree and the great cat shared the moment as it gave each a sense of calm and sustainability. Then on went their meticulous plotting of courses of action, deep into the afternoon, sliding into evening.

***

On flew Dekel and Kayfin as they journeyed through the mountainous woodland in search of Oreighnthia. A pair of lightning bolts they were, as if the mighty god Zeus had hurtled them across worlds. Whence they reached a small pool of ill-colored water at the southern edge of the Bridge, Kayfin became slightly unnerved and confused. But being a quick thinker and trusting her blue bird friend at her side, she simply blinked her faerie eyes and upon reopening them, she could see the train of a magikal air wave that Dekel was following intrinsically from memory. As a younger drisolek, Oreighnthia had once invited Deki inside to continue their playful introduction. Using the adrenaline of obvious war at hand pumping through the blue bird's body along with this single, brief memory of ages ago, Dekel was swiftly leading the two right to the home of the very creature capable of finding Dorian's prison.

After the initial plunge through the questionable pool, it was not long past the surface that they found their selves standing on solid ground in a vast air pocket. The water was simply a ruse; only going as deep as maybe thirty feet then breaking open into an underwater village of drisoleks, without the water. As the water dissipated closer to the village, Deki's and Kayfin's bodies naturally eased into an upright position so they landed erect upon a solid, grassy mound. The terrain was much like that of the original Minaleth. Vibrant colors, exquisite aromas and a lovely prominence of full-bodied trees. There was no sky but the small pool of water in which to enter this hidden land reflected its ripples downward, casting upon the drisolek village a mirage of dancing light. The village beneath the water, called Ensumei, was in no way a world of its own. Still within the realm of the Core World, it was simply a haven for the drisolek village; hidden for the purpose of avoiding conflict. There was no danger in entering Ensumei unannounced but the unanticipated arrival of a faerie and a blue bird did raise a few eyebrows nearby.

"Sir," Deki began asking an older drisolek meandering the dale, "Do you know where I can find Oreighnthia, daughter or Loreuhnd?"

The elderly drisolek readjusted his poise with a simple grin and pointed to a Banyan sapling Oreighnthia was gingerly tending to.

Both Dekel and Kayfin nodded with smiles of gratitude then made their way over to express their urgent need.

"Old friend," Thia cried when she noticed Deki coming toward her, "what time has gone by since we last frolicked with one another!" A tender embrace was shared, somewhat awkwardly considering the difference in size and species. But Deki was too aware of the urgency of the matter and quickly went into an explanation of her presence in Ensumei. Once the details had been fully clarified, Thia took no time expressing her commitment to help.

"Please believe that my father was acting only as he was ordered to do." Oreighnthia humbly pleaded as the three started off together.

Kayfin replied with a sense of calm and understanding, "Do not fret, new friend. We trust that your father meant no harm to Dorian. But much time has faded by now so you must lead us now with great speed to your father and our beloved warrior." And with that, running as swiftly as the other two were flying, Oreighnthia led them to the very place her father advised her to go only with extreme caution.

Chapter 13
Restitution

Slowly and quietly they crept along the path Loreuhnd had taken to get to the cluster of trees. Oreighnthia was successfully tracking her father's route and as the footprints became fewer in number, the three girls realized they had reached the place they so voraciously sought. A silent hush took over as the necessity for stealth swept about each girl. Deki, now somewhat nerve stricken, trembled at the thought of not having planned a course of action any further than this. Thia, too, had partially frozen in place, peaking ever so diligently past every shrub and tree for a sign of entry...or possible foe. Kayfin, however was composed, astutely aware of the surroundings and currently interpreting her sense of the source of magik being hosted by Dorian and eluding the griffins. In other words, Kayfin could see remnants of a magikal trail she could only assume came from Dorian. Using body language to communicate her scheme, Kayfin was able to direct the unimpressive rescue team to the base of a similarly unimpressive tree. It was skinny and bare, rather pathetic amidst other, somewhat more lustrous trees. But Kayfin confidently hovered to and fro amongst the branches until she seemed fixated on one in particular. Ignoring the exchanged glances of uncertainty Kayfin knew the other two were sharing, she continued her discrepant flight then finally came to rest on a branch midway up the tree. Dangling her small legs over the edge, looking curiously at the branch, then at the tree, then at the branch again. She then motioned for Thia and Deki to come to where she was. With Kayfin's influence, on the silent count of three, the girls pushed down on the branch the faerie was currently sitting. With a few dangerously noisy snaps and creaks, the branch came down while the tree tilted in a congruent direction, opening up into the ground.

Crude steps turned into a tunnel that travelled beneath the ground in unison with the many tree roots already lain. Cautiously the girls crept through the shaded course towards what they hoped would be the place Dorian was being kept. Having no light to guide the way was far from a concern as Thia had superior vision in all measures of light and Kayfin, of course, could use her magikal eyes. Unknown time went by as their pace gradually drew them nearer to their destination. Finally a flicker of light caught their attention and they suddenly came to a halt in order to assess what lie ahead. Hushed, with ears attuned, Oreighnthia took the lead and directed the other two to duck low and keep silent while she went slightly further ahead, acting as a periscope to evaluate potential danger. The flicker was from a single candle in a holder protruding from the wall, seeming to be a marker for the entrance. Thia tentatively pushed against the wall of the tunnel which had come to a dead end. A very miniscule amount of soil broke loose from the tightly compacted dirt surrounding the wooden door (which was more the size of a trap door) as it slowly opened to a dim-lit oval room. Momentarily disheartened, Thia quickly but thoroughly observed the area but noticed no evident reason for or continuation of the room. She signaled for the Kayfin and Deki to join her and there they stood, looking all 'round for some answer, some clue. Raising her head, Kayfin spotted another bit of dirt crumbling from the ceiling. She grabbed the attention of Thia and Deki and pointed to where the dirt fell from, then, moving her raised finger through the air, traced the outline of what could only be a way up and onward. Understanding the next necessary steps, Thia took to standing fully erect at six and a half feet tall and gently pushed evenly upward within the outline. More dim light poured through the cracks and Deki took the cue, using her tiny head, to peek through and relay pertinent details of the new room. Eyes widened in apparent terror, Dekel lowered her head back down.

"Your father." She said...eyes now enlarged black orbs of fear, in a whisper to Oreighnthia.

***

Dark had settled in Minaleth – sinister shades of deep ocean blue smudged and smeared against black and deathly rouge. Those at Redwood Wall had taken to rest for they knew the chances of a detrimental attack in the oncoming hours and wanted to retain as much energy and strength as possible. A company of dragonflies, led by Strike, cased the region as security while the

Brights slept trusting their breath would not be stolen from them in their defenseless slumber.

Meanwhile, as Dorian clung to the hope that she would certainly be rescued from this purgatory, Atorik the shadow entered the room with an ostentatious air about her. Her malicious grin and narrowed eyes hinted to some falsely benevolent scheme most assuredly underway. Dorian raised her fatigued head with tired eyes as Atorik's clawed, winged arm raised the warrior's chin ever so slightly. She glared at Dorian, still grinning, then with a jolt of cruelty slapped the girl across the face. Her numb, crusted face now oozed with fresh blood. With her head still turned to the right from the force of the blow, Dorian spat the liquid life-source accumulating in her mouth then turned to face Atorik once again.

"Why do you so torture yourself, warrior?" The shadow asked.

Blood dripping down her pasty left cheek, into the corner of her mouth and continuing down her chin, Dorian answered, "I assure you," she took a breath, "I am torturing no one."

Atorik's eyes narrowed further.

Unafraid of the consequence, "I believe you have yet to hear of where your precious Nitris is." Said Dorian.

The notorious strike of Atorik's claws once more drew blood from the unmoved warrior.

"You, your friends," Atorik spoke disdainfully with such quake of evil in her voice, "your beloved Minaleth…they will all succumb to Nitris." She sadistically stroked Dorian's face and pushed a strand of hair behind the girl's ear. "You fail to see the complexities of the situation. Your world, Dorian, will end."

Her head hung low, Dorian wished not to feed into any rue expected by Atorik. She did not respond but only let herself dangle, lifeless yet ever full of spirit. She refused to give in to ask what Atorik meant specifically but she could not negate the deep feeling of concern she felt pulsate through her body. The magik of the world had kept her coherent this long but now she was feeling the full weight of fatigue, concern, hunger and oddly, loneliness. Dorian wanted above all else now just to embrace the kindly Serian, sweet Grenig and inspiring Fayden. She wanted to bury her face in their magnificent coats with her arms fully encasing each of their robust necks. A single tear escaped the trenches before Dorian caught herself.

With a final statement, Atorik left, "You are no warrior. You are just a child."

***

This night was proving unending to everyone caught in the trials of war. While the Brights at Redwood Wall were resting and regaining their strength, and while Dorian was slowly and unintentionally giving in to Atorik's debauchery, Dekel, Kayfin and Oreighnthia were demonstrating their prowess and stealth beneath the unseen treachery wrought by Nitris' minions. Seeing Loreuhnd disheveled as he was, beaten and bloody, sent waves of hope and adrenaline through Dekel's little body as she descended back to the other two to relay the information. Immediately upon hearing of her father's condition, though thankful to have found him, Thia exhumed from her soul a rage contrived purely for this manner of discord; to manifest as determination and agility in order to rescue the only individual intimately connected to her heart. Absolute resolve gleaming from Thia's opaquely copper-toned eyes expressed enough inclination that the other two subsequently understood what was to follow this mindful exchange of speechless heroism. Prepared for what consequences lay ahead in the next moments, Oreighnthia cautiously approached the trap door and raised it only so much as to quickly glance at the exact position of her father and with a scrupulous breath in, she pushed open the door entirely and stepped through onto the decrepitly-wooden floor without so much as a creek. Being so silent, Loreuhnd did not take notice to his daughter now carefully making her way toward him. His body was slumped to the floor in a heap of blood, bruises and filth. One of his massive legs was folded in at a bit of an awkward angle while the other lay outstretch with a slight bend. His head hung low and to the side, as his body leaned to the right, his shoulder drooping, appendages limp, drool oozing from the corner of his swollen lips and his spiked hair badly chopped down. It pained Thia to see her great father so impaired, especially to see the chopped spikes of his hair for drisolek hair was not simply upon the head but attached, as bones, so she knew the pain he must have endured during the wretched procedure. The room he was kept in was stingy and odorous with leaks and molds upon the walls and ceiling. The door, faintly to the left, was opened just a touch and Thia could make out the outer edge of a griffin wing. She got a bit closer to fully evaluate the threat only to find the fool snoring in his so called watchful guard. She decided to ignore him for the moment and crept over to her father. She knelt down and gracefully pet Loreuhnd's distraught face with the back of her hand. A moan. She now cradled his face in the palms of her hands and whispered an inaudible phrase, words exchanged only between them in past times, and Loreuhnd's puffy eyes opened ever so slightly. It took him a moment to focus but he was soon peering into the beautiful eyes of his beloved daughter whom he believed he would never see again. Tears poured to his lap as he and Thia shared a moment of pure, heartfelt gratitude.

"Papa," she spoke softly, "I'm here. You'll be ok now." Her precious smile was overwhelming to the broken, in body and spirit, drisolek. His tears continued to flow as he recalled the very reason for his being in such a horrible position.

His voice cracked with emotion, "I...that poor girl...surely she is..." weeps and groans of remorse immersed his speech, "...Dorian. I brought her here. I betrayed her." His head fell low again, sobbing in the shame of having captured such a brave and noble spirit.

Oreighnthia shook her head and spoke gingerly to her pain-ridden father, "Papa, it's ok. We believe she has yet to breathe her last breath. What you did no longer matters. We need to find her and get the two of you out of here. Papa, do you know where they are keeping her?"

Sniffling, catching his breath and looking woefully, he raised his head to nod and turned his head to the right, towards the door. In broken-patterned speech he described the room Dorian was kept was through the door, down the hall a bit and to the right. He was unable to remember any more specifically than that.

"This griffin outside my door here," he went on, "...he is a careless fool and should not be much difficulty. But there are at least two more elsewhere, as well," he paused, fear emanated from his eyes and voice, "there is a shadow of great evil. She goes by the name Atorik. She is dangerous, my love."

Now Dekel and Kayfin moved closer to the drisoleks, "We will protect you, Loreuhnd." Said Kayfin. Then Deki added, "We came to rescue you and Dorian and we will not relent to any shadow or griffin."

With a sweet smile across his daughter's face, Loreuhnd trusted the words of the young girls and nodded in accordance with their determined strategy. They helped him to his feet, though weakened as he was the presence of his daughter and her friends gave him a rejuvenated sense of strength. Grasping the iron medallion 'round his neck, Loreuhnd let his mind sink into the magik of world, his eyes closed and his breath slow, and a moment later awoke from the minute trance to explain the griffin outside the door was the only foe they need be concerned for so far. While Thia, Dekel and Loreuhnd remained still next to the far wall, Kayfin moved forward to the door as she pulled an arrow from her quiver and set it to her bow. She let her wings carry her just above the doorway and slightly to the side to give herself a crystal clear shot to the beast's skull. With the exception of the twang of the bowstring releasing, Kayfin was but a ghost, unseen and unheard. Having not a clue that an arrow had penetrated his head, the griffin remained speechless, motionless, breathless, forever in his vile dreams. Now safe to leave the room, Kayfin took the lead out of the door, followed by Dekel then Oreighnthia with Loreuhnd trailing behind. The dingy hallway failed to accommodate the height of the drisoleks, forcing both Thia and her father to duck, somewhat, in an uncomfortable fashion. Each step they took seemed to sink into the floor, as if the floors were so saturated with water, blood, excrement, bile…utterly revolting. Though it left footprints of the band it also worked in their favour as it quieted each of their steps. Torches were lit along the walls on alternating sides but they failed to provide adequate lighting as they flickered in and out of fuel, casting moving shadows that forced the rescue team to take extra precaution as they trekked on. Two doors lined the right wall, both closed, both locked. They went unchecked this time however for Loreuhnd assured the group that Dorian couldn't have been through either of these doors. It's true that he was unable to remember specifics but he knew that the sweet warrior had not been kept so close. He was more than certain that they would find her through another door further down the hall a little ways. Clutching her iron medallion, Thia abruptly jerked her head toward her father with fear in her eyes.

"Papa..." she said. Bringing his eyes down to where his daughter motioned and seeing her hand clenched tightly around her necklace, he quickly took hold of his own and immediately grabbed Kayfin and Dekel by their tiny, dangling legs and held them back. Quite unappreciative of being held back by their legs, each girl turned, with their eyes glaring, ready to attack with vicious rhetoric concerning manners. But as they saw Loreuhnd and his daughter frightfully shaking their heads, each holding their necklace, they understood that danger must have been afoot. Shuffling to a nearby corner, Loreuhnd ever so quietly explained that Atorik was nearby, as was Dorian. Swiftly, a plan was drawn up between the four should the tyrant shadow attack. Agreeing and understanding their roles, they moved into the hallway once more and, reaching the end, made a right turn to find a single wretched-looking door at the end of another hallway much too small to really be called a hallway. A single lantern hung from the ceiling just above the doorway, bequeathing an eerie light to hover in the cold yet densely humid air. A terrible stench struck their noses as they came to the door. Sulfur. Loreuhnd signaled for the group to disperse and take their agreed positions. Upon doing so, Loreuhnd retrieved his hilken dagger from its holster and held it out, prepared to strike if need be. On the count of three...two...he released the latch holding the door closed and nudged the door open. Kayfin, upside down atop the door jam, conjured a simple enchantment of dust to engross the room; the intention being to suffocate the enemy's breath and vision. As soon as she released the enchantment, Loreuhnd pushed the door open wide and moved in toward the right with extreme caution. Oreighnthia moved in next but to the left flank. Dekel remained as she was, yet to demonstrate her role in the rescue. Kayfin moved along the ceiling like an insect and waited patiently near the far left-hand corner for her moment. All was silent and only Kayfin had the ability to clearly see through the dust cloud. She saw Dorian hanging lifeless against the wall adjacent to Loreuhnd. He hadn't realized she was so close. Nothing more seemed to be in the foul room. But that thought was quickly extinguished when Kayfin shifted her eyes to the ceiling ahead of her own position.

There, hanging as a bat, was Atorik. The others hadn't noticed as their attention was not naturally drawn to the ceiling but Kayfin could not wait for someone else to see the shadow and react. The brave faerie quickly took up her bow and instantly had it set with an arrow. Needing only a split second to take aim, she raised it and fired but at first, appeared to miss. The arrow flew beneath and past Atorik to the opposite wall. But it seemed to be a part of the plan as Atorik took it as her cue to engage, thus relinquishing her position to the others. The shadow turned in response to Kayfin and started toward the faerie but was abruptly cut short of her path by an unexpected weapon. Kayfin's arrow had not arbitrarily flown past her intended target. No, she aimed not for the enemy but for the warrior. The arrow stuck straight through the left side of Dorian's chains, indicating her whereabouts to Loreuhnd. Without hesitation he thrust his hilken through the chain with such force the chain shattered! Stunned by the blow, Dorian shook her head to wake up and seeing Loreuhnd next to her where the chain had broken, she immediately concluded that he could not have truly been an enemy and thus gave him a tender smile of gratitude and forgiveness. Atorik was caught off guard by the passing arrow and took to pursuing the shooter, not realizing that Dorian's chains had been broken. A rush of evil came at Kayfin but her size and agility worked in her favour. She dodged the attack while skillfully stringing another arrow to her bow. A quick tuck n' roll then she fired, scraping the shadow's left wing. Atorik was now hunched on the floor buried within her wings. Growling and hissing in anger as perhaps an alligator would, she slowly spread open her blood-red wings but as her head came up, her eyes went wide. Standing before her, blade in hand and ready to strike with precision was Dorian. Atorik just stared blankly at the warrior, trying to conceive a way to take control of this potentially fatal situation.

The dirt and blood that caked Dorian's face crushed the innocence now buried deeply beneath and gave her the demeanor of a malicious killer. She did not wish to so viciously destroy such a vile creature. Atorik was outnumbered and surrounded – the scene was set for slaughter rather than a noble battle. *This,* thought Dorian, *is not what I want. Is not right.* But as Dorian contemplated the continuity of her character and the evil she suffered, Atorik cleverly observed and noticed the loosed grip Dorian now had of her katana. Understanding the crucial opportunity couldn't possibly last long, the beast lunged to the left of Dorian just out of sword's reach but her demise now became all too clear. When Atorik made her move, Dekel had been intently watching, waiting, for the right moment and this was definitely it. It took the blue bird only a split second to burst forth in a rage of energy fueled by the adrenaline of rescuing her dear friend and irreplaceable warrior. As Atorik started with the clear intention of clawing at Dorian, Dekel flew in and pierced the bat-like shadow with her devastatingly sharp beak, unbeknownst to all around her. The shriek of Atorik as her right eye fell to the floor in a bloody mess caused everyone's ears to ring as such a pitch had never before been heard. Furious but struggling, Atorik managed to clip the tip of one of her wings to Deki's tail but before the charming and surprising bird could be mutilated, Dorian's sword had already sliced so cleanly through the shadow's neck that its head was able to balance freely for a moment, with an expression of amazement glued to her features, before toppling over.

Once the fatal confrontation with Atorik had come to its end, Kayfin and the others were ready and desperate to get back home but Dorian was unwilling to ease her desire to unleash the captive Hawk Lords. That was the very reason she had risked so much to come to this place. After a little convincing, the broken and bruised warrior got her way and before deserting the haunting stench of her three day prison, the remaining Hawks still gripping to life were found and unshackled. They were urged to join the others in their return to Redwood Wall but the dozen or so Council members reassured Dorian that their wounds would be best cared for in the confines of their nests with the healing magik of the Hawk shaman. As the clan made their way from the haunting arena, Dekel took an extra moment, as she was in the rear of the caravan, to caution the noble birds.

"War is upon us," the blue bird began as a few of the contingency became attentive, "...it would be wise to gather all the hawks and retreat to a place of secrecy and protection, while the events synchronized and orchestrated by Nitris play out." Said Dekel in a low, powerful whisper of warning.

To Deki's pleasant surprise, the nearest Hawk Lord glared into the bird's eyes, "O, trust me, Sweet Blue," he croaked out in a deep, hoarse drawl of justice, "this war was upon us ages ago and its conclusion is at hand."

Another more aged and bitter Hawk added, "Nitris and her followers have perpetuated the demise due unto them. Now that we are released, hellfire shall descend upon the crowns of those Shadows and griffins acquainted to those of whom we were so unfortunate to meet. The Hawks of Minaleth will bring forth an eclipse of life, of power."

There was nothing more Dekel could contribute to such a profound proclamation from such a wise and mystic entity of a race born competent of the world's magik. Deki bowed her head in farewell and flew to catch up with her departing friends. A sense of confidence accentuating her little face.

Chapter 14
Governance

At last Kayfin had the young, mighty warrior in her protective sight. A sigh of relief escaped her mouth as she serenely soared through the air next to Dekel and above the others. The refreshing air moving past her face felt as though a whirlwind had taken over her tiny body. Briefly she let her eyelids fall and in her self-produced shade she let her senses absorb every bit of the sweet, magikal air. It was dawn and the glorious skyshine displayed exuberance like none other, to Kayfin. The emotions electrifying her body made her feel as though a family member had been returned to her. The group had travelled in a steady pace through the night and was now approaching the Bridge. They would arrive finally to Redwood Wall late in the night. If it were not for Dorian and Loreuhnd's weakness they may have been able to reach Redwood Wall by nightfall but their fragile bodies begged for rest. Within a burrow, perhaps the type a badger may dwell, they found refuge. Though it was a snug fit for the two drisoleks, none could complain for the joy of being safe, with the captives now free, brought a savory sense of calm and strength. Gently the group drifted into rejuvenating sleep, kept safe under the watch of Dekel, more than willing to keep guard. Despite the pains Dorian was faced with while captive under the torturous, sadistic Atorik, she let her mind sail upon the waters of an ocean accessible only to her. A sea yet riddled with magnificent waves; simply still and vast, offering an escape. A treaty of endurance and rectification, sealed with the protection of the almighty Poseidon.

The night had passed and morning was creeping along when Redwood Wall came into sight to the small clan. Each let loose a sigh of relief to see their precious home finally so close. For Dorian, it was as if she was returning to the home she had always known...not her home of another realm. As the group approached the fringe of the haven, Serian and Grenig came trudging toward the weary travelers. Despite her severe wounds, Dorian held her head high as her friends got closer and as the distance between diminished, she stretched her arms out as wide as she could at the moment and wrapped them tightly around the lion's massive torso. Without shame, Serian let part of his head sink into the crevasse of her shoulder while sweet tears rolled from the corners of his magnificent cat-eyes down his snout to drip upon Dorian's slightly exposed back. Next was Grenig's turn to embrace the damaged warrior with a genuine, irrefutable love for one whom he considered akin to his heart. Dorian braced the tiger's glorious face in her palms and let a soft stream of tears flow down her face. As she lost herself in his deeply tender eyes, she heard the resonant voice of her dear Wise Bright call her name. So gingerly. Without shame or disappointment. Grenig smoothly stepped to the side to allow Dorian pass by towards the Cherry Tree. His small yet pronounced button-like eyes were a welcome sight to the emotionally and mentally exhausted young lady. The ancient Bright stretched wide his arms to receive his beautiful, other-worldly granddaughter and in reciprocation, she moved in with her arms ready to fit together the two puzzle pieces. Feeling in no way odd for quite literally hugging a tree, Dorian let Wise Bright pull her, with his strong and sturdy arms, closer until their bodies were forged into one impenetrable connection.

"You knew." Dorian whispered to the small tree.

Without relinquishing his hold, he responded, "I heard you. You truly hold wisdom beyond your years, child."

Together they released each other and let their eyes meet to exchange an intimacy that was more of a treasure than that of the famed City of Gold. Once the moment had passed, Dorian began to wonder where the Commander was and before she could inquire, Wise Bright intrinsically knew the girl's curiosity and twitched his head in Fayden's direction. Dorian smiled and looked over to see her standing beneath a tree, the shade and skyshine casting shadows and highlights in such a way that the marvelous tiger looked as a watercolor. But in the tiger's eyes Dorian could see the struggle, surely to do with disappointment of the girl's actions in the days prior. It seemed as though Fayden was simply waiting, sitting erect with power looking Dorian's way, her being piercing Dorian's heart. She calmly walked over to the Commander and came to a halt beneath the tree, beneath the great tiger's maw. There they stood, speaking to one another with their eyes. Fayden chastising Dorian for such foolish and selfish actions, while sending forth a blessing of gratitude and relief, knowing the warrior had succeeded in her personal mission. Meanwhile Dorian, pleading for forgiveness as well as subtly inferring the accomplishment Fayden so quickly dismissed possibility of. It was clear the relationship they possessed had become tainted and as each realized this they unlocked their shared gaze upon one another and went about debriefing each other of the recent events.

It was an odd feeling Dorian experienced once the two had become saturated in conversation of the events likely to unfold in the oncoming days. Devious was the sensation crawling just beneath the surface of Dorian's skin. Respectfully, and cautiously, the warrior listened and participated in the discussion but as Fayden shifted conversation to the girl's understanding of *Wise Bright's* intentions, she decided to investigate her suspicions. Something was out of place with the tiger, specifically a particular intensity of her eyes, which gave the Commander an unnerving ferocity, personally sprinkled with a learned humility.

"If Wise Bright wishes me to have understanding of *his* intentions as well as wishes *you* have understanding, he will surely approach us separately to discuss matters personally." Dorian ended with a stern expression.

Fayden off-handedly muttered in agreement of the girl's statement, further arousing Dorian's suspicions of the Commander. As Fayden tilted her head, muttering under her breath, the young warrior caught a more enlightened glimpse of the tiger's eyes, for in just the way she tilted her head, a brilliant ray of skyshine shone through the green canopy to make sparkle those orbs of power. But therein lays the subtle rhythmic dysfunction that Dorian was keenly aware of. For the Commander's eyes were not glowing with the usual emerald zest of vigor but rather a muddy, green haze of encumbrance. Dorian regarded the phenomenon but decided now was not the time to openly press the matter. Morning had drifted into the past as mid-day was being welcomed with the tantalizing aromas of luncheon meats, cheeses and fruits. Fayden, feeling a loss of trust from Dorian, wanted the uncomfortable moment to pass anyway and so turned to the girl.

"Ought to be indulging in such glorious sustenance, should we not?" She asked in sync with a nod of her head indicating the noticeable aromas.

Dorian took the opportunity to end this particularly odd encounter, "I am quite famished and something does smell delectable!" She added a smile for good measure and the two went their separate ways.

***

Nika was a faerie that resided within Redwood Wall, having carved out a cubby in a trunk. Nika was of the few faeries capped with a brilliant, deep red hue of which was enchanted with the ability to become as flames, as much of a defensive tactic as an offensive one. Of course, her magnificent mane and wings only looked as though consumed by fire…in reality it was a mere illusion wholly contrary to the very nature of Nika. She was a kind-hearted, gentle faerie with profound, protective instincts toward all, particularly her beloved son and daughter. The average day could only dream to awaken the fury dormant beneath her surface; ready to erupt, to caste a moltenous river of protection around those dear to her heart. It was her homely cooking responsible for permeating the air with such an extravagant deliciousness intended for whoever desired.

These very traits are the origin of perhaps the most pertinent piece of a jigsaw, becoming more complicated with each turn of events. As time passed in the days and weeks of Dorian's company, Nika, observant and perceptive as she was, initially noticed a slight variant in Fayden, the powerful Commander. Assuming it was the result of the stresses of war wrought by Nitris, who had evaded all by simply vanishing, the faerie decided to forego investigating, however; she was inclined to take note of those subtle manipulations whenever they grabbed her attention. As it was, Nika had discerned from the beginning what those in more advantageous positions had yet truly discovered. Understanding the precarious circumstances now hovering in the vicinity of her very home, a home she had already been exiled *to*, the defiant red faerie was far from letting this opportunity pass her by.

"Dorian!" She called to the girl wandering in her general direction.

The young warrior was unable to pull her attention from the fiery faerie as she altered her direction, still intoxicated by the aromas, "Hi, there!" Dorian said gleefully as such a shade of color had absolved from her mind the nagging confusion.

"You remember me, of course?" Nika asked with a hopeful smile.

"Of course I do! Nika, right?" Dorian reciprocated the cheerfully friendly exchange.

Pleased, and trusting her insight, Nika went ahead with her idea and offered Dorian an array of perfectly prepared entrees of impressive variety, "Please, help yourself." Spoken with sincere generosity.

Half starved and anxious to indulge in this magnificent smorgasbord so graciously displayed in front of her, Dorian did not hesitate and swiftly began skimming the arrangement for what her belly wished to consume. After a moment of uncouth though justifiable gorging, Dorian raised her attention once more to Nika, "Thank you so much! It's all so wonderful!" She squeezed through food-filled cheeks.

"You are more than welcome, dear warrior, but I must confess I have alternate intentions for you." Nika leaned nearer to the girl, as Dorian did likewise, understanding immediately a need for privacy, though uncertain as to why.

In quiet tones, Nika went on, "The Commander, I fear she is amiss in some way."

Dorian nodded, unfortunately agreeing, now very curious to what this faerie had to say.

"I have been obligated by concern since the time of your arrival to Minaleth to discreetly observe Fayden, for since that time, she has undergone subtle alterations of demeanor and personality that I find I can no longer hold to my own thoughts..."

Dorian waited...

Nika went on, "...I believe our Commander is becoming, if not already, a threat to us...to the Brights." The fear of such a notion being true was evident in the tremble of Nika's gentle voice and apparent as her icy-blue eyes dilated.

Dorian was obviously aware of what Nika was speaking about and knowing the dangers of a tiger of Fayden's stature, she asked the faerie to divulge what information she could, sparing not a single detail. While rhythmically, with as much etiquette as one raised with such expected manners, selecting, savoring and swallowing the overwhelming flavors and textures Dorian became aware of an intense feeling of satisfaction within. Not unlike the sensation felt when one has had their fill of their favorite cuisine but this was something far beyond that common fulfillment. She was feeling rejuvenated to the *nth* degree; a fresh and abundant store of energy flooded the warrior's body, saturating every cell, rapidly healing the wounds and aches causing her aggravation and fatigue.

"Nika…" Dorian began through her meat-clenched teeth.

Knowing already the direction of the warrior's thoughts, the faerie broke in, "It is an enchantment. Sustainability is what you require now thus at the blessing of Wise Bright I infused this spread with magik."

"So I will be stronger, now, with more power and such?" Asked the girl.

"So to speak," was Nika's reply, "it is not an enchantment of false magik; a mere illusion of what one actually needs…you will not be impossibly powerful or have the strength of a mountain. You still have *your* gifts and abilities but a surplus of such."

Dorian nodded her head, "I can last longer." She surmised.

"Precisely!"

***

In the time Dorian had taken to indulge in understandable gluttony, Dekel took the initiative to brief Wise Bright of her private encounter with the Hawk Lords. The Cherry Tree of Old carefully absorbed what precursors to the Hawks' intentions he could from "Sweet Blue's" explanation. Adamantly he asked Dekel to repeat the description, over and over, verbatim including the subtle prosodic shifts that she could recall.

Wise Bright pensively spoke aloud the ponderings of his mind, "It would seem – Sweet Blue (he added a wink) – that what we can expect from the Hawks is nothing short of magnificent. Let us trust that our choreography of battlement will fall into sync with their own." Deki escaped into her mind for a moment as she contemplated that trust. Wise Bright tracked the bird's thoughts as she tried hiding the subtle dissipation of a smile as thoughts of Adalei entered her mind.

"Have you any word from your lost friend?" Wise Bright inquired with compassion.

Deki was thankful for the Cherry Tree's concern but it pained her to consider the question. "I have not. No longer do I feel her kinship as the two of us once shared. I do not doubt her destined cohesion to the Shadows."

With the desire to prevent the bird's obvious decline into sorrow, Wise Bright made a suggestion, "Perhaps, my friend, you could go to the faeries? Inform Flutter of the potential aid from the Hawks. Lord Tukiund, too, should be aware so as to lend any insight."

"Of course, Sire!" Dekel said without question. With a smile, she was quickly off and Wise Bright was left in the wake of subsequent possibilities of which influenced his deep decent into meditation…to consider the current events of the Core World in retrospect. He was witnessing the changes in his beloved Fayden and knew the kind of tricks Nitris was capable of enacting. Time was running short, he knew, to overturn the situation.

***

"What news of Lord Tukiund?" Serian called out to Flutter from a short distance away. He had coordinated strategies with the Giants and was currently making his way to confirm tactics with the grostels.

"His wounds are quick to healing as he is feeling ever more prepared for battle." The magenta-painted faerie shouted back with joy, busying herself with a mixed group of warriors doing checks on nirfins and sherzirs.

"Good word." Said the lion, pleased to hear of the improving condition of a royal member of the Order of Hawks. "And you are feeling confident of the regime Ralkan has been given command of?"

Flutter responded with an accomplished smile, "Without doubt, sir. He and his two hundred fighters are standing by at Willow Plateau for the command to engage. Ralkan is a competent, strong young faerie who has demonstrated his loyalty and dedication to those around him. The boys he is leading trust and look up to him for direction and protection as brothers of blood do."

In a low, imperative tone Serian gave Flutter the order to send for word to have Ralkan's regime move ahead as a scouting company. They were to send recon upon reaching the Bridge but Flutter was to remain at Redwood Wall. The authoritative faerie left at once in search of Kayfin, whom she wished to have deliver the message. As Flutter swept her small body through the warm air and trees, her path proved to run perpendicular to that of Dekel, and with a thud the two interceded and a new plan was drawn on the fly.

"I am to have Kayfin send word to Ralkan to move forward and recon once the Bridge has been reached. I want you to remain at Willow Plateau to provide relief for Kayfin, for when she travels with word from the Bridge, she may be in a great rush and will surely appreciate help for the last leg." Flutter asked for confirmation of understanding with her eyes, provoking Dekel's response.

The blue bird answered with determination, "Of course, miss," she added the salute of a wing, "I'll not leave that post until I have received word from Kayfin and when I do, with seldom-matched haste will I fly to your position to pass word on."

Flutter smiled and with a nodding confirmation continued on her way to find Kayfin. As the expansive thermals of the Core World lifted her ever higher through the airy wisps of vibrancy, she was caught by the sheen of Fayden's magnificently decorated body. Slowing her pace and descending through the thin awning of leaves, Flutter came to rest on the grass just ahead of where the great tiger sat in contemplation.

"Commander," the gentle though bold faerie began, but Fayden stopped her.

"You have a task to complete at this time?" Fayden asked.

Flutter nodded, not taking her eyes off the tiger, whose eyes were not shifting from the ground.

"Go," said the commander, "you haven't the luxury of redirecting your concern. Go."

As Flutter turned to leave without arguing, she could not hold in what she let escape her lips, "*We* do not have the luxury of having a commander distracted in her thoughts." With that, the faerie flew off and Fayden could only glance up through misty eyes to see the girl's wake disappear into the meadow.

***

Flutter found Kayfin busying herself with final prep and packaging of supplies for a group of elderly Brights making their way from the Lake. She offered help to Kayfin while explaining the situation at hand and what the younger faerie's role was for the time following. Once the sacs of food rations were tied and placed into the travel trunk that was being packed, Flutter and Kayfin said their farewells to the group of Brights and went on their way towards Ralkan and the others while Flutter gave a few final words of instruction and protection. After only a few moments of flight, Flutter looped over and back towards Redwood Wall. Kayfin barrel-rolled through the influx of air caused by Flutter's maneuver and darted off to carry out her duty. Upon reaching the battalion of young, gruff faerie warriors at Willow Plateau, Kayfin delivered the message for the two hundred, plus one, to march on to the Bridge. Having instruction to move onward, Ralkan excitedly shouted the command to those within ear's shot to move out, then with a great and glorious sounding of a nump, the small portion of a tree root turned into a horn, Ralkan, Kayfin and the fervent regime started off at last as the preamble to what would surely be Minaleth's greatest tragedy.

PART THREE
THE PUZZLE

Chapter 15
The Beginning or the End?

Perched upon a branch not far from the ground Dekel sat ever vigilant of the surroundings, patiently waiting to run the next leg of the race. Singing to herself a soft tune, watching the copper and periwinkle skyshine jump from vine to vine through the willows, she was startled when the branch below her fidgeted with weight. The blue bird looked down to investigate and was shocked again to see another blue bird perched on the lower branch, seemingly unaware, or inattentive, of Dekel's presence.

"Adalei!?" Dekel shrieked, scruffling her feathers before hopping down next to the recently *lost* Bright.

Adi didn't speak, only stared straight ahead. Dekel gave it a second attempt, "Adi? What happened...?" Deki tip-toed closer to Adi's right side, then gently bounced to the left side, "...are you OK?" Deki's quick head twitched this way and that as she eyed her friend, waiting for some response. Before Dekel had a chance to react, Adalei whipped her head to face the unfortunately clueless bird and with her powerful beak took a firm grip of her friend's delicate neck. What should have been a quick snap instead crackled and fractured as a living branch frays rather than breaks in the hands of another. Dekel's head hung limp then as in the preceding moments, Adalei heartlessly jerked her head and body to the side, tossing Deki's lifeless body from the tree to fall heavily to the turf below. Blinking erratically, scanning the area, the blue bird with breath still in her lungs gave a flap of her wings to stretch then a twitch of her tail and with a final tilt of her head to view the fallen Bright, she leapt from the branch and lifted herself through the willows. To the east.

***

After having an exponentially fulfilling meal with Nika, Dorian returned to her cabin for a quick revamping of thought and energy. Easing out of her armor, for she was still suffering from open wounds and wanted not to re-awaken the streams of blood, Dorian slipped into the basin of warm water that had already been drawn for her. Her toned, milky body emancipated from its crusted surface the remnants and stains of the recently passed ordeal. Quickly the water dulled to a murky red and she released the drainage cork, after which she dumped the awaiting remaining buckets of warm water into the basin and continued to soak, now enjoying a few added oils and extracts of Minaleth's healing flora. When she felt she had reached the threshold of refreshment provided by the bath, Dorian stood dripping for a moment before redressing in her armor. Outstretched upon her hammock, wondering of her parents, the recovered heroin was interrupted by Fayden in a rather guarded and peculiar manner. The tiger surreptitiously stepped into the cabin, sniffing and listening for the tiniest details. Dorian made to speak but was cut short by the Commander's brash motion to be silent. Seeming confident of their safety, Fayden let the words slip past her great maw, just as when the wind is drawn through a curtained window, "I found Dekel's body." Her eyes were narrow, indicative.

Dorian stood with her jaw clenched, her right hand instinctively to the hilt of her sword, and her eyes letting loose tears of grief, rage and disillusionment. "How?" The single inquisition croaked from her throat.

Fayden's answer stayed simple, "Snapped neck."

Immediately wary of the potential for very real danger lurking, hiding, around every corner, Dorian chose to alleviate what reservations she had for Fayden. The tiger had been withdrawn in recent days but she hadn't the physical capability to have been the one to kill Deki in such a clean fashion.

"Where is Wise Bright?" Dorian asked.

The fur on Fayden's lower back became erect with caution while her massive ears lay flat to her head as she glanced outside, "He is just outside here with Flutter. There is a faerie regime en route to the Bridge now to provide reconnaissance; Serian is with the grostels and I believe Grenig is still with Klum and the giants."

Dorian swiftly finished tightening loose laces and fastening buckles then she and Fayden left the cabin to discuss the situation with Wise Bright and Flutter. Unless some manner of attack had taken place near the Lake, Serian and the grostels were in need of warning that Redwood Wall could be on the verge of infiltration. Grenig also needed to be found and put on alert. Lacking the time to further discussion and debate, it was decided that Dorian and

Fayden were to remain together as they traversed the meadow along the riverbank to reach Serian while Flutter was to soar the perimeter in search of Grenig. Once regrouped they were to send word of so via soil. Wise Bright made his way to the Council's meeting place to wait in calm as his loved ones journeyed on once again. The Cherry Tree slipped into a meditative state of magik as his essence mated with that of the Core World to reveal to his senses what dangers lay in wait. He could feel deep within his being the gentle steps of Dorian along with the heavy-footed impressions of Fayden. A gust of wind stirred the blossoms of Wise Bright, carrying away the loosed ones in an airy swirl.
***

The Commander and warrior were wary of the hazard of time's passive-aggression and so treaded the cashmere flooring with great care in order to avoid distasteful expiation. Their conversation was minimal as both were occupied with sustaining their situational awareness. Fayden was not quick to crouch at the sound of every snapping twig, a clear over exertion and misplacement of alertness; rather, she was calm and sure of the identity of the various sounds tickling her sensitive ears. Only a handful of times did the Commander silently call for Dorian to stay still and silent as she scanned the proximity with her supreme cat senses. As they approached the Lake they could see Serian gathered with a group of grostels while another group, a much a younger group, splashed about in the water nearby. While Fayden made her way to Serian to deliver the news of Dekel, Dorian slipped over to the water to indulge for a moment in the youthful innocence.

"Do we know what happened?" Serian asked remorsefully.

The Commander shook her head and with a furrowed brow, "No. But I hold no doubts that Nitris is afoot. What troubles me is that the menacing shadow that *is* Nitris has been eluding us all this time, even her own army, and we appear clueless as to what she and her followers are plotting."

"I think we know more than we realize. That girl, Reilly, is surely a pawn in this game; the idea has been churning in my mind for some time now, admittedly to no avail, but I do not believe she is here by coincidence..." Serian paused for a moment as he studied the tiger's behavior, "...Fayden, you needn't let your mind get so wound up. We are all prepared for whatever may hit us."

"Are we...?" was Fayden's sullen response.

The lion wasn't entirely sure of how to interpret the unusual behavior, "Commander...?"

Fayden shook away the fear she felt an obligation to conceal and pressed the conversation forward to avoid further detriment to her integrity. She shifted her focus to view the young grostels at play with their warrior and immediately felt her vigor redeemed as a thought bombarded her mind, "Send Dorian to the Valley!" were the words she excreted in a half-whispered, spoken thought.

Serian's features seemed to be manipulated by an outside, unseen source playing with modeling clay. He was crossed between anger at the absurdity of such a dangerous conception and confusion that Fayden would even suggest such a course when she was so disoriented by Dorian's first action to leave the so-called safety of the Brights' territory. "Commander, I'm not sure..." he began but was interrupted by the tiger's enthusiasm.

"Dorian!" Fayden called and the girl excused herself to answer the Commander's beckoning. She jogged to where they had been standing and gave her attention. Serian tried again to damper the hurried idea but the tiger was too quick. "Child, can you go back to the Valley?"

Dorian looked to Serian for clarification but he could only shrug and direct their attention back to the Commander, who seemed to be losing her mind.

Fayden reiterated, "Are you willing to go to the Valley?"

The warrior had no idea what kind of plan this question was preceding but the girl felt pulled to trust her friend's prowess and wisdom. Her eyes darted to and fro in contemplation, quickly analyzing reasons for going to the Valley, various scenarios and outcomes, even considering the likelihood of seeing her world again. A smirk pulled itself through to the surface as Dorian glanced up with a slight nod and was met by Fayden's own devious grin. Serian was far from incapable of deciphering that the girls were now in cahoots with one another with a possibly brilliant or devastating plan and he needed to understand the premise of the situation before rash decisions were made. He was becoming irate with the level of secrecy and suddenly lost the ability to withhold his frustration; a thunderous rumble quaked about Dorian's senses then broke into a full-bodied roar, drawn from the lion's deep belly. Fayden and the girl held their breath and stared wide-eyed for a moment in terrified confusion.

"Enough of this! We must work together; if I cannot be the recipient of your respect and trust, from the Commander and from our beloved *warrior*, who can? The deceptions you create, the truths you hide, will only erode your core – your soul – until you are no more than a shadow." Serian's upper lips were snarled and his ears were pulled back in discontent. His ears and whiskers, and tail, twitched intermittently as he took deep breaths to gather his composure.

Fayden moved closer to the lion, her eyes cast down, her voice ready to break, "Serian, I apologize…you…"

Serian cut her short, "I know you struggle now and have been struggling. We have all witnessed changes in you and as we all experience change, concern has not been raised, until now. I fear for the growing rage of your heart. You are the Commander; you *must* channel it first through reason, or risk decisions that will leave the rest of us in the smoke of a disaster."

"Serian," Dorian started but again he broke her words.

"What is it the two of you plan?" He was after a straight answer with which to move forward.

When Fayden and Dorian had concluded their alternating explanation of the subliminal plan they shared together, Serian sent word to Wise Bright, informing him of the new, highly dangerous, plan of action. Though specific details must be spared while using soil-tracked communications, Wise Bright was able to interpret the basic concept and return his consent, relieving a portion of Serian's anguish.

***

Meanwhile, Flutter had cased the region and was currently rushing through the long grass along the northern fringe of the meadow not far from the Rainfalls. She spotted Grenig and Klum walking south with a small gaggle of giants, seemingly following a trail of sorts. She opened her wings to gain resistance and with moderate speed descended to a moss-eaten boulder a yard or so ahead of Grenig. As the faerie came to rest, Grenig and Klum smiled pleasantly at seeing their friend but those smiles soon dissipated when Flutter shared the disheartening news and what remained were solemn expressions of loss. Klum's demeanor appeared more affected and he struggled to sequester the escaping tear from the corner of his eye. The drop was noticed and Flutter gracefully hovered to the giant's face and wiped the confusion away.

"I feel so naïve," he choked out, "I did not believe any of us would truly lose our lives."

Grenig spoke softly, "Klum, my friend, you were confident in our friends' abilities. Do not feel ashamed for that. Dekel is…was…a smart bird and was obviously duped in a manner that could not be anticipated." Klum nodded in accordance, took a deep breath and regained his composure. Flutter sweetly smiled and embraced Klum's pained face then did her best to smoothly transition into a discussion of tactics. She asked about the tracks they were following and was enthused to learn the inconspicuous foot prints were small and human in form. All agreed at the obvious possibility of their belonging to Reilly and Flutter relayed the new information to Wise Bright. Grenig then inquired about Dorian and Fayden and what may be the decided course of action. Unaware of the newly formulated plan to send Dorian back to the Valley to draw out Nitris, Flutter could only assure the tiger that Fayden's decisions could be trusted and when she learned of their intentions, would certainly inform Grenig. Without that knowledge, there was really nothing more to say and Flutter knew Ralkan and his regime would be nearing the Bridge by now and so left the tiger and giant to continue searching for the nefarious human while she flew ahead to the Plateau to receive Kayfin's incoming recon.

Watching the colorful faerie gain distance, Klum's mind started churning and he turned to Grenig, "What of Loreuhnd and his daughter? Are they not to assist us?"

Grenig's eyes fell as he answered, "He and Oreighnthia are returning to Ensumei. The drisoleks are neutral and now that they are once again out of a shadow's clutches, they feel it is no longer their duty to intervene. It is not that they wish disaster upon the Brights, they simply do not wish to be involved."

Klum nodded in understanding but could not help but shake his head in frustration in what he believed to be misconstrued morality. With his mind clear of current ponderings, Klum laid his eyes upon the ground again, following the impressions, as he followed in toe the fresh prints of Grenig.

***

Quickly and with excitement Dorian found a small stick and began drawing out her version of the shared vision she and Fayden were eager to get underway. She started with a basic layout of Minaleth, referencing for exactitude the map the blue birds had made then distinguished their current position, the nest where she and the Hawks were imprisoned and the place where they collided with Reilly. Dorian went on to describe what she believed would be the logical certainty of Reilly's travels, contingent, of course, upon the assumed desire to follow the warrior and/or her group of friends. At the conclusion of the demonstration, Dorian placed Reilly, being the culprit in Deki's murder, at Willow Plateau in recently past hours and within reasonable proximity of their current position.

"She is guaranteed to follow as I will be heading into the embers of her comfort zone. She'll be incapable of resisting." Dorian finished with a smile of excitement with one quick addition, "I believe she is Nitris."

Serian raised a brow, uncertain of this *guarantee*, "Dear girl, though I agree of the incomprehensible reason for that other girl's being in the Core World, I fail to see the proof of your theory that she is behind Deki's death as well as in commission for your life as Nitris."

Fayden was quicker to respond, "That deceitful human claims to have felt pulled down here…"

"And our warrior followed a few flowers." Serian flatly stated, forcing Fayden to reconsider her argument.

Dorian jumped in again, having quickly contemplated the lion's perspective, "Serian, you're right. I don't have proof but I trust my instincts and right now they're telling me that Reilly, whether or not she is Nitris in disguise, is a menace and getting to her will at least shed enlightenment on the situation."

All three stood momentarily deliberating the idea to their selves. The wise lion could not argue the girl's logic, despite its not being entirely sound. But he was unable to overlook a crucial detail, "What of the army? They need a commander, Commander."

Fayden's eyes glistened in the ever-changing skyshine as she looked from Redwood Wall to the Valley and back again. She knew the necessity of a commander over an army and felt the sting of guilt even as she merely considered the thought. But she also knew the strength of the Bright army and wisdom of her friends. Dorian, however extraordinary in various and numerous aspects, was not immune to the delicacy of her heart and Fayden saw that. "Friend," the Commander mustered the humility buried within her thick skin, "Serian, would you do me the honor, do the Brights of Minaleth the honor, of leading our army as I accompany our warrior to the Valley to face with her this danger, side-by-side?" He could not refute the passion and determination seeping from the great tiger's being. Serian shook his head, confused, unsure, but wanting desperately to end this malevolent time. In all the years the lion had known Fayden, he had come to recognize an expression of solidified love the tiger had adapted to be perceived as sternness. He now witnessed that very expression as he watched his dear friend observe Dorian. And inward chuckle of disbelief put a smile on Serian's hulking face, "Go" he said simply and with that single syllable, Fayden and Dorian, bonded as they were by a mysterious love, dashed off to what Dorian did not know would be a last battle.

Chapter 16
Into the Valley of the Shadow of Death

Serian worked hard to diverge his concentration from the fatal danger Fayden and Dorian were now *running* into. Incidentally as he rushed in return to Redwood Wall he spotted Grenig and Klum and released a slight roar to announce his company.

"Friends," he huffed though far from out of breath, "am I mistaken to believe from the looks of your actions that you are in the midst of tracking?"

Grenig affirmed the observation, "We think the girl Reilly has been in the vicinity. Perhaps she can provide a little clarity regarding the situation."

"And what of the Brights?" Serian asked as he did not stop his motion toward Redwood Wall.

"All are gathered within the safety of the Wall; Ostel is with the regimen of youth standing-by at the Rainfalls. Grostels are stationed at the Lake and Strike informed me earlier that the Dragonflies shall be the fiery stars of our sky; that the 'rain of daggers shall curtain the eyes of our foes'; that his name will become his purpose and should we need him unexpectedly, a nump will summon his aide."

Serian gave a single nod of approval accented by a solid expression, "Excellent. Call to Wise Bright, should you discover the other girl, but if darkness sets before that time," he now hopped over a tree root as he concluded the encounter with Klum and Grenig, calling back from a turned head his final instruction, "you two must return to the Wall!"

Grenig and Klum silently accepted the instruction without question, watching their friend bound through the meadow, together analyzing and interpreting Serian's behavior to reach the understanding that Fayden must have given command of the Brights to the lion. When they had each drawn the conclusion and begun following their directed path, Grenig quickly realized that in the brief exchange with the lion, explanation of Fayden and Dorian's current road of travel being into the heart of Minaleth was overlooked. Not that there was anything either could do at the time for the danger-bound duo but Grenig couldn't help but feel that a little information pertaining to the direction of Fayden's course would have been a relatively useful reference regarding his own course. The opportunity had passed however; so with a wave of his head in the direction of their plotted path, Grenig and Klum continued on – completely unaware that they were being duped. Like a cloud being pushed and pulled by the force of wind, so, too, were these two Council members being manipulated by an unseen force. Nitris, through the power of fear, derived not of love but of control, had caused the entanglement of an entire world.

***

Fayden and Dorian wasted no time and while Dorian's pace mingled not far from the tiger's, Fayden knew their journey could be trimmed with the girl upon her back. Ever grateful of the respected friend's generous offer, Dorian gently climbed aboard the beautiful, hulking tiger, mindful of the hidden tender spots. Not wanting to be a burden to Fayden, Dorian asked several times of the certainty of the offer but Fayden's final response was simply, "Child, you weigh that of a grape; now hold on." That said, with a shared smile, Dorian gripped the nape of the creature's neck and together now they galloped onward. The sky was marbled in deep pastels of caramel and burgundy – the day dissolving into what Dorian hoped would be the end of this nonsense – and there was an abnormal chill in the air, abrasively reminding Dorian that the Core World was no longer the quintessential embodiment of righteousness but an illusory encampment fighting an incoherent foe. With incredible speed did they reach the fringe of the meadows and even as Fayden utilized the momentum of hopping here and there to move steadily up a hill of the Bridge, she and Dorian were admittedly startled when from a distance not far to the south they heard the sounding of Ralkan's nump. Knowing the faerie was only signaling his battalion's arrival at the Bridge, Fayden did not let the noise siphon her concentration, and so continued on without pausing to consider the possibility that perhaps, once again, Nitris was at work.

A steady pace took them beyond the Bridge and far into the northwestern mountains, a fair distance off the common path, using the trees and brush as cover. Though the route added unavailable time to the girls' quest, wise Fayden knew wrapping around the mountains rather than cutting through into the Valley would counteract the time constraint with the element of surprise. Further and further Fayden's sturdy legs brought the warriors into the region of Minaleth few Brights had ventured to since the segregation. Plant life was bare with death, eradicating their cover and leaving Fayden and Dorian open to the Shadows and Griffins of the land. But their worry was sedated as dark violet, maroon and navy now glazed the sky, providing the simple cloak of twilight darkness. Hours had gone by in their trek from the meadows so they paused at last to refresh but now was not the time to relax and immediately after alleviating built-up fluids from their bodies, the Commander and warrior were back to a steady, though now more cautious, pace through the trees.

***

Meanwhile, when Fayden and Dorian heard the sounding of Ralkan's nump, they were not hearing the mere signal of a destination reached, for Kayfin travelled with the regime as a *living* signal to carry the news back to the Willow Plateau thus eliminating the need to sound the nump. Rather, the faerie leader was sounding an alarm. Coming from the southwestern mountain range, on the inner fringe of the Valley, Ralkan spotted a cluster of Griffins heading east. His enchanted eyes revealed to him the clever ruse of the Griffins; unlike natural birds, utilizing the lift generated by the leader of the V shape in their flight, the militia of beasts formed a single line behind the leader to create the illusion to onlookers ahead that only one Griffin approached. Their strength was enough to overcome the windy resistance. But the faerie caught the slightest glitch in synchronization and at the blast of the nump, every warrior under Ralkan's command raised their eyes to the darkness, piercing through it as butter with their magikal icy eyes. Immediately upon visual confirmation, each faerie withdrew his weapon; those manning the sherzirs and nirfens repositioned to more advantageous positions and anchored the weapons. Each flank was equipped with a sherzir and two nirfens held the center position. A risky strategy in mind, Ralkan zipped over to center position to the faeries manning the nirfens to give his instructions.

"Be still until those brutes are just shy of being overhead then fire the nirfens in succession. Hopefully the majority will fall and the rest will diverge to attack us." Closer now were the Griffins and Ralkan drew his cherished sword from its sheath.

Kayfin was hovering at the faerie's side, "Ralkan…"

"Go now to Willow Plateau!" He declared and she was gone.

The Griffins moved with impressive speed so the hulking masses were soon in the faeries' proximity. In mere moments, Kayfin was out of sight and a soldier concealed in a tree near the left flank called out with an eerie echo, "They're approaching!" Ralkan rushed to center position; quickly inspecting the set angle of the lethal apparatuses then with a bolt of aggression he breached the control of his voice, "FIRE!" The word scraped his throat and engorged his veins. A cloud of enormous arrows bombarded the Griffins causing a great number to fall to the waiting faeries below and the rest to scatter in confusion. The captains of the smaller crews operating the weapons waited for their cues and as if choreographed to the perfection of trapeze artists they executed with precision timing the launch of a second down-pouring of fatality. Another flock tumbled from the sky to join their fallen comrades in combat, unaware of the electrifying gates in their path. One by one the foul mules tried to penetrate the perimeter but the sherzirs adequately cooked the beasts to a frightfully shocking death. In the wake of the deathly bursts of energy, one Griffin discovered the advantage of flying over the area of shock but below the range of arrows, and those clever enough to notice were soon successfully hopping and ducking their way into the hostile territory.

"Get those bastards back!" Ralkan shouted, noticing the infiltration of the left flank. A nearby bowman instinctively turned and fired a series of arrows - each striking an enemy to leave it critically wounded, capable of nothing more before being decapitated by a rushing horde of faeries. While the faeries were quick with their senses, there was no denying the brutality of being caught in a whirlwind of sulfur. One Griffin exhaled with fury from within and swept up a number of Ralkan's warriors. Another accepted one of the large arrows through its side, forcing its dissension but unfortunately as it tumbled to its death it landed to impale itself upon a part of the left flank's sherzir. The post of the sherzir struck into the broken creature's right thigh, through its rib cage and out, only to be further embedded into the left side of its jaw. Removing the mass was out of the question thus leaving the weapon rendered useless.

As the left flank now fought to maintain control without a sherzir, the right flank was having no picnic of its own and all the while center position was double-timing it in an attempt to prevent chaos. In all the mess, only a few Griffins flew past the blockade toward Redwood Wall – a threat although doubtfully detrimental to the integrity of the Wall. What did cause concern was the glimpse of one tactful Griffin Ralkan saw fading out of sight behind Kayfin. The sound of battle around him muted and he gripped his sword ever tighter as tunnel vision crept in. He did not bring his eyes back to the battle scene but sprang forth with increasing speed – following the trail of life Kayfin unconsciously left behind – and the malicious, repulsive odor of the beast following her.
***

All illuminating light was smeared over in the night hours of plum, blackened-evergreen and sienna. Dorian was now heavily relying upon Fayden to use her superior vision to guide them out of the midnight thicket. Gradually the forest disappeared into ash and dirt until finally the friends' travels brought them to the tundra of the Valley. Side by side they stepped silently along the road, Dorian's vision useful once again from the occasional lit torch along the way. Her heart was calm, thinking of how safe she felt in the protection of this muscular, towering tiger of such experience. She placed a hand upon Fayden's soft back in grateful affection, conjuring a purr from the prolific Commander. But the sentimental moment was cut short by the ear-numbing screech of a creature not far. Dorian looked to Fayden for an explanation but Fayden could only shrug as she, too, was unsure of the sound's origin. Again they heard the awful screech and this time the trespassers halted completely in a crouch as each scanned the area for danger. Dorian's vision in the darkness was nowhere near that of the enormous cat next to her but she was able to catch slight movements here and there between insignificant shrubs and burnt trees.

"Shadows?" Dorian asked in a whisper.

Fayden's narrowed eyes darted to and fro as did her ears, "Yes. Stay quiet and close. Be ready but do not draw your weapon unless I say."

Dorian understood and they slowly crept forward, making their way to the marketplace where Reilly was first met. The Shadows around were clearly unimpressed with the intruding Brights but none felt inclined enough to pass a true threat. A couple gruff beasts made eye contact with the Commander, teasing what present little fear with aggressive flaps of their wings or a snarl. But Fayden was having none of it and continued leading her sweet friend to their destination. With cautious steps they continued to tread until at last Fayden recognized the surrounding and upcoming region to be the end of the marketplace (in their case the beginning).

"We're here" Said Fayden.

Dorian acknowledged with a nod and scanned around for a place of cover. To the right Dorian spotted a large boulder nestled with a couple of bare twigs posing as trees. It seemed that was their best bet so pointing out her find, Dorian made her way to the sad covering with Fayden in toe. There they sat, their eyes wide with awareness as they now waited, hoping Reilly would, as Dorian anticipated, feel an irresistible pull to follow them into her own territory. While Dorian's theory and plan had been sound, enough so, to will Fayden into the idea, it was not enough to overcome the unfortunate reality that Reilly was in fact far from the Valley in the midst of misdirecting Grenig and Klum.

***

As dark had fallen over the world of Minaleth, Grenig and Klum heeded Serian's advise and turned back to Redwood Wall since they had failed at finding the rogue human. The two Council members with their entourage of giants reversed direction and picked up a steady pace back to the Bright haven. The trail was still aside from the occasional breath of wind creating a shudder in the trees. They walked on along the reeds of the riverbank north of the meadows thinking nothing of the natural borne sound. Suddenly without warning, one of the giants, a smaller one, was violently snatched into the air and carried away. Instinctively a number of the giants rushed off to follow their friend while those remaining broke into a momentary panic. Grenig was quick to thinking and immediately ordered in a roar for the giants to use their faulnies. A couple managed to pull the weapon from its place and have it at the ready but the rest were just incapable of using the device; either pinching their fingers between the wooden blocks or accidentally snagging another giant. Klum ran to his comrades and did what he could to help them but again a Griffin swooped in for a victim. A giant was caught in the beast's painful grasp and lifted up, up but not far enough, not fast enough, for Klum had acted quickly enough to toss his faulny to the air. At just the right moment he yanked the rope attached to the airborne blocks as hard as he could, jerking his body a little to the left for torque. The weapon worked perfectly, the wooden pieces coming together with such force against the Griffin's hind leg that it was instantly mangled. Klum held tight to the rope as the beast let loose horrifying screams of pain. But in a rage, before the captured giant could wiggle free of the deathly grip, the Griffin held the Bright to its face, growling, then without mercy raked at the victim with his remaining hind-leg. His talons were too much for the giant to endure. With each pass, more of the poor Bright's flesh was torn off and dropped to the ground. Terrified for their friend, the giants near Klum all grabbed hold of the rope and pulled with all their might. Slowly the deadly creature and the now limp, lifeless Bright giant was brought closer until finally another giant came in from behind and with his club knocked the head clean off the Griffin in mid-air. Its body and victim fell to the ground in a messy heap. Hoping for life, Klum bent over his torn friend to check. The dying giant, gargling and coughing, looked to Klum one final time but was unable to speak. Within a few seconds Klum was looking into the memory, no longer the life, of a friend.

Meanwhile, Grenig had taken to the pursuit of the first attacker as Klum had taken control of the second situation. The tiger sprinted at full speed through the dark, very quickly overtaking the giants ahead of him. The poor soul that had been snatched was screaming for help, screaming for the Griffin to let go. In a daring move, Grenig gartered even more speed and launched himself from a mound into the air. Claws out and teeth bared, the crazy tiger anchored himself to the beast, stabbing deep into its flesh. The bundle of beast, tiger and giant sank lower and lower until the beast could no longer continue holding onto the giant with a tiger concurrently clawing its back. The giant fell to the ground, acting as a kind of weight release, for Grenig and the Griffin gained more altitude. Together the great cat and malicious creature wrestled and fought in the air, Grenig losing his grip of the beast more than once only to maneuver and grab better hold. The tiger was unable to keep his body from the vicious stabs of talons nor did the beast spare exhaling his sulfuric breath. Grenig's eyes were now red and burning causing him to tear up thus eliminating his vision. His lungs, too, were burning as he became disinclined to breathe. Holding his breath, furious at what was happening to his world, to his friends, Grenig thrust one of his hind legs, claws straight and true, right into the Griffin's belly. He continued to push his back paw into the beast's entrails – twisting and gouging – then as the creature wailed in agony, Grenig utilized the opening as a step. With his newly developed leverage, Grenig thrust his body upward while pushing the beast's shoulders down and sank his massive K-9's into the exposed jugular and clamped his mouth shut, locking his upper and lower teeth. He then jerked his body with all his might, tearing and ripping the beast's throat apart, as the two tumbled from the night sky. With a thud they hit the ground, creating a small crater; the dead body impacting first as a cushion for the badly wounded tiger. The giants Grenig had passed now caught up and rushed to the heap of flesh and blood. Two attended to their deceased friend while the other two went to Grenig's aid. He was struggling to stay conscious as an inch-deep gash stretched from his side to his belly. The pain was monstrous enough without the added burning of his eyes and airways. The two giants gently lifted the tiger together, while the other two hoisted the giant's body, then they mournfully continued on to Redwood Wall as quickly as they could.

Now only Klum and perhaps five giants stood amongst the reeds of the riverbank. Two grotesque piles of death lay near – a threat to the tender hearts of the giants. Carefully watching the skies for further Griffin attacks, Klum and the giants unfortunately fell into the abyss of deception of which Nitris was so opportunely creative. She had not given any order for the Griffins to infiltrate the Bright territory – that was of their own accord – but as she had become aware of the current events, she could not resist the opportunity to devour inferior life. Without effort the malignant, tyrannical Shadow went to the battle site between the less than intelligible foes and snaked herself through the river, watching what she considered amusing. When the fight seemed to have ended, as the giants stood clueless to their demise, Nitris slithered from the water and reeds to stand as a vaporous Shadow, invisible to the dull-giant eyes. Unhooking a whip-type instrument from her waist, Nitris casually strolled to the center of the stench of innocence and raised her arm in the air. With a sinister, malevolent chuckle, the giants' eyes lifted from the *real* danger, Nitris brought her arm down, snapping her wrist in unison. The whip shot out in front of the Shadow and she spun to increase the momentum of the strike. Twice she spun 'round 360 degrees, her razor-sharp whip slicing everything in its path. No blinks. No screams. One moment Klum and the giants were peering up into the dark sky, on guard for another Griffin attack, and the next they stood momentarily balanced before their halved bodies crumbled into heaps.

***

Kayfin sped through the meadows and was now in sight of Flutter. The faerie leader could see that not far behind the young faerie was a sadistic looking Griffin on the verge of catching up. Quickly she set her bow and took aim but what she did not know was that Ralkan, too, was in the chase. Ralkan was just as near to the beast as it was to Kayfin and with his bow readied in mid-flight, the warrior aimed, catching a glimpse of Flutter in the distance just a second too late. At the same moment, Flutter and Ralkan released their arrows – Flutter's aimed high to the head, Ralkan's aimed to the heart. He screamed for Flutter, incidentally causing the Griffin to raise his head and shift his body, as Flutter's arrow pierced right through the skull of the creature, dropping the body from the sky. Ralkan's arrow continued in its path directly in line with Flutter. Kayfin had ducked upon seeing Flutter ahead with her bow but now as she raised her head from her arms, she watched Ralkan's arrow sail cleanly through Flutter's right shoulder.

"Flutter!" Kayfin screamed in terror as her faerie leader hovered for a moment in confusion then fell to the ground. She turned to see Ralkan rushing toward her, shouting as he came nearer that he couldn't see Flutter. He slowed upon reaching Kayfin but she was up and speeding to Flutter's side.

"Oh, Flutter! Flutter, are you OK?" Kayfin frantically asked.

Ralkan set down panting and erratic, "I didn't know you were there! I didn't see you 'til it was too late! I'm so sorry, Flutter, I'm so sorry!"

Flutter lay on the grass with her eyes closed, moaning, and an arrow protruding from her flesh and cleanly through her shoulder. Kayfin gently called to Flutter without answer.

After several moments, Flutter mumbled something that sounded like, "You...moron."

Quizzical, Kayfin bent lower, "Miss?"

Flutter ever so slightly lifted her left arm to swat Kayfin to the side as she glared Ralkan down, "You moron" she said defiantly, slowly pulling herself up with Kayfin's help. Sitting up, coherent, Flutter tilted her head to see the wound and made a half-hearted attempt to tug at the arrow shaft.

"Please forgive me, Flutter. I didn't see you until after I had fired." Ralkan pleaded.

The wounded faerie winced in pain as she tried flapping her wings but it was no use. The arrow punctured through a nerve of her right wing depleting its functionality. Sighing in frustration Flutter looked to Ralkan, "Tell me the status of the Bridge."

He quickly sputtered out a report of the infiltration of Griffins through the breach of a sherzir and his knowledge of the few beasts that surpassed the blockade. "If you have not seen those Griffins then they must have been overtaken in the meadows or turned back."

"Go," Flutter ordered, "get back to our warriors and find those Griffins." She looked down at her shoulder, again attempting to pull the protrusion out without success, "Kayfin...are you able to help me back to Redwood Wall?"

"Of course, Flutter!" Kayfin reassured her leader.

With a nod of approval, Ralkan sped off back towards the Bridge while Kayfin lifted Flutter from the ground; Flutter's arms wrapped around her friend's neck for support, and carried her back to the safety of the Wall.

***

Fayden and Dorian were now losing their patience and becoming anxious to know why Reilly had yet to be seen. It wasn't long before Dorian realized the situation and understood the degree of manipulation to which she was standing against.

"Damn it!" Dorian exclaimed at the dénouement of her thought.

Fayden turned to acknowledge the growingly outraged girl.

"We've been had…" she went on, choking on her disappointment, "Reilly's not here, not coming here. We have to get back to Redwood Wall, now!"

"Get on my back!" the Commander ordered fervently, "and hold on, we're going to have to go straight through Minaleth then cut north to the river." There was no time now to be cautious. Fayden was going to have to use all the speed she could muster, for she knew all time was lost in the insurance of the Brights.

Dorian was concerned but understood the detrimental circumstance that had befallen them. There was no telling what move Nitris had made in this clever though treacherous game of chess and the only way of knowing her next move and deterring it was in learning what she had already done by getting back to Redwood Wall. As the two determined warriors thundered through the trees Dorian could concentrate only on the rhythm of her adrenaline-saturated breaths; the deep, belly-based inhales and exhales of the great tiger beneath her. The rustling of the trees and underbrush as they sped through Minaleth tickled Dorian's ears. The deep shade created by the massive conifers of Redwood Wall was coming into view at the horizon, just beyond the tall grass of the meadow. Fayden veered to the left, north to travel along the river into Redwood Wall in hopes of travelling under the Shadows' radar.

"Fayden…" Dorian said grimly, unable to find further words.

Profoundly distraught at the grisly sight of the slaughtered giants among the reeds, the tiger slowed to process the massacre but upon seeing the mutilated body of dear Klum Fayden released a blood-curdling, vengeance-filled roar that shook the immediate ground beneath them.

Eyes dripping with pain, Dorian grit her teeth, "We'll get her. Let's go."

Pushing past the immense rage that now anchored their hearts to the demise of Nitris, Dorian and Fayden stepped through the bloody reeds and continued east along the river's shallow bank. Towards what they now desperately hoped would be the end of the terrorizing Shadows' endeavor to eliminate the Brights. The malevolence poisoning the splendor of Minaleth was now far outweighed by the love and justice consuming the hearts of the two friends, now furiously hunting the murderous tyrant, no longer searching.

Chapter 17
The Banyan Tree

Ralkan's little body, solid as it was, was shaking with concern, dread, as he neared the Bridge where he had left his fellow faeries in the midst of a Griffin attack. Expecting fully to be pulled further down to despair at the sight of slaughtered kin, Ralkan was slapped in the face with relief as he could now see a strong majority of the faeries rejoicing amongst a swarm of dragonflies, shrouded by dust…all that remained of the Griffins. Strike and a few others noticed Ralkan approaching, "Ralkan!" they called, "Ralkan!" Strike called as he flew to meet the faerie.

Now among the group of Brights, Ralkan was just about encircled and turn by turn, the faeries and dragonflies excitedly recounted the battle that had ensued at the Bridge. Despite their losses and wounds, they felt joy in the small victory and were eager to end the war Nitris had wrought. "Have you word of Serian and Grenig?" Strike questioned when he had a chance through the many voices.

Ralkan hadn't been sure of the felines' whereabouts for some time now but what he did know was still worth hearing, "I haven't; however, Kayfin and Flutter have made their way back to Redwood Wall together for protection and mending and my intel indicates the Griffins that had gotten past our blockade have been eliminated."

"What should we now?" came a call from the crowd of Brights.

Strike and Ralkan looked to each other for assurance. Discreetly Ralkan drew a fact to Strike's attention, "Technically my friend you are the present Council member, so it is your word we should follow."

With a breath of responsibility to fill his tiny body, Strike brought his eyes from the ground in thought to scan the whole of the newly formed regimen of faeries and dragonflies. All ears waited respectfully for the direction of their leader. "Friends!" he cried out to the crowd, "Return to the Wall! Ralkan, take the faeries back along the river and have Ostel and the grostels at the Rainfalls return to the Wall as well." With care and tenderness in his voice, Strike added a final word, "Gather our fallen along the way", his eyes locked onto Ralkan's before they exchanged a nod of understanding. Ralkan signaled the faerie warriors to follow him and in a bat-like swarm they launched into the air and flew swiftly out of sight to the northeast.   Strike informed the dragonflies that they were going back to Redwood Wall through the meadows and each was to mark in their mind the place, if seen, of any downed Bright so a party of larger, more dexterous, Brights could return to the spot to have the remains brought back. As the two parties now departed in different directions to reach the same destination, both Ralkan and Strike privately took a moment, as they led their respective clan, to send to the winds their collective confidence and strength.

***

Not a far distance behind their smaller-sized, flying friends, Fayden, with Dorian still straddled to her back, bounded through the paw-deep river's edge while both played ignorant to the searing, throbbing pain nagging at their muscles and bones. A short distance east beyond the Bridge and across a narrowing of the river a creek split off to run parallel but behind the river. So as Ralkan's company made its way east along the river, Fayden and Dorian trekked shortly behind and to the left along this creek, neither party aware of the other's location.   Each step the wondrous tiger made seemed to compress Dorian's lungs and steal her breath. Something bored through her heart urging her to open her eyes to what was really in front of her. All at once the Core World trembled and shook with great ferocity while a powerful gust of wind twisted and flowed across the breadth of Minaleth and all to the Eastern Absent. The land quaked and churned in chaos while the sky became doused in a molasses-thick cloud. Serian, Grenig and those already safely back at Redwood Wall braced their bodies with shouts and cries of terrified confusion. The grostels in the lake and the youth with Ostel at the Rainfalls scattered through the water in fear, casting a brilliant array of iridescent sapphire beams every which way, until the thick, malevolent sky covering dissipated the light used to cause the defensive display of radiance. A small network of underwater caves lay beneath the Rainfalls, so Ostel, concerned of the increasingly unexpected and dangerous situation, took the young grostels in his care below for safety. A line of bubbles became their breadcrumb trail as the Brights swam through the narrow tunnels to stay safe where they converged to form an air pocket no larger than a small gymnasium. Counting to ensure every young grostel with him was now in the safe zone, Ostel was unable to conduct a perimeter check but one of the young creatures knew this needed to be done and took it upon himself to do it. Unfortunately and with absolutely no warning a large, cloaked shadow, in between tangibility and a misty entity, stepped forth from a concealed depression on the perimeter's wall. Like the Grimm Reaper, clad in death and unwilling to show any mercy upon those with whom he has chosen to take, the shadow moved forward and began engulfing the grostel in its smoky blackness. A life-ending scream burst from the grostel and Ostel was only just able to place the scream in time to witness the youngster disappear *into* the shadow. The shadows had unintentionally burrowed their way beneath the Rainfalls in their attempt to reach the surface. Clearly completely off the calculated course of the dig, the shadow in charge of the fleet of approximately 50, became internally irate with humiliation and determined to satisfy its rage as productively as possible. Thankfully for the evil bastards the walls of the air pocket had somehow been brandished with indentations that created optical illusions, perfect for each shadow to hide in. Unbeknownst to Ostel, his small company of small soldiers was now surrounded by these shadows, led by one intent on personal restitution. In a moment of realization as he caught the movement of a couple of shadows move from their concealment, Ostel's heart sank in understanding of the immediate detriment he had unwittingly fallen into with his young friends. Screams of terror sprang out all at once as the grostels became aware of the situation. In an instant a number of youth were consumed by shadows that were now fishing for Brights from the depressions of the wall. All at once dozens of wakes formed in the shallow water as everyone took off in a rush at an attempt to survive. A few more prepared, unmoved grostels were quick to bravery as they chased down the shadows after their friends and worked together to block a shadow off before flaunting the blinding light of their sapphire undercoats. In the split second of visual confusion for the shadow, the grostels pounced and smothered it to its last breath. The small victory however did not last and failed to reach the hearts of the others in view. While a number of other grostels were able to pool together to maneuver the same attack, the strength of the pressing shadows was too much for the young Brights and one by one each young grostel met the same ghostly fate. As the children of his friends fell victim to the evils of Nitris' followers, Ostel was darting to and fro as quickly as he could to do anything he could to save the young grostels. With about a dozen youth still frantically trying to escape the death trap, a shadow caught just enough of Ostel's tail to retract it and pull the Bright closer. Ostel's being fell to oblivion; his jewel-like body empty of life sank to the floor. The terrified youngsters that witnessed the act, still swimming for their lives, became weakened in heart and overwhelmed with fear. They came together as a single small group, clutching each other so as not to face the inevitable alone. The shadows encircled the grostels and drew closer and closer until finally enveloping their little bodies. The caves beneath the Rainfalls had been empty and untouched for ages and now they remain strewn with the shells of Brights too young to hold their ground alone.

The lake was nearer to the safety of the Wall than the Rainfalls allowing those grostels the opportunity to retreat to safety, though they hadn't yet abandoned their delegated post. When Ralkan and his soldiers met with the lake, they were glad to see their friends still alive and well.

"Have you knowledge of the welfare of Ostel and his group at the Rainfalls?" Ralkan asked as he and the faeries approached the grostels.

A grostel amongst the crowd called out, "We were hoping you could tell us."

Immediately concerned for the events unfolding before him, especially regarding the grostels unaware of their comrades, Ralkan lowered his hover in order to scoop a handful of soil to communicate with Wise Bright. To his dismay, at that very moment the insurgents of shadows from the Rainfalls appeared in the midst of the faeries and grostels. Without hesitation, Ralkan and his faerie warriors were to arms while the grostels broke away in every direction, immediately utilizing their blinding undercoats. Within a mere few moments of the ambush, a handful of shadows lay empty of life while only a single grostel tasted death. Ralkan's message was received and Wise Bright sent Serian in an instant along with Flutter, whose wound was already healing with the magik of the Core World, to help push back the shadow infiltration. As the two Brights hastened to aid their friends Wise Bright sent a message of his own to the Hawk Lords via Lord Tukiund, who was now feeling strong enough to fly to the Order's rally point. It was time for our noble companions to save the day, thought the Cherry Tree.

***

Unintentionally, Fayden and Dorian had travelled a route that took them directly to the Banyan tree Dorian once gazed upon while in a discussion of magik with Wise Bright. The recollection of that insightful day warmed the dimensions of the warrior's soul as she pulled the conversation from her memory. Her heart began palpating as her mind churned with the idea that perhaps, should she survive this war and fulfill her honor and obligation to the Brights of Minaleth she could find a world, a realm, more suitable to her spirit. The Core World was extraordinary but torn from its potential for true beauty by the distinct segregation between darkness and light. Dorian's thought was abruptly interrupted by an ever-growing shade in the sky above, different from the ill-omened cloudiness clearly representing Nitris. Fayden and Dorian raised their heads and let their eyes process.

"The Hawks have come." Fayden concluded with resolution before the girl could question the event.

"They're heading east..." Dorian commented, sighting their flight path.

"...to Redwood Wall for protection. The Brights are safe." Fayden said conclusively.

With their heads still held to the sky Nitris crept her way slowly, unseen, to within a few feet of the warriors, standing slightly behind a tertiary trunk of the Banyan. Coldly, mimicking the sensation of a cube of ice on the small of your back, the shadow spoke with an unnerving subliminal tongue, "You do not belong here."

A deathly chill crawled up Dorian's spine as she turned to face not a ghostly mass of being but a small, unintimidating adolescent human. "Reilly," Dorian acknowledged.

"Ah, sensei," the girl sarcastically began, "did you miss me, friend?" she teased.

"Why would I miss someone who is far from what she seems? You're no more than a lowly shadow of Minaleth, bored with your disdain for a world you've polluted with enmity." Dorian responded defiantly.

Nitris took the moment after Dorian's words to transfigure from the girl playing the façade of Dorian's contemporary to the malicious, empty-bodied shadow responsible for the manipulation and perversion of the Core World.

"What was the point?" Dorian questioned the twisting mist.

With a sinister chuckle, "Of deceiving you with a disguise in your own world?" finishing the warrior's thought. "Well don't you see? Your spirit is unlike that of most in all the worlds. Not to say you have the right to gloat of your magnanimity and passion, as you are not alone. The difference is in the darkness I have seen you face each day within your heart. Your compassion has wavered with each dagger aimed at the delicacies of your soul. Properly mentored I knew you could be a vassal of power with or against me in a new Minaleth. I needed to evaluate you; study you to find a way into the recesses of your mind where you conceal the malignance to distinguish if it could be manipulated and extracted."

Dorian could only blink in disillusionment as she listened to Nitris' delusional explanation. "So I guess that means you're a terrible analyst then" were the words Dorian squeezed through a patronizing smirk creeping along her face. She could see the irate anger flush the shadow's face and took that as her queue to continue her observation, "If you had *properly* studied and evaluated the inner workings of my heart and mind you would have discovered that while yes, there is a part of me surely capable and guilty of such atrocities committed by the most evil of individuals but, my heart beats for the collective moral and ethical righteousness that drives the civil progress of the world, or worlds. Universal love is the constant variable in every equation that runs through my mind. Even I have tried but it cannot be eradicated because what it comes down to is whether or not I want to make the world I live in better or worse. I could relent to the selfish, vile fantasies and desires I keep locked away in my mind but to what avail? I was given breath and with that breath I will always strive to make a positive difference."

Nitris felt the defiance and irrefutable determination of Dorian's words but nothing seemed to affect the shadow's desire for control. Her despicable face twinged as she realized the improbability of using Dorian as a tool. Fayden caught the disappointment in Nitris' eyes but was distracted by the idea of Dorian being used. Her claws spread and gripped the ground in an attempt to prolong the release of her overflowing contempt.

Meanwhile, the scene at the Lake was rapidly unfolding as Flutter charged in, sword in hand, eyes aglow with fury. Serian was only seconds behind, bounding into the mess with a bone-chilling roar. Ralkan was busy in mid-swing of his sword when the sweet, magenta faerie appeared next to him, matching his swinging force and ferocity. The pair attacked and parried valiantly side-by-side while in the sky above the Hawk Lords began circling in formation in a manner appropriate to that of vultures. As their encircled course continued a gradual wind picked up in the air around them; the distorted skyshine now dim and discolored swirled and groaned in a storm condensed according to the Hawks' parameters. Dense, dark clouds gathered and encompassed the area above the Lake and churned the consistency of the storm into thick, consuming custard. Curious as they all were, not one shadow or Bright could risk breaking their concentration from the concurrent combat despite the growing interest for what this tornado-like creation could accomplish. Serian focused his attack on a pair of shadows wincing from the radiance of a single grostel exposing its undercoat. They had no chance of surviving as the lion's nearly 1-ton body descended upon them with unyielding force. Before they could even think of a defense, Serian's jaw was already ripping at the throat of one and all four legs were raking at the other. The grostel darted away and quickly entered into another scuffle while Serian lifted his blood-dripping maw from his victims.

Dorian didn't wait for a definitive bell to initiate the fight. Swift with finesse Dorian reached to her back and unsheathed her Masamune katana. In a warrior's stance she stood, her knees bent and sturdy, her center of gravity established and controlled and sword forward, inviting Nitris to join the martial ballet about to ensue. The shadow fingered something at her side then let drop the coiled whip that had so cruelly mutilated the giants, including Klum. In an instant the whip and sword were clanging and scraping against each other and Fayden bolted to the opposite side of Nitris to gain the advantage but the shadow was ready with a second whip out and was now swinging both arms wildly and viciously.

***

Strike and the dragonflies were now back at the Wall and helping to fight off the few Griffins trying to infiltrate the haven. In the intervals Strike had between defending and attacking he tried to locate Ralkan or any of the faeries his company had so recently disbanded from but could not find them for they hadn't made it back to Redwood Wall. From the safety of the massive trees the Brights could see the ominous storm unfolding, suffocating the fringe of the meadows at the Lake. None of the Brights could do anything about what they knew was certainly an act of malevolence from Nitris. They could only hope and trust that their precious warrior would eradicate the circumstances and abandon Nitris to the emptiness of her much favored control. In their cooperative campaign Flutter and Ralkan together proved to be a devastating force of tactic and fury. But in a moment of a shadow's dissipation, Flutter barrel-rolled to avoid an oncoming missile of dark magik and in her motion was unaware that Ralkan had been deceived, the dissipated shadow invisible but blocking the faerie's special vision. Ralkan couldn't see that the beast was still before him, casually unraveling a short cord with a delighted and relaxed look on its disheveled face. In an instant the cord shot from the shadow's hip, wrapping around the blade of Ralkan's sword, and recoiled in a blink to bring the hilt straight into the hand of the shadow. The faerie's valiant life ended with a swift thrust through his little heart. The shadow dropped the sword upon Ralkan's body before actually disappearing to cause havoc elsewhere without even a glint of remorse when it read the inscription on the faerie's sword. Ralkan's blood soiled the ground beneath his body, staining the blade of his sword with what remained of all that he had.

Growls and grunts spilled from the tiger, girl and shadow as they shuffled and fought with every ounce of their martial integrity. Dorian and Nitris bartered in sync to the intuitive choreography of their weaponized tango. The metal of Dorian's katana and that of Nitris' whips crashed and scraped together in a disorienting orchestra until unexpectedly and suddenly Nitris simply vanished. On their toes at the ready with constant movement Fayden and Dorian circled in anticipation of the shadow's reappearance. Sensing the entity, Dorian trusted her instincts and rushed forward before sliding to the ground with her sword thrusting forward into the empty air. Her keen instincts did not fail her as Nitris manifested clutching a gouge in her side but this sent her into a rage and a enchantment quickly muttered upon her whips turned them searing red-hot at the tips. A twirl of the whips above the shadow's head warned Dorian but to her dismay she was not quick enough to block or move. The molten cord shot at Dorian, embedding into the exposed flesh of the warrior's right arm for a second, then ripped free, revealing the fresh brand. The pain of the burn, even just the impact of the whip on her skin, sent Dorian into unmitigated agony and emotional dissolution as she howled at an incomprehensible frequency. The girl lay against a boulder, writhing and clenching the melted muscle and skin of her wound while the screams echoed across the meadow, sounding carried by the river. In a breath Fayden jumped upon the shadow with overwhelming ferocity and managed to wrangle a whip from Nitris' hand, well, she took the whole hand. The disgruntled Nitris grabbed at the air where her hand would have attached to her forearm but with nothing there the moral dissention clouding the world and driving this war, along with the unwavering dedication of Fayden and her dear friend, compounded and drove the shadow into momentary concealment in order to re-strategize. With the shadow temporarily out of sight Fayden rushed back to tend to Dorian. Pale with shock, drenched in tears of pain, Dorian looked into the Commander's eyes, "Help me" she forced out, "so we can end this." Fayden knelt lower and gently placed a paw at the shoulder joint of the injured arm for stability. She dropped her head and began licking the burn, evaporating the bacteria and sealing the wound. Just the gentle touch of the majestic tiger warmed Dorian's body and eased the pain.

When Serian was lifting his head from the shadows he had mauled, he heard the blood-curdling scream of his beloved warrior and bounded off, fearing for her safety as well as Fayden's. In his expedient trek to go to the rescue Serian was intercepted by Flutter, who had also been unable to ignore the scream and the two together now raced to be by their friends' sides. In no time, as Fayden was nearly finished cleaning Dorian's wound, the intrepid lion leaped clear over the river and came stampeding through the reeds just behind where Dorian now lay, bringing a brief smile of relief upon Fayden's face. Flutter, too, was now hovering at Fayden's side, calmly and quietly speaking encouragement to the hurt warrior, adding subtle Silethin words of strength to the whispers. In the presence of such caring and inspirational friends from a world she had known for a limited time, Dorian felt rejuvenated enough to stand and retrieve her sword. Flutter handed it to the warrior as Dorian braced herself with Fayden and Serian aiding her from each side.

Nitris was aware of the new cavalry next to her intended victim and now stood unabashed facing the quartette with every expectation of finishing this endeavor as victor. But no one expected what happened next. The growing storm created by the Hawk Lords had reached its pinnacle and from the clouds emanated a sumptuous sound irresistible to the shadows' taste for pleasure and control. All the shadows and griffins in the vicinity of the storm were drawn from their combat and lured to the blanket incurring them to be consumed with pleasure. Entranced by the Hawks' magik, subjugated by their lesser senses, one-by-one the attacking shadows abandoned their battle and stepped into the cloud entirely unaware they were stepping into a net. The Brights were stunned with perplexity of the Hawk Lords' ingenious tactic as they watched their opponents dissipate and make their ways to the shrouded trap. In the absence of the shadows the Brights had a moment to breathe and ensure those around them were alright.

Nitris however, was adept enough at the powers of the Hawk Lords that she was keenly aware at the sight of the cloud that her witless followers were walking into a trap. Feeling the possible loss now that the Brights were relieved of their individual battles, Nitris fumed and in a flash altered her appearance to look like

Atorik, in an attempt to shake Dorian's courage. Seeing the minion that had tortured and maimed her to within inches of life failed to have Nitris' hoped affect. Instead, Dorian felt empowered, knowing that she had slain that evil beast and what stood before her was no more than a façade of terror. No longer could she stand the idea of this malicious entity having anything to do with life. Without a second thought Dorian rushed the shadow, coming straight on, her katana forward but gripped in just a way to allow it to spin at Dorian's wish. Nitris stood ready, her handless arm at her side, her other arm - whip in hand - gathering momentum. She snapped it out and it caught Dorian's blade but she could not retract just the sword. Rather, Dorian held tight and went with it, right into facial contact with Nitris. Impressively resisting Dorian's counter pull with only a single arm, Nitris was in fact able to withstand only so much. Dorian felt the twinge of weakness in Nitris' fighting arm and instantly acted on it, reaching for the tip of her sword to utilize her two-armed advantage, and gripping it, unhindered by the painful gash brought by such hand placement, and forced it beneath the shadow's chin. Dorian was successfully pushing Nitris back through the water and nearly had her against the Banyan but with a clever jerk of the cord, Nitris was able to finally able to get a push on Dorian. The warrior had no choice but to release the hold she had as the gash was now on the cusp of slicing through nerves and Dorian knew she had to keep the advantage of having all her body parts. Intuitively connected to her friends, she did not have to verbalize the plan ready to unfold. Standing at the ready behind the warrior, Fayden, Serian and Flutter anticipated their required moment of need. With a cry of bridled hate, Dorian suddenly slipped her feet from under herself, dropping to the ground and crouching while sweeping the katana wide and to the right. The unexpected movement caught Nitris off guard as her legs were sliced at the knees but what really startled her was the charging tiger now soaring through the air in her direction. Over Dorian's covered body, Fayden flew, with a powerful tackle straight into Nitris. The magnificent enemies pushed and howled at each other against the base of the Banyan hip-deep in water. Dorian quickly recovered to see Nitris kick one of her legs out right into the Commander's stomach. This forced the tiger back just slightly but Flutter was already there, flying too fast for anyone to realize she was in fact lashing the shadow's legs together. Catching Nitris' eyes, Dorian looked fiercely into those orbs that had once been those of a Bright, and offered her final attack. Nokun terr reyh yevir kuna vodan; nokun corris reyh yevir kuna terr. Kelden reyla bej ihn rol wilrev, Dorian spoke to herself. She sought for the right opening between Fayden and Flutter to ensure maximum effectiveness. Dorian then leapt from her position, actually launching from a part of Fayden's back, and thrust her katana into the right of Nitris' chest. The force and gravity of the leap pulled the two into the water, submerging them from sight. Beneath the surface, Nitris and Dorian wrestled and fought but with a sword through her chest and the realization that her legs were tied, Nitris began to panic. Fearing Dorian would drown in her desperate attempt to end Nitris, Serian dove into the water to pull the girl out but she would not relent. She continued pushing with all her might on the sword, forcing the duo deeper, ignorant of the breath leaving her lungs. At what couldn't have been anything but the final expression of life in the shadow's eyes, Dorian sent a final thrust through the length of the sword, pushing it through the shadow's body all the way to the hilt. When she raised her eyes from the defeated shadow she was mystified at the sight of a subtle current travelling up into the trunk of the Banyan. Nearly out of breath, she reached for her sword to draw it free of Nitris' corpse but struggled as it had been so deeply pushed. Serian's plunge into the water created a large wave under the water that pulled Dorian from where she was, releasing the sword from the body but pulling her into this bizarre current. Serian saw the warrior and the odd current she was heading towards. Unwilling to learn the hard way, Serian swam to reach Dorian, grasping one of her boots in his jaw to pull her from the danger; he unfortunately had no way of knowing the strength of Banyan's pull and together they drew closer to the roots. Expecting Dorian and Serian to come back up any minute, Fayden and Flutter waited at the bank. The wait would last, as the wise lion and brave warrior had unknowingly, unintentionally been pulled into the water flow and up into the hollow Banyan trunk. The tree of course was more than just that. It was the link to other realms, to new worlds. Awakened with the truth of what actually occurred at the river, Fayden and Flutter went back to

Redwood Wall with the story. Wise Bright had assumed in secret the nature of the Banyan tree and with his explanation of the magik the Commander and faerie leader felt a warming confidence that wherever the magik had taken their friends was where they belonged. They trusted that Serian's wisdom and Dorian's passion would keep the two safe in whatever adventures awaited them in a new world.

Epilogue

Dorian's ears tingled in the salty splashes on the shore of a beach. Bits of her hair had matted to her cheek against the sand and she could feel the coarseness in her mouth, particularly irritating her palate. She pushed her tongue along the roof of her mouth to remove the grains then smacked her lips a few times to push them out. Dorian's eyes were crusted shut so she tried opening them as wide as she could until the upper and lower lids broke free of each other. She blinked a few times, gathering what information she could. She still lay on the ground with her right side exposed to the elements and this severely limited the scope of her sight so she started to push her body upwards, starting with a push-up and moving into a kneel. It took a moment but Dorian now stood upon a beach of cashmere sand stretching for miles in either direction looking out at an ocean of a remarkably clear, pure blue that nearly brought tears to the girl's eyes. That was when she noticed Serian in the water, partly submerged and rocking gently with the waves. Dorian delicately stepped through the shallows toward her friend and upon reaching him, brushed his tangled mane to the side and whispered gently in the lion's ear, "Serian?"

At first he gave no response, frightening Dorian momentarily, and then slightly swished his tail to and fro with an inner grumble.

"Are you ok?" she asked Serian gently while he slowly raised his huge body from the water to stand on all fours.

"I believe so" he groaned with a stretch and a good shake, "Are you?"

"I think so," Dorian answered, "other than the burn Nitris gave me." She poked the wound, wincing only a little, and rubbed it amazed at the healing touch of Fayden's feline tongue.

"That will scar but it will heal quickly." Serian commented.

Dorian nodded as she looked out across the ocean and beach, squinting in the sunlight, turning her head for a panoramic view. Unsure of the world she was in, she could not discern the directions but opposite the beach was a field of think, partially long, green grass. This field was several miles wide and stretched deep, building into hills and converging with rather treacherous-looking mountains with steep peaks and sharp edges. These also spread infinitely to the right and left and were only the front of a series of subsequent ranges. Also flanking the field and ranges on either side were sparse trees that grew denser, building into rich forests. Looking out her eyes started to water as she was still adjusting to the spectacular shine of the sun stinging them. Serian, too, was adjusting to the brightness of the very earth-like sun while slowly scanning the surroundings – observing the types of visible terrain – and taking into account the feel of time and the climate. A light, refreshing breeze passed by, gently brushing the warriors' faces and cooling their skin.

"Well, my girl, I would guess that it is likely between the hours of late noon and evening. What are your thoughts?" Serian asked.

Dorian agreed and considered herself for a moment. She felt weakened but not weak; unsure but confident. Once again she found herself in a new, unfamiliar world that could hold any number of possibilities of threats, joys and adventure. Serian watched as Dorian's eyes glistened with intrigue in her contemplation. Exhausted as she was from the trials of Minaleth, the warrior at heart could not resist the magnitude of her desire for new adventures. She looked straight ahead, her vision narrowing in on the monstrous, jagged protrusions beyond the empty field, and then surreptitiously glanced the lion's way. Serian smirked understanding their unspoken cahoots with each other. Equally curious, though a little more cautious, he gave a wink and started forward, motioning for the girl to come along. Dorian smiled gratefully with excitement and picked up her feet to walk beside her wise friend toward unknown territory in an unknown world. Fear of the unknown tickled her heart briefly but then she remembered and whispered to herself that remarkable, empowering phrase she learned in the Core World: *Nokun terr reyh yevir kuna vodan; nokun corris reyh yevir kuna terr. Kelden reyla bej ihn rol wilrev.*

The End

Made in the USA
Columbia, SC
03 November 2018